ANNA E. COLLINS

A
LIFE
IN
BLOOM

A Life in Bloom
Red Adept Publishing, LLC
104 Bugenfield Court
Garner, NC 27529
https://RedAdeptPublishing.com/

This is a work of fiction. Names, characters, places, and incidents either are the product of the author's imagination or are used fictitiously, and any resemblance to locales, events, business establishments, or actual persons—living or dead—is entirely coincidental.

---

1.   http://StreetlightGraphics.com

To all the teachers in my life—

gardeners of the mind,

planting seeds that grow into possibilities

PART 1

CHAPTER 1

If I were a color, I'd be gray—or so my mother told me once when I was fourteen. Not her nicest assessment of me perhaps, but also not the worst. Besides, at this very moment, with a cruiser's blue-and-red lights spinning in the rearview, I hope it will serve me well as I try to blend into the clay-hued cloth of the passenger seat.

"Fudge puppets," Patrick mutters, hands at ten and two. He tilts his face to the ceiling, nudging his glasses off-kilter. "That's going to be another one hundred thirty dollars. Told you we should have stayed home."

"Or stuck to the speed limit," I whisper to my window. It's his second ticket this year. One more, and he'll be a carless traveling IT consultant. Awesome.

Three sharp knuckle raps on the window, and Patrick lowers the pane. "Hello, Officer."

The hint of a smile in his voice is cringeworthy. He doesn't even have the decency to be embarrassed about this.

"License and registration, please." The officer's deep voice has the haggard drawl of a teacher at the end of a long day of wrangling unruly teenagers. I would know.

Patrick starts digging for his wallet.

"I clocked you twenty over the limit," the officer says. "In a hurry?"

Patrick hands him the documents. "Well, sir, we're late for a family get-together. Her mother's birthday." He pats my leg and ends with a possessive squeeze that makes me want to sidle closer to the door. I'm not ready to end my invisibility here. I don't want to be pegged as an accomplice. Yes, we're going to see my family, and sure, I didn't tell him to slow down, but that doesn't mean I'm to blame.

Since, deep down, I know guilt by association is not a thing when it comes to basic traffic offenses, I allow logic a win and will my baseless anxiety back in time for the officer to lean forward to look at me. I force the corners of my mouth up and give him a small nod. The muscles in my face twitch with the effort.

He disappears back to his car, and an edgy silence follows as we wait for the verdict.

"You know I can't drive you to work now that I don't have first period free," I say, after a tense minute has passed.

Patrick loosens his tie and glances in the rearview. "It'll be fine."

"I'm just saying—"

"Don't."

"But one more—"

He shoots me a glare. "Oh, for God's sake, Kris. It's a ticket, not the end of the world."

I turn to face the roadside again, a lump forming in my throat.

One ticket, two tickets, three tickets.

I close my eyes and swallow.

Golf outings with his buddies, new game console, smartwatch, gym membership never used, that stupid fantasy football league.

With each item recounted, my heart pumps faster, gradually dissolving the obstruction in my windpipe and replacing it with resolve. The bushes outside come into focus again, and I flex my fingers. I should do it now—say the words that have been percolating in my head since New Year's when he was too drunk to either kiss me at midnight or drive us home as he'd promised. I let my lips form them without sound—*I think we should break up*—then try out a few other variations on the same theme at my reflection in the window. My pulse settles, and my shoulders come down. Slowly, the threat of a breakdown recedes.

Once Patrick receives his ticket, we drive the rest of the way in silence and within the speed limit. The words stay on my tongue, sweet like gumdrops. They want out, but I bite down, until all I taste is the metallic flavor of blood. That's how it has to be right now thanks to this morning's discovery. I need time to think, and today I'm pretty certain that's not going to happen.

As if the universe wants to congratulate me on a conclusion adeptly reached, at that moment we pull into my twin sister's pristine driveway to see my mother come running out of the house dressed only in a terry robe and a yellow feather boa. As you do.

"Kristin! Patrick! I was so worried. You should have been here a long time ago."

My mother is out of breath, and splotches of pink appear on her sagging cheeks.

"Hi, Mom. Happy birthday."

She grabs my shoulders and kisses the air by my ear before doing the same to Patrick.

"We hit a traffic snafu on I-90," Patrick says, his tone not inviting any questions.

I want to remark on the irony of his speeding making us late, I really do, but then my sister steps out onto the front porch, and as usual, I'm rendered speechless.

Shannon is two whole minutes younger than me, married seven years, with two well-adjusted kids, a career in nursing—part-time, but I'm not allowed to point that out—and a golden retriever named Lucky. She rolls out of bed each morning with a smile and a song while precocious forest critters dress her in crisp cotton wear—organic, of course—after which she admires her perfect reflection in the newly washed windows. At least I'm pretty sure that's what happens. Basically, she is everything I'm not. Needless to say, we're not identical.

She hurries toward me, arms outstretched, wearing an apron complete with frills, buttons, and complicated straps, the scent of baking bread trailing behind her, and I nearly get back in the car. I say *nearly* because I'm a grown-up, one with a full-time, serious job even, teaching other people's kids how to be productive citizens. I no longer act on every impulse to flee that enters my mind.

"Shannon," I say instead. "The yard looks wonderful."

"Aw, thank you. Thomas has worked so hard."

We embrace, and I suppress the urge to sniff her shirt. My stomach rumbles. I only had cereal and a bagel this morning, and it's been what, two hours now? That morning sickness I've read about is starting to come on, I think, a flutter of something that could be excitement, fear, or possibly acid reflux running through me. Though maybe that's too early. I only just found out.

I glance at Patrick wrestling our overnight bags out of the trunk with my mother hovering. His face is a darker red than usual, and I can tell from the way he holds his arms that he's starting to sweat despite the still-cool May air. I can't help but feel a bit guilty. He didn't want to come, but I convinced him with the promise he could skip Fourth of July when I know he would rather be with his buddies anyway. I hate driving the two and a half hours from Chicago to Madison by myself, and I need someone in my corner in situations like these—i.e. family get-togethers. Plus, since he is likely soon to be the father of my child, sticking together seems like the right thing to do.

"Come inside," Shannon says, interrupting my reverie. "I made scones."

Of course she did.

A few hours later, we've settled into the second guest room, given the kids their mandatory gifts, played with said gifts, admired the new deck, and collapsed into plush, bug-spray-smelling deck chairs underneath the radiant warmth of several patio heaters.

Thomas has fired up the grill and stokes the coals, or whatever it is men do when they are in charge of The Meat, while regaling Patrick with a story or two from the golf course. My mother and I sip our wine in companionable silence for once, and I have time to think *this isn't so bad* before she asks, "Has he proposed yet?"

As if sensing a disturbance in the Force, Patrick looks up at the other end of the deck, meets my gaze, then looks away again, laughing at something Thomas said. My eyes linger at the back of his wide neck.

"I promise I'll tell you if he does."

"If? You mean when?"

"Sure. When. Mom, do we have to—"

"What is he waiting for?" she asks, more to herself than to me. "Doesn't he know you're thirty-five?"

Here we go again. "I've told you before. Our relationship is just as committed as Shannon and Thomas's."

"Tsk."

"Don't tsk me."

"Do you have a ring on your finger? Kids I don't know about?"

My thoughts shift to the stick I peed on earlier. "No, but—"

"No. Thomas popped the question after he and Shannon had dated one year. To the day. You and Patrick are well into your second."

"Mom."

"What? I don't understand what's taking you so long. Look at this." She makes a sweeping gesture to incorporate The House and The Husband in all their splendor. "You can have it too. I know you can."

She's right. I could. It's supposed to be the next step now that I'm nearing middle age and apparently have a baby on the way. Only, the thought of it is about as exciting as getting into college after twelve years of grade school. Then again, I did that and lived.

"You should have someone to take care of you."

She puts such an emphasis on *care* that I look up. For a split second I think I see something unfamiliar flitter across her face, but then it's gone, and she drains her drink.

"Where's that bottle now?" She looks around. "Thomas, could you be a darling?" She holds her glass up in the air.

He comes over and pours her a generous helping of chardonnay.

"Thank you, dear."

"Anything for you, Jane." He winks and clinks his IPA bottle against her glass. Then he turns to me. "So how are the kids, Kristin?" He rocks back on his heels and eyes me expectantly.

I know what he means—the kids at school, my students, work—but the way he asks it has me shift in my seat so that my arms cover my stomach. I should have worn the oversized blue sweater instead of this clingy white one. Though even if I were full-on, for sure, one hundred percent, five-months-or-so pregnant, I doubt anyone would be able to tell. I willingly admit I'm still carrying some holiday weight. I less willingly concede it's likely permanent.

"Kids are good," I say with exaggerated enthusiasm. "In a teenagery way, but good. I *love* my job." As soon as the words cross my lips, I frown, not sure why I sound like an infomercial. Neither, it appears, is Thomas, for he blinks twice and returns to the grill.

My mother squints, her gaze boring into me. "You're being weird," she says, petting the yellow boa she's still wearing.

"Thanks." I take another sip of my wine, almost choking on it as an image of the baby-grain being showered in alcohol enters my mind. It shakes its fist at me while opening an umbrella. I suppress the urge to spit the wine out but set down my glass all the same and decide to ask Shannon for some sparkling water. Where is she any-way? I realize suddenly I haven't seen my sister since our arrival.

"Is Shan inside?"

"No. Hayley has ballet, and Zach needed a present for a birthday party. They should be back soon."

So the house is empty. I peer surreptitiously toward the guys, but they are busy admiring the trampoline Thomas recently assembled for the kids.

"Got to powder my nose," I say to my mother, and then before she can respond, I walk into the inviting stillness of my sister's im-maculate home.

Shannon's house is decorated in white and pale yellow to contrast gleaming dark oak floors. The HVAC hums as I make my way through the kitchen into the walk-in pantry. This is my guilty plea-sure—other people's pantries. I know it's super weird, but they make me feel relaxed and at home. I only have a shallow closet in my own kitchen, but Shannon has the queen of pantries with floor-to-ceiling shelves, a wine fridge, a small table for prepping, and even a narrow window with a view of a flowering magnolia tree.

Stepping inside, I scan the canisters and boxes, lift packages of protein bars and shuffle the big bag of dog food to the side to peer behind it. An unopened package of Girl Scout cookies is hiding in the corner, and I do a jubilant fist pump at my luck. After peeping out into the kitchen to make sure I'm still alone, I sit on the floor and lean against the wall. With one Thin Mint in my mouth and another in my hand, I close my eyes and inhale the musky scent of cumin and cloves, garlic, and bread. I love it here.

Too soon, a sharp bark disturbs the peace. Zach throws open the door to the pantry and tumbles in, followed by Lucky, who is having the best day of her life, judging by her exuberance. I shrink into the corner, but Zach's shrewd four-year-old eyes find me in an instant.

"Aunt Kristin, what are you doing?" He peeks around the table to where I'm sitting, cookie halfway to my mouth.

"Um, hi, bud," I say, scrambling for a plausible explanation. "Cookie?"

"No, thanks. Mom says it's dinnertime."

The little freak. Good thing he's cute. "So it is," I agree, shoving the cookie into my mouth. "Listen, don't tell any—"

But Zach, having found a treat for Lucky, is already on his way out. "Later, gator," he hollers.

"Zach, no running," Shannon says before she comes into view through the open pantry door. "Tell the others we'll eat in ten. They're all outside."

I hold my breath as I wait for his response. *Come on, Zach. You saw nothing.*

"Not Aunt Kristin. She's in the pantry."

My face flushes. I have a second, maybe two, so I scramble off the floor while brushing the cookie crumbs off the front of my shirt. Then my sister is there.

Her eyebrows are raised as she takes in my figure. "Again?"

"What?" I push past her. "It's not my fault you have an awesome pantry."

"True." Her head bobs in the direction of the deck. "Did you need a break?"

I don't know how she does it, but Shannon always makes me feel as if she's the big sister. We couldn't be more different, yet she totally sees through me.

"I guess. And I really like it in there." I point to the pantry. "You can design mine when we get a bigger house."

"Deal." My sister opens the fridge and pulls out a tray filled with veggie kabobs, plus two bowls with salsa and guacamole. Both home-made. "And... do you know when that'll be?"

"Please, not you too. I've told you before, I don't need a ring on my finger. We're good. I'm fine. I'm happy."

Shannon sets a basket of bread on a tray and looks at me, brows furrowed. "Are you, though?"

"Wha—?" I blink. There's no way she knows I'm having doubts. "Yes, of course."

"Okay," she says, hands raised in surrender. "I won't ask again." She walks past me and gives my shoulder a little squeeze. "If you're happy, I'm happy." She opens the patio door and calls out, "Meat al-most ready, hon?"

"It's ready," Thomas says. "Everybody, grab your plates."

I am stuffed like a Build-A-Bear in the hands of an overly enthusiastic preschooler.

Scraps of food are left on my plate, yet I don't feel even a minus-cule inkling to touch another bite. My belly is distended and labor-ing to digest the massive amounts of steak, sausage, baked potatoes with trimmings, grilled veggies, chips, sparkling water, and birthday cake I've consumed, and I have to suppress a groan as Hayley hugs me from behind. She and Zach have been busy playing with bubbles for the past fifteen minutes, but now they're bored.

"Please, Aunty Kristin, come play tag with us," she begs, her skin-ny six-year-old arms squeezing my neck.

"I'm sorry, sweetie," I muster. "I'm too full to move right now."

She giggles and pokes a finger into my stomach. "You look like you have a baby in your belly."

"Hayley!" Thomas snaps under his breath next to me.

"It's squishy," Hayley continues, oblivious of the social faux pas she's committing. She pokes my belly some more. "I love it. Squish, squish, squish."

I know my face is bright red. I could not care less that my niece is announcing my flab to the world, but it's that word again—*baby*. It's on repeat in my head, and I stare at Hayley's hand, completely fascinated with what it's doing. Her cousin is in there.

"Hayley, that's enough," Thomas says, louder this time, and grabs her arm. "Why don't you take Zach inside for a bit? Maybe do some Legos, huh?"

Hayley looks up, her lower lip trembling as she turns from her dad to me. I want to tell her it's fine, that she can poke my belly anytime, but instead I give her a smile to let her know she's done no harm.

"I'll play with you later, okay?" I say.

"Okay." She calls out to her brother, and the two of them disappear into the house.

"I'm so sorry, Kristin," Shannon says from across the table. "She didn't mean anything by it."

"No, it's fine. I don't care." I venture a quick glance at Mom, expecting her to pounce at the mention of offspring, but her gaze is locked somewhere far away as if she hasn't heard a word.

"Yes, really," Patrick chimes in. "She doesn't care. I love your squishy belly, too, babes." He leans in and pats my belly while giving me a sloppy kiss on the cheek. His breath smells of beer and onions. "See."

I push him back into his seat with my elbow and flash Shannon an apologetic smile. "Okay, that's quite enough about me," I say with a self-deprecating snicker. "Dinner was delicious as usual. Thanks, guys."

"A baby," Patrick mutters to himself. "Pretty sure science would be baffled considering we hardly ever—"

"Yes, happy birthday, Jane!" Thomas raises his glass, thereby sparing everyone an awkward moment.

We all do the same, nodding and smiling like a group of bobbleheads. I shoot Thomas a grateful glance. I don't know what's gotten into Patrick. He must be drunker than I thought. I glance at him, but he doesn't look up.

After we set our glasses down again, Mom seems to startle back to the present and clears her throat. She's been unusually quiet throughout the meal over at the head of the table. Now, however, she looks at each of us in earnest.

"Yes, thank you both," she says, indicating Thomas and Shannon. "And thank you, Kristin and Patrick, for making the drive up here. I know you all have your own lives, so I really appreciate us being here together as a family for my birthday today."

Shannon and I look at each other in confusion. What the duck is going on?

"Now that the children have gone inside, I have a bit of news I want to share with you all."

Shannon's brows furrow. "Is something wrong?"

Mom raises a hand. "Please let me do this without interrupting."

"Do what?" Patrick asks. There's a slight slur to his speech, and I glare at him icily enough to make him sit back in his chair. Yeah, he's my boyfriend, but the man has the worst timing.

"Well." Mom wrings her hands, catches herself in the act, and forces them into her lap on top of the boa. "There's no easy way to say this, but I'm sick."

"Sick?" Shannon leans in closer to Mom.

I'm frozen in place and can do nothing but stare, completely transfixed, as she continues.

She looks from Shannon to me. "Well, yes, pretty sick. Ye olde cancer." She gives a nervous giggle then falls serious again. "Actually," she says, raising her chin, "I'm dying."

CHAPTER 2

The house is quiet and dark. The kids have been put to bed, Patrick is passed out in our room, and Shannon and Thomas have retreated to their main suite. I'm alone in the sprawling family room, tucked under a blanket on the couch, still trying to make sense of my mother's news.

Sick.

Ovarian cancer.

Dying.

Goose bumps prickle across my skin, and I wrap the blanket tighter around me. I've always thought of my mother as strong and healthy. Sure, she partakes of the occasional drink or three, and she loves her chocolate, but other than that she has few vices. She goes for daily walks, she doesn't smoke, she's never been hospitalized. My mind rages against the fallacy of logic. How can my mother be dying?

"Kristin, is that you?" Mom's voice reaches me from the hallway. She's shed the boa now and is wearing only a full-length nightgown. It makes her look like a little girl.

"Hi, Mom."

She doesn't say anything else but comes over and sits down next to me. When she takes my hand, the first tears start burning behind my eyelids. Her warm palm is unfamiliar to my skin.

"None of that nonsense," she murmurs, squeezing my hand a little tighter.

I hear her swallow and do the same, forcing the lump down. "Are you sure there's nothing they can do?" I ask, my voice weak and desperate in the silence.

She shakes her head. "I already told you. Stage four is late in the game. It's spread... everywhere."

"But you could... There's treatment. I know there is. Maybe chemo or—"

"No." She pulls her hand away and forces me to meet her gaze. "I don't want to go that way. Months of agony for a sliver of a chance."

She leans back against the cushions, shrinks into them like a small child, except this birdlike figure has deep shadows lining her eyes, tight tendons protruding from her neck, and the skin on her hands is like crimped parchment. I know we only see each other a few times per year, but I can't believe I never noticed this before. It's like her mom veneer has come off, leaving a normal, vulnerable human being before me, and it's the worst epiphany I've ever had. I would take a million fights, put-downs, and disappointed sighs over this.

"Shannon said there are experimental treatments, and—"

"No." She closes her eyes. "It's not up for discussion. This is my life, and I've made my decision."

She pulls a pillow to her, and my chest tightens with something I'm not used to feeling around my mother. I know I should put up a fight—a good daughter would—but this is the longest uninterrupted time she and I have spent together alone since I lived at home. I don't know what words to use with her or even what language to speak to make myself understood. I'm in uncharted territory, and from her guarded stance, I can tell I'm not the only one who's wary of overstepping.

Somewhere inside my head a whooshing sound ebbs and flows. *Like our sprinkler when we were growing up.* Mom used to get up extra early during the summer to turn on the water before heading to one of her many jobs. I would lie in bed and listen to it move back and forth until the sun peeked through my curtains. Our house wasn't much, but the yard was always the greenest on the block. I haven't thought of this in years.

"Mom."

She opens her eyes again.

"How long?"

The tip of her nose reddens, and she clears her throat. "Four to six months is what they said."

The air escapes me. "Four..." I pause and focus my gaze on one of Shannon's family portraits on the wall. She'll be gone before the baby is even born. *My baby won't have a grandmother.* It's a while before I think my voice will carry again. "And with treatment? Maybe you'd have longer. A year at least, or more?"

Her jaw sets. "I'm. Not. Doing. Treatment. At this point it would only delay the inevitable. Now, I don't want to talk about it anymore."

The finality of her words hangs and swells in the air between us, accompanied only by the occasional thump of the air ducts in the basement. The blanket is too heavy, suffocating me, and I throw it aside then tilt my head back against the cushion and look at her.

Mom's eyes are pale-gray wells in the dim light. A small tilt flutters across her lips as if to take the edge off her words. "It'll be okay," she says.

I scoff. "How is you dying okay?"

She draws in a long breath. "Yes, it fucking sucks, doesn't it?"

My eyebrows jolt up. I don't think I've ever heard her swear before.

She smirks, clearly satisfied at my scandalized expression. "In life you pick your battles. I know one I can't win when I see it."

At this seeming capitulation, a poem by Dylan Thomas I teach in my sophomore literature class forces its way into my head about raging against the dying of the light instead of going gently into the good night.

She's not raging.

Maybe it's not as bad as it seems, a small voice in my head says. If it was, surely she would tear up heaven and hell. Maybe she'll get better. Doctors can be wrong. Shannon will have her get a second opinion, and Mom will be proven right in one thing at least—it'll be okay.

"So what happens now?" I ask, having reasoned myself into a safe place.

"Now?" She stretches, yawns. "We'll go to bed, have a good night's sleep. Tomorrow is another day. Oh, and you need to ask Patrick to marry you." The clever gleam in her eyes I've come to know so intimately over the years is back.

I almost laugh with relief. She's still my mother. I do an exaggerated eye roll because that's my part to play, and maybe she'll appreciate us falling back into our normal patterns as much as I do after the upheaval of the evening. Her mouth turns down in instant disapproval.

"I'm not joking, Kristin. I'll be damned if you're still alone when I go."

I throw my hands up. "I'm not talking about this now."

"Don't you want more for yourself?"

"I said I don't want to talk about it." I send her a warning look, willing her to stand down.

A voice from the stairwell saves me. "You're still up?"

It's Shannon in her matching pajama and robe set. She pads down the stairs and cinches the belt tight around her waist before she sits down in one of the wingback chairs across from the couch. Her eyes are still red rimmed from earlier. "I thought I heard voices. Have you been down here long?"

"Long enough." Mom yawns again. "Talk some sense into your sister, will you? I'm going to bed." She pushes herself off the cushion.

"What was that about?" Shannon asks when Mom has disappeared into the darkness of the second floor.

"Nothing." I rub my eyes until they hurt then face her. She's inherited Mom's penetrating gaze and has it cranked to high on me.

"More of the same? No treatment?"

Sure, that's all. I nod.

She lets out a low "hmm" but doesn't say anything else. I don't speak either, and together we let the silence envelop us.

"Ice cream?" she asks in a strained voice just as the lump in my throat threatens to burst.

"Please."

She is gone and back in less than a minute, carrying two pints of Moose Tracks. She hands me one and sits down next to me.

"What are we going to do?" I ask between spoonfuls. "Mom is—"

"I know."

"And I'm—" I want to say *pregnant*, but choke on the word. The thought of Patrick looms heavy in my heart. If I break up with him now, the baby will have neither father nor grandmother.

"I'm not ready either." Shannon stabs the tip of her spoon into the carton.

I rub at my brows and stretch out my legs on the low coffee table. "Tell me you already have a plan."

Shannon gives my woolly-socked feet a dirty look but doesn't comment on them. "Well, yeah. Obviously, she'll move in with us. That's a given. She can't stay in Rockford. It's too far from both of us, but between Thomas's practice, my work, and the kids' activities, I won't always be able to be here. You really need to take a greater interest in her, Kris. You know, the time she has left." Her voice cracks, and reality comes crashing back.

There is only one problem. "She doesn't want my help. I'm not you."

Shannon scoffs. "That's ridiculous."

"Is it?" *Shannon, help me find a dress to wear. Shannon, send me the recipe for that apple pie. Shannon, can you help with my tax return? Shannon, set me up with your hairdresser. Shannon, Shannon, Shannon.* Shannon can do no wrong in our mother's eyes. She was a happy, popular child, a happy, popular teenager, and is now a happy, popular adult with the kind of all-American life Mom always wanted.

"Just because she doesn't approve of your living situation doesn't mean she doesn't want you around."

I roll my eyes. "You make it sound like I'm some sort of a degenerate."

"You know what I mean."

I do know. I also feel like being difficult.

"Kris, come on."

"Fine. Sorry. But don't be mad at me if she turns me away. What do you want me to do?"

"Um... every other weekend?" She squints, as if bracing for my reaction.

I bolt upright. "You're out of your mind. I can't—" Before the words are out of my mouth, I stop myself, a deep burn flushing my face. Whatever objections I might have had in the past no longer apply. In a calmer voice I say, "Won't it be unsafe for her to drive back and forth in her condition?"

Shannon smacks her lips in disapproval. "What I meant was, you would come here."

"Every other weekend?"

"That's what I said."

My palms start to sweat, and I wipe them on my thighs. That's a lot of traveling, too many miles of road to cover for my taste. The more you drive, the likelier you are to become a victim of pileups or road pirates or hydroplaning. What if the AC dies or I forget my cell phone at home and get stranded or there's a tornado? Oh, I really, *really* don't want to. But how can I not? She's my mother. Surely I should be able to overcome whatever small discomforts come my way to help ease her much bigger one. As her daughter, do I not owe that to her for, if nothing else, giving me life?

I draw in a deep breath. "Okay."

"I know you and Mom have your differences, but it's time to step up. What's it going to take for you to understand that? I can't do everything myself and—" Shannon pauses, her eyes darting to mine. "What did you say?"

"I said okay. You're right. It shouldn't all be on you."

Her brows knit. "And you're fine with it?"

"I didn't say that, but I'll give it a go. For her."

"What about Patrick?"

"What about him?"

"Will he mind you going?"

Will he mind? I glance toward the stairs and realize I'm not sure. I suppose it's entirely possible he, too, has felt the strain of time on our relationship, only I haven't considered it before.

"Don't worry about it," I say. "Just let me know when you want me here."

"Wow." She relaxes into her seat.

"You're taking her to the doctor, though, right?"

"Of course, that's a given. I'll make her get a second opinion if it's the last thing I do, but you know Mom. Once she makes her mind up about something..."

It's true. In a battle of wills, Mom is the undefeated champion.

"Do you remember when Mike Benanti asked me to prom senior year, and she told him I couldn't go if he didn't also get a date for you?" Shannon giggles at the memory.

"How can I forget? You refused to eat for a week and made life hell for all of us."

"I snuck food at night when I thought you were sleeping. Later I found out Mom had deliberately stocked the pantry with my favorite snacks. She knew I was full of it."

"Lucky Mike." I smirk at her, but she ignores me.

"What was his brother's name again who you went with?"

I search my memory for the short freshman who'd escorted me into the den of depravity that was the school gym. "Angelo, I think."

Shannon's eyes widen. "Oh my God, really? Michael and Angelo. Michelangelo. Are you serious?"

My lips twitch then burst wide. It feels odd after tonight. "I guess, yeah."

"Man, some parents..."

I quirk a brow at her. "You should talk. You almost named Zach *Zebulon*."

She shudders. "That was Thomas. I made him see sense, thank goodness."

For a few minutes we lapse again into silence, focused only on the softening ice cream and the ghosts of the past.

"I didn't want to go, you know," I say when I can't eat anymore. "To prom."

An odd expression comes over Shannon, and for a moment I think she's going to scold me for making her go through with the hunger strike for no good reason. Instead, she folds one leg underneath her and says, "That's not what your journal said."

The words come out so quietly that at first I think I must have heard her wrong, but the guilt is unmistakable on her face.

The muscles down my spine tense. "You read my journal?"

"Only the one time."

I'm afraid to ask what part she read, but since she's not meeting my eye, I think I already know the answer.

"It was an innocent teenage crush," I say, my hand skimming across my mouth and settling underneath my chin. The apparition of my high school bestie, Alice, flitters through my peripheral mind. Asking *her* to prom was unfortunately not an option. "Nothing ever happened."

Shannon finally looks up. "Did you ever tell her how you felt about her?" Her voice is stronger now, laced with curiosity.

"No, we lost touch after graduation. She went to Stanford, I think, and I— It was stupid, anyway." I put my empty carton and spoon on the side table. "Do we have to talk about this? Don't we have more important things to deal with?"

"So you've never since had feelings for—"

I silence her with a glower she knows to heed. "It was a long time ago."

"Mm-hmm."

"And how about 'Sorry I went through your stuff, Kris'?" I toss a pillow her way to lighten the mood and steer us off this path I never intended to go down.

She offers half a smile. "I am sorry. I promise." She clutches the pillow close to her and rests her chin on it.

We talk a little while longer before Shannon heads back to bed, but as soon as I'm alone again, panic sets in. I just committed to driving to Wisconsin every other weekend to be in close proximity to my mother and sister. I moved out on my own my senior year in high school for a reason—to get away from the drama, to not constantly feel like the third wheel, and to not incite in Mom that singular look of displeasure mingled with bafflement she had reserved solely for me. What if I make things worse? Make *her* worse.

I stay on the couch with my thoughts until morning, only drifting into a fitful rest right before dawn. When I wake up, I am still none the wiser.

CHAPTER 3

My cat, Morrison, greets us when we finally get home late afternoon the next day after almost four hours on the road through the flat Illinois countryside. The muscles in my back are like tense coils, my mind drained from being in the midst of moving traffic for so long with no distractions. Patrick is never good company when he's hungover.

As soon as we step in the door, he makes himself scarce in the guest room that doubles as a game den of our duplex.

"What about the bags?" I call after him.

"I'll get them later."

With a throaty hiss, I head back to the car and grab them both. I consider leaving his behind, but wouldn't it be typical if there was a car prowl tonight and someone took it? You can never be too sure. I pick up my bag to bring it to the bedroom, leaving his on the hallway floor. I give it a small kick for good measure and take disproportionate pleasure in seeing it tip over. "You're welcome," I mutter.

I feed Morrison, who magnanimously lets me sit with him while he eats, and then I heat up a slice of the leftover spinach-and-feta quiche Shannon insisted I bring home. Occasional bursts of TV gunfire erupt from the closed door down the hall to accompany my meal. The sound nags me even more than usual today. I want to talk to Patrick about Mom, but his seeming indifference to her news doesn't exactly invite conversation.

I look around the small pantry-less kitchen and try to picture it the way Shannon's was this morning. Scents of coffee, pancakes, bacon, eggs—Thomas was at the griddle, aka the indoor grill, of course—the kids running around in their pajamas, Lucky on their trail, Mom reading a review of a new art gallery aloud to anyone willing to listen. To look at her, you would never know anything was amiss, and when Shannon started fluttering about her, damp eyed and doting, Mom was quick to put an end to it with a sharp "I'm not on my last leg yet, girl."

By comparison, my kitchen is so quiet, so lifeless. Gray linoleum floors, IKEA cabinets, a single pot of basil on the windowsill.

"Pat," I call out.

No answer.

"Patrick?"

The volume on the TV grows more faint.

"Did you say something?" he shouts.

I walk down the hallway to the closed door.

"Kris?" he calls again.

I push the door ajar. "I was wondering if you want some quiche. Join me in the kitchen?"

"Oh." He rubs a hand over his face. "I'm kind of in the middle of something." His finger already hovers over the volume button on the remote, ready to turn the sound back up.

I tilt my head. "Can't you do that after? Come hang out."

His gaze cuts from me to the screen and back, then he reluctantly places the controller on the armrest. "Fine. Ten minutes."

Win!

"How much do you want?" I ask once he's seated at the table. I measure out a piece of cold quiche with the knife. "Is this good?"

"A bit more."

I heat up his food and grab him a beer from the fridge.

"Thanks." He takes a deep swig and lets out a low belch. "That hit the spot."

I let him finish a few bites before I start talking. "I can't believe Mom has cancer."

He shovels another forkful into his mouth. "Yeah. That's rough." He reaches out a hand and strokes the back of mine before returning to his food. "You holding up all right?"

I blink at him, not having expected the question. "I guess. Sort of. Do you think it's weird that I'm not more"—I circle my hands in front of me in search of the right word—"I don't know. I feel like I should be crying all the time or something. I mean, she's my *mother*. It doesn't seem real."

Patrick polishes off the last bite on his plate and sits back, beer in hand. "Yeah, I know what you mean. When my grandpa had his heart attack, I was the same way." He bobs his head several times, drinks.

I cross my arms over my chest. "Weren't you eleven, and he survived? That's not the same thing."

"Just saying. If you ask me, there's nothing wrong with *not* being emotional."

My skin heats. I have a sip of my water and another bite of my quiche. The food has lost its flavor, but I force it down. "Anyway, I'm going to be helping Shannon take care of her." I launch into the details of her plan to get it out of the way.

Patrick listens until I'm finished, but when he speaks it's as if the lid has come off a pressure cooker. The disbelief in his voice borders on offensive. "You're going to drive three hours there and three hours back, by yourself, every other weekend? You hate driving. And what about me? 'Cause don't think I'll be tagging along."

There's a spinach leaf stuck in the corner of his mouth, and I focus on that to keep from raising my voice. "Believe me, this is not my first choice. But she's my mother."

"You don't even like her." He takes a swig of his drink. "This will never work."

"Thanks for the confidence."

He scoffs. "You barely tolerate each other on a good day. What makes you think this will be different?"

"I'll make it different. I have to. She's dying." I will my voice to hold and cross my fingers that I'm right. I think I read somewhere that people see things more clearly when they are close to death, that they feel a need for reconciliation. Who knows? Maybe this will bring us closer.

Patrick's expression softens, and he puts his beer down. "I know, and I'm sorry about that. Is this the answer though? Shannon and Thomas can manage, can't they? Your mom is not going to want to be babysat twenty-four seven, and if you're gone on the weekends, I'll never see you."

"*You're* gone on the weekends," I say, thinking of his fantasy football league. "What's the difference?"

"Not all day, and I like coming home to you."

"You like me waiting around for you, you mean." Appetite now completely gone, I push the plate aside. My tongue tastes oddly metallic.

"What? No, don't twist my words." He leans forward across the table. "Think about it, okay? You don't have to commit to anything. See how it goes. Play it by ear."

I'm about to respond when I feel bile rise in my throat, and before I know what's happening, I'm rushing to the bathroom and barely making it to the toilet in time. When I'm done, I sit against the shower stall and wipe my eyes. I'm out of breath, and my stomach is cramping.

Patrick hovers right outside the open door, concern and disgust warring on his face. He's a major germophobe.

"You all right there?" he asks.

I close my eyes and tilt my head all the way back against the cool tile. "Fine," I say.

"What happened?"

I award him a glare. "I threw up. Probably something going around," I add before he can ask any other questions. "Can you get me a glass of water?"

He scurries off and returns with a glass that he hands me from as great a distance as possible.

"Thanks." I take several deep gulps before getting off the floor. Patrick still watches me, and for some reason, this remote act of observation rubs me the wrong way. A helping hand would be nice, a reassuring stroke on the back. He offers nothing, just stands there while I brush my teeth.

"I'm going to bed," I say when I'm done and push past him.

"What about this whole thing with your mom?" he calls after me down the hallway.

"Whatever." I slam the door to our bedroom shut.

He doesn't come after me, and a few minutes later I hear the game start up again in the other room. I'm not ashamed to admit I'm relieved to be alone. The barfing has set my thoughts on a completely different track because I was under the impression morning sickness, by definition, is supposed to only happen in the morning. I open my laptop and do a search for it, from which I resurface, educated and appalled, thirty minutes later. There's so much I don't know. Such a scary world out there.

CHAPTER 4

At the end of the week, I'm in the bathroom in the teachers' lounge because I overslept and didn't have time to do much other than wash my face and grab a protein bar from my pitiful pantry. Normally, Patrick wakes me up in the mornings, but he's been in Milwaukee for work since Monday, and the snooze button is my enemy.

I'm applying mascara like a ten-year-old, clumps everywhere, and I'm not sure why I'm even bothering considering how, in the last few days, the ice wall inside me has somehow magically melted, and I now break into tears at every thought even remotely related to my mother or Patrick or the baby. In fact, at the mere thought of crying, I have to pinch myself hard to make my tear ducts cease and desist.

My colleague, partner-in-crime, and confidant, Aimee, saves me from a self-inflicted bruise as she pushes open the door and enters, whistling the *Dora* theme song.

"Hey," she says, yawning with exaggerated flair. "Happy Friday."

"Ditto." I lean in to study my skin closer in the mirror. I need to buy some concealer for these circles under my eyes or people will soon start running away from me, fearing the zombie apocalypse is here.

Aimee disappears into a stall, and I glance at her sneakers underneath the door. Someone has doodled blue and red crayon all over one of them. The sight is the final straw that breaks my resolve not to tell anyone about the baby until Patrick knows.

"Hey, Aimee," I stage-whisper through the door even though no one else is around.

"Yeah?"

"I need to tell you something."

"Can you wait until I'm done peeing?"

I bite my lip. "Sorry." I run the faucet to give her some privacy.

"Everything okay?" she asks as soon as she comes back out.

"Mm-hmm." My lips tug upward, and when I catch a glance of myself in the mirror again, the zombie has turned even more terrifying with its face flushed and a wild gleam in its eyes. "I'm pregnant." It bubbles out of me before I can even attempt to stop it, and my grin gets wider at hearing the words out loud. "I'm going to have a baby."

Aimee shrieks then clasps a hand over her mouth. "Oh, Kris!" She pulls me into a hug. "That's awesome."

"Right?" I knew she would approve. "It is, isn't it?"

"Of course. Oh, so many questions! How far along are you?"

I laugh. "I don't know exactly. About eight weeks, I think." Knowing there were only so many weekend nights Patrick was home in March narrows the window of opportunity.

"Doesn't matter. You're pregnant!" She hugs me again. "You must be so excited. What does Patrick think?"

I free myself from the embrace. "Um…"

Her expression falters. "He doesn't know? You haven't told him?"

I squirm under her inquisitiveness. "Well, technically, no."

"Technically?"

"It's complicated."

Her eyes narrow. "You *were* trying, though, right?"

"Well…" Oh, I should have never told her. What was I thinking? My lower lip starts trembling. "It was an accident," I admit. "We were a bit drunk and forgot the… the thing. But it could be a good thing. I think. Maybe a sign? I want a family. I want to be a mom." The first tear spills over and runs down my cheek.

Aimee makes hushing noises as I cry into her shoulder. I knew the mascara was a bad move. Now it will be stuck to her shirt the rest of the day.

"Of course you do," she coos. "You'll be a great mom."

"Will I?" I pull away and wipe my nose on my sleeve. "Because right now I'm not so sure. I mean, you heard—I haven't even told the dad."

"Are you afraid he doesn't want the same thing?"

My mind goes blank. Then the tears start up again. "I am now!"

Aimee hands me a paper towel and pats my back as I let it all out. "It'll be fine," she says. "That time at my house he'd had a few drinks. I'm sure he didn't *really* mean having kids would be the end of the world. Just tell him."

I dab at my cheeks, though it's a vain gesture. "Right." I can feel her watching me as I open the faucet and splash water on my face. The last remnants of my makeup swirl down the drain in a slow spiral.

"There's more, isn't there?" Aimee hands me another paper towel, eyes not leaving me.

I lean back against the sink, ball up the paper, and toss it into the garbage can.

"Are you worried about the baby? Because that's perfectly normal."

My face contorts into a grimace as new tears spring forth.

Aimee immediately pulls me to her again. "What's wrong? You're scaring me." She strokes my back until I calm down then watches as I clean up for the second time. "Tell me what's going on. Is it Patrick?"

I turn to her with a deep sigh of resignation. "I... I don't think I love him anymore." My voice trembles, and a chill runs through me upon hearing the words out loud. "But how can I leave him when I'm about to have his baby?"

Aimee is quiet for some time. "How long have we known each other?" she asks eventually.

I count in my head. "About five years."

"Five years. And we're good friends. You know I love you, I'm here for you, and I only want what's best for you, right?"

Unsure where she's going with this, I give her a shaky nod.

She cocks her head to the side on an exhale. "Maybe the question isn't *How can you possibly leave him now?* If you don't love him like you say, maybe the question is *How can you* not *leave him?*"

I start at her words, and she continues before I can respond.

"Don't you owe it to yourself and your baby to be happy?"

"But—"

"Do you see yourself happy with Patrick?"

My jaw clenches, Mom's words echoing in my mind. "We've been together a long time—long enough to get married. We live together, I'm expecting his child, and I've seen how hard it was for Mom to be a single parent. Why would I do that to myself?"

"But are you *happy*?" Aimee raises her hands in exasperation. "I'm not telling you what to do, but as your friend, I'm not going to stay quiet when I think you're headed toward a mistake. You told me a minute ago you don't love him anymore."

"Who needs love?" I spit out. "Maybe love isn't for everyone." I pull off a paper towel from the dispenser and blow my nose with a loud honk, accompanied by the first bell.

"You don't believe that."

A tired laugh escapes me. "I don't know what I believe. Sorry I brought this up. I have to get to class." I hoist my bag onto my shoulder and move past Aimee to the door. She doesn't try to stop me, but I can feel her gaze burn at my neck until I'm out of sight.

Ugh, sometimes insightful friends can be such a pain.

Aimee and I both teach English Language Arts and Social Studies at McKellan High in Rosemont. I've been here for over ten years, so I mostly know what I'm doing. This year, I'm also the assistant coach for the swim team, which is laughable because I sink like a rock as soon as my feet don't touch the bottom. Aimee is the head coach, and I'm doing it because she asked me. Little do the swimmers know my preferred stroke is dog paddle.

Today, I am less than a stellar educator, though. The morning's conversation with Aimee looms over me like a wet woolen blanket through *Animal Farm* and *Maus*, argumentative essays and sonnets, and not even Ben Roman using the trash bin as a basketball hoop provokes enough of a reaction in me to get out from under the weighty shroud.

I don't know what to do.

If I break up with Patrick, I'll be a single parent and quite possibly send my mother to an earlier grave than she's slated for. If I don't, I have to keep living with him. Possibly forever. As much as I don't want to admit it, Aimee is right. I'm not happy with him. And I don't think he's happy with me.

As soon as the final bell rings, I'm out the door and into my car, forehead against the steering wheel. I need a plan or a sign or something.

Voices nearby make me straighten. I place a hand on my still-flattish belly and sit like that for a moment, focusing all my attention inward on what's going on in there. Will I be able to give the little grain what it needs? How am I going to cope? There is so much to do—make a doctor's appointment, plan a nursery, pick up prenatal vitamins, shop for maternity clothes, and probably put daily walks on my schedule so I can keep up with the baby once it's born. I should just tell Pat tonight when he gets home. Maybe a joint effort is what we need to make it through our slump.

Yes, I decide, the baby could be the answer. Tonight I'll make his favorite, spaghetti Bolognese, open a bottle of Shiraz, and... I give myself a mental slap. No more wine. In fact, no more spirits at all, no smelly cheese, no sushi, no—what else? I'd better ask Aimee. So much to think of.

At least I have a plan, and with renewed spirits I start the car and head home.

CHAPTER 5

I know as soon as I put the key in the lock, the evening will not turn out as I imagined. I shouldn't be surprised; I'm thirty-five and should know by now that human plans are there but for the amusement of whatever higher powers watch over us. Not to mention it's Friday the thirteenth. So at the sight of two extra pairs of shoes in the hallway, I merely sigh.

A game is on the TV in the living room, and as I enter the kitchen with my grocery bags, three male groans arise in disapproval of whatever play just occurred. I shove aside an empty pizza box that's been left on the counter to make room.

"Kris, is that you?" Patrick calls.

I walk into the hallway and peer around the corner. "It's me. Hi, guys, how's it going?"

Rashid and Jared—Patrick's best buds since college—wave at me in greeting, but Patrick's eyes are glued to the screen, where someone is about to attempt a field goal.

"What time did you get back?" I ask. Knowing Milwaukee is almost two hours away, I wasn't expecting him until later.

Patrick glances my way then returns his gaze to the screen. "About an hour ago. The power went out at the office, so they sent us home."

"Nice." I shrug out of my jacket and fold it over my arm. "How was your week?"

"Fine. Hey, do we have any more beer in the garage?"

My jaw sets at the curt response, and my fingers curl. I give him another chance to look up, but when he doesn't, I stomp back to the kitchen without answering. To my great annoyance new tears burn behind my eyelids, and that only fuels my anger. How about *I've missed you, Kris? How was your week, Kris? Sorry I'm a selfish asshole, Kris.* When my toe catches on one of the kitchen chairs, I kick it over with what can only be described as a roar, and it makes a lot more noise than I expect.

Patrick comes through the door, a bewildered look on his face. "What's going on? Are you okay?"

I want to yell at him, tell him how stupid his sports are, that he could stand to drink less for his health, and what a horrible father he'll make.

"I'm fine," I say instead. "I wasn't looking. Chair got in the way."

"Oh." His eyes narrow, and for a moment I think he's going to come to me, ask what's really wrong, but then it passes, and he turns to leave. "Your mother called, by the way," he says, walking away. "She said to give her a ring."

The Bolognese ingredients taunt me from the bags on the floor. A can of pasta sauce has rolled out and lodged itself under a cabinet. Looks like our life-changing evening is on hold.

"You girls are high if you think I'm going to come live with you" is how my mother greets me when I call. "Your sister has called me every day this week and only stopped when I threatened to disown her. You know what she did? She had Hayley call instead."

Judging by her tone, this is an infraction of unspeakable gravity, and I can tell she wants me to agree. I don't. In fact, I don't say anything, which is a trick I've learned with age. Don't speak until you know what kind of trap she's prepared. If only my poor teenage self had been so wise.

"Kristin?" she asks. "Are you there?"

"Mm-hmm." I press my lips together.

"Oh good. I thought your phone ran out of battery again."

I don't remind her I'm calling from my landline. The battery excuse is a handy one to have up my sleeve.

"Nope," I say.

"So, Shannon tells me I'm moving in with her and that you are going to help 'take care of me' every other weekend. Really, Kristin, what were you girls thinking?"

I can't keep silent any longer, not with a direct question hanging in the air. Instead, I do the second-best thing and throw my sister under the bus. She'll survive. She always does.

"I thought Shannon had talked to you already. It was her idea."

"Well, of course it was." Mom scoffs. "It would be quite out of character for you."

Ouch.

"I have a home where I'm perfectly comfortable, thank you very much. I have my friends here and my babies. Thomas is so allergic."

I'm pretty sure the invitation to stay with them did not extend to her three Persian cats, but I keep that to myself.

"You have to talk some sense into her. I don't need her help. And who would water my plants?"

"But Mom," I say, before I can stop myself. "You might need *some* help. Won't there be lots of doctor's appointments and stuff? And what about when you—" Oh, dangerous ground. How do I put this? "Um, later on. You feel strong now, but that could possibly change. Right?"

She's quiet for so long I'm starting to think *she's* hung up on *me*. She lets out a sharp breath and a hum. "I don't want to talk about it," she says. "Not right now."

"Okay." I fiddle with a spoon that's been forgotten on the kitchen table while I wait for her to continue. "Why not?"

"I'm not ready for that." Her voice is softer than before. "Maybe later. Much later."

Again, that lump in my throat. Pregnancy hormones are no joke. I come close to telling her about the baby-grain, about becoming a grandmother, but choke on the words as the image of a shared future goes up in smoke. Shannon's second set of doctors confirmed the diagnosis, so unless they are all wrong, Mom won't be here for that—no first Christmas, no birthdays, no getting spoiled at Nana's house. A sob escapes my lips then another one, louder this time. I cover the receiver with one hand to mute the sounds, but she's on to me.

"Do *not* cry," she says, her voice back to stern normal. "No tears. Seventy years is a long enough life, and I plan to go out with a bang. In fact, I just read you can have your ashes turned into fireworks, and I think I might do that."

I laugh between the tears because it's so her. Always marching to the flashy beat of her own drum. It's not easy, having that kind of personality for a mom, especially since there was never a dad in the picture to balance her out, but I must respect her, nonetheless. She's always been herself, regardless of others.

"Sounds good," I say. "But promise to let us know if there's anything we can do."

"Ugh, everyone's so sappy today. Now, before I change my mind..." Her voice trails off.

"What?"

"I do have a small favor to ask of you."

"Of me?"

"That's what I said." Her tone is snappy again, and I welcome it. "I want you to help do my bucket list."

"Your what?"

"My bucket list." She says it with exaggerated patience. "You know, things I always imagined doing before I died, places I want to see. It seems like I've run out of time, so we are going to do them together."

I laugh. A big snorting guffaw. "Yeah, great idea." I adjust the pillow behind my back.

"I think so. I can't ask Shannon, can I? What with her kids and all. And my doctors have made it clear the way I'm feeling right now— Well, let's just say my sell-by date is fast approaching. You're my only option."

"Mom." I close my eyes and rub two fingers into the sockets. "You are out of your mind."

"How is that? Tell me."

"Well, first of all I can't afford going anywhere on a teacher's salary."

"I'll pay for everything. I'm not cruel."

"I have work."

"We'll go during summer break."

Grasping for straws, I blurt, "Patrick won't have time off."

She scoffs. "Patrick's not invited. What else?"

I frown. "What do you mean he's not invited?"

"I'm asking you, Kristin, to do this with me. Not the two of you." Then she mumbles, "Of course Patrick doesn't have time. He'd miss all the silly boy games he plays."

I'm taken aback by her tone, and so, it appears, is she because she lets out a slight cough as if to smooth over her words. "I want you to do it by yourself, that's all."

No, not so fast. "I thought you liked Patrick. You've been pushing for us to get married like it's an Olympic sport."

She clicks her tongue then says with an air of dismissal, "Oh, he's nice enough. You can still get married after." There's a pause on the line. "So, we've covered cost, work, and Patrick. What other arguments do you have that I can shoot down?"

I roll my eyes. "Mom, I'm not doing your bucket list with you."

"Why?"

"You know why."

"I know no such thing. This is your dying mother's last wish." She emphasizes each word. "You'd better not tell me it's because of your silly fear of traveling."

Her words echo on the line, leaving a suspended silence in their wake.

"Well..." I squeak.

"Kristin."

What am I to do? At the mere mention of traveling, I have started to sweat, and the butterflies in my stomach are waking up, warning of an imminent sprint to the bathroom. I don't travel. *I. Do. Not. Travel.* Heck, even driving the three hours to Shannon's house by myself is a stretch. I would do it if I had to, but I'm secretly relieved that the every-other-weekend scenario is out the window.

"I'm still waiting," she says, and I panic. At least that's my only excuse for saying what I say.

"I can't do it because I'm pregnant."

My sudden reveal hangs in the air between us for a long moment, and then my mother lets out a soft glottal sound I am not familiar with.

"You're pregnant?" she whispers.

I stutter something unintelligible, wishing I could take it back. This is bad. So, so bad. I might as well have shouted it from the rooftops.

"Oh, Kris. That's wonderful news. Not that it changes anything, but I'm very happy for you both. Surely now Patrick *must* propose."

I'm about to say something snarky about her wedding obsession when the implications of her words sink in. "What do you mean *it doesn't change anything*?" I ask. "Of course it does. I'm growing a human in my belly. I can't be gallivanting around the globe on some silly quest that—"

"Yes, yes, it's all very special. Do you know what I did the year I was pregnant with you girls?" She doesn't wait for me to respond. "Your father, of course, left at the first mention of a baby, so I moved from New York back to Illinois, worked three jobs, slept on a friend's couch for two months, fixed up the duplex I finally found to rent—including replacing some faulty wiring in the basement, might I add—enrolled in night school, and made all my doctor's appointments."

I know what comes next. My mother loves telling the story of my birth. Over the course of my thirty-five years, it has morphed and grown into a legend in its own right—the story of the story—and it doesn't matter how many times I ask her to please, for the love of all that's holy, not to tell it again, she always delivers. The twenty-seven hours of labor, up two from last year's twenty-five. The misplaced epidural, the drunk nurse, the broken tailbone, the pain, the agony, the torment. Oh, how she revels in its gore, in the horrified faces of her captive audience, be they Bunco ladies or school kids on a field trip. And that's not even mentioning the part about how my blood-curdling howl short-circuited the doctor's hearing aid and scared a second baby out of Mom's already fatigued uterus—because *that's* how twins are made.

Having heard this story many, *many* times before and knowing how it ends, I cut in the first chance I have.

"Okay, I get it."

"Do you?"

I glare at the ceiling. "It's still not going to happen."

She's quiet for a long time, and I hear a low rustling on the line as if she's folding up a piece of paper. Then she clears her throat and turns her voice as soft as silk. "Very well. Now, tell me more about my new grandbaby."

It's terrifying. To anyone who doesn't know her, it would appear she's given up, but I know better. I know this was only round one, and she'll strike again when I least expect it.

As if reading my mind, she says, "Oh, and I'm driving down there tomorrow, so we can talk then. I should be there around noon."

She does this all the time, announcing her plans without asking if it works for me.

My shoulders slump in defeat. "Will you be staying over?"

"Ha! Last time I slept in your guest bed, I couldn't walk for a week."

Always glad to know our hospitality is appreciated. "Okay, then. I'll see you tomorrow."

Like I thought—round two is imminent.

I wouldn't be surprised if the battle is already lost.

CHAPTER 6

"She wants you to do what?" Patrick's mouth is full of bacon he's temporarily stopped chewing.

"She wants me to complete her bucket list with her." I have a sip of my fruit-and-spinach smoothie, and my tongue curls. I hear leafy greens are baby-grain cocaine, so I'm all for incorporating them into my diet, but my taste buds are not quite on board.

Patrick cocks an eyebrow. "Right. She must be losing it."

I don't know what it is, but even though I essentially agree with him, his words make me put my glass down too hard on the table, the green liquid sloshing onto my hand. This could have made for a great start to a tirade about his lack of compassion, but instead I'm forced to get up and grab the paper towels. I glare at him while wiping my hand.

"What?" he asks, still chewing. I can see the mushy meat between his teeth.

"Close your mouth," I say under my breath.

"What was that?" *Chew, chew, chew.*

"I said, please fucking chew with your fucking mouth closed!" I yell, slamming my paper-wielding hand onto the wood surface. I'm breathing like a bull, but I'm not sure what to do next, having had little experience with rage up until this point in my life. I contemplate storming off, but in the time it takes me to do so, the anger drains out of me, and I sink back into my seat. "Sorry. A lot going on right now."

Patrick stares at me, his fork stuck in the air between his plate and his mouth.

"Really, I'm okay." I push a strand of hair out of my face.

He wipes his mouth on a napkin, not taking his eyes off me. "You sure?"

"Yup."

Patrick resumes his eating, if with tentative movements, now making a deliberate effort to only open his mouth enough to insert a forkful every now and then. It's oddly satisfying.

I stir what's left of my drink with the straw. "For the record, I don't think she's losing it. She's just being Mom."

"Is there a difference?" he asks under his breath.

"Hey!" I yell.

He startles and looks at me again like I'm a few bricks short of a pile. "What?"

"Do you have to say things like that?"

"Sorry," he grumbles. "But you told her no, right?"

I press my lips together for a beat but then concede. "Of course. Though I doubt she's given up."

He snickers and shakes his head. "You, traveling? With your hodophobia, you must admit it's a bit far-fetched."

Patrick is the only one who uses the real name for my fear of traveling—something he took up in our early days of dating when explaining to other people why we never did weekend getaways or vacations. I wish I knew where it came from, but I don't. Could be something scared me during a car ride when I was a baby or I saw a plane go up in flames on the news during my formative years. Could be I was born this way. It is what it is.

"I bet Shannon and Thomas would love to do it. Why doesn't she ask them?"

I smile sadly into my plate. "'Cause of the kids."

"Right." He scrapes the rest of the eggs from his plate with a piece of bread. "Man, when you have kids, that's basically it." He gets up and sets his dishes on the counter with a "This was delicious. Thanks, babes" then heads toward the bedroom.

I still have breakfast left, but I'm not hungry anymore. From my seat by the window, I can hear him go into the bathroom and turn on the faucet. He has a ten o'clock tee time with his buddies and a game to watch after, so I know I won't see him until later tonight. I look down at my stomach and set my fingers over my belly button. Aimee's voice echoes in my mind, "Don't you owe it to yourself and your baby to be happy?"

I wish it was that easy, but Shannon and I used to imagine a dad when we were kids, jealous of our friends who had them. So to choose going at this alone from the start is not as simple as acting on my feelings for Pat. It's about more than me right now.

Mom shows up promptly at midday, exiting her car with a scarf wrapped around her head like an old-time movie star even though she drives a beige Saturn.

"Hi there," she calls as if she's surprised to see me and didn't just drive here to do exactly that.

I head outside. I want to ask how she's feeling, but she's been firm on being done with that conversation, and I don't want to start a fight. Instead I say, "Everything go okay?"

"Never better. How is my grandbaby? Any morning sickness? Here, I brought us some sandwiches. It's important that you eat." She thrusts a take-out bag into my arms and walks past me indoors without waiting for an answer. Without hesitation, she grabs plates and napkins from my cabinets and places them on the table.

"Um, I'm good. We're good. What if I had prepared lunch for us?"

She stops what she's doing and looks at me. "Did you?"

I take a seat, unwrap the paper of my foot-long. "No." I have a swig of the pop she's opened for me. Aside from that one episode, I've had no more nausea. I could eat all day every day and still be hungry. "Thanks."

"Where's Pat?"

"Golfing."

"Oh, I was hoping to congratulate him in person."

I take a big bite of bread and turkey to avoid answering. She doesn't need to know I've yet to tell him. Warfare 101—don't give the enemy ammunition.

"The best venues book up years in advance, so let's hope he has something up his sleeve we don't know about. Preferably before you puff up."

I keep chewing, tuning her out as she regales me with plans for wedding cakes and bridesmaid dresses that don't end until Morrison enters the room, marches straight up to her, and rubs himself against her pants leg.

"Aw, that's a nice kitty," Mom coos, picking him up. He curls into a ball on her lap and starts purring, which I'm aware is perfectly normal cat behavior, except if I or anyone else did that to him, they'd be torn to shreds before they could say *claws*. I'm still staring at the pair of them in bafflement when, in the middle of a purr, I swear he opens one eye and winks at me. What a traitor.

We've both finished our food by now, and aside from Morrison's engine, the only other sound is the jackhammer ticking of Mom's old wristwatch. I shuffle my pop can around, waiting for her to bring up the list, but instead I'm met by her best impersonation of innocence—wide eyes, head tilted, and ill-hidden amusement playing on her lips.

"So," I say.

"So." Mom scratches Morrison behind the ear but keeps her gaze on me.

"Was there something else you wanted to talk to me about?"

"Like what?" Mom's smirk grows bigger.

This kind of power play is her lifeblood, only today my brain is too jumbled to make for a worthy adversary.

With a deep sigh, I hold out my hand across the table. "Give me the list."

She instantly lifts Morrison down, digs around in her purse, and produces a folded sheet from a striped notepad. "If you insist," she says, handing it to me.

"Don't think I'm agreeing to anything," I say, unfolding it. "I'm just curious."

"Mm-hmm." She leans forward, elbows on the table. "And what if I told you I asked someone else?"

My gaze jumps off the paper to meet hers. She has a decent poker face but one I've known for thirty-five years. There's no one else.

"Oh, that's fine." I adjust my own features. "I just wanted to know what was on it. No biggie."

"Ha!" My mother lets out a cackle so loud Morrison flees the room with a distraught *meow*. "You forget I gave you life. And with considerable effort, I might add."

Here we go again.

"Don't roll your eyes at me. Now read it. You know you want to. I'm going to make some tea."

While she busies herself by the stove, I do as I'm told. Some items are written in blue ink, some in green. The last one is in red and hastier penmanship.

To do before I die in any order:
1. Learn to do a handstand
2. See La Bohème *on stage*

3. Learn to knit
4. Get a tattoo
5. Climb the stairs of the Eiffel Tower
6. Do a ropes course
7. Paint the sunset at Butterfly Beach
8. Apologize to Bart
9. Have a painting displayed at the Louvre
10. Fall in love again
11. Ride a hot-air balloon

I set the list down on the table before me and stare blankly ahead. She truly is nuts and not only for asking me to do even two of the things on her list but for wanting to do them in the first place. Climbing the stairs of the Eiffel Tower? I'm pretty sure there are elevators. Ride a hot-air balloon? Ever hear of the Hindenburg disaster? And who the heck is Bart?

I read it through once more. When did she start this? And why hasn't she checked any items off? Question upon question builds in my mind, making me light-headed.

The sun has moved since we first sat down, and the rays tickle my cheek, their warmth settling me somewhat. Mom has found a packet of sugar cookies to go with the tea and sets a plate and a steaming mug in front of me. Without a word she flips open a cooking magazine from the stack at the end of the table and puts on her reading glasses. She stirs her tea to dissolve the honey I know she's added, eyes glued to the pages. With each exacting movement, she pushes my buttons a little further.

"Mom," I say when I can't take it anymore.

She finally looks up. "Huh?"

I hold up the list. "Can we talk about this?"

"It depends." She takes her glasses off. "Am I going to like what you have to say?"

"You mean, am I doing it? Of course not."

"Then I don't want to talk about it." She turns another page with demonstrative flair. Unable to think of another option, I snatch the magazine from her hands, surprising us both. I immediately apologize but don't give it back.

"When did you start the list?" I ask.

Her lips are set, and she glares at me. "Not important."

"Where's Butterfly Beach?"

No response.

"Have you been there before?"

She starts polishing her glasses with her shirt.

The juvenile inside my head jumps up and down, screaming profanities, but I silence it with a haughty look. Two can play at this game, and I've learned from the best.

"Fine." I make to leave the room. "I'll tell Pat you said hi. Have a nice drive back."

I reach the foyer before she asks where I'm going.

"I have errands to run. Grocery store. Make sure you lock up when you leave."

I'm about to open the door when she comes around the corner. "It's in California," she says. "I went there once in the seventies, and I haven't seen a sunset like it since."

I let go of the handle. We regard each other for a long while, a silent battle of willpower, that—holy smokes—I win.

"Don't go," she says. "I'll answer your questions if you stay." On some level, Mom must know the stakes in this little battle are higher for her. She's the one wanting something from me.

I pretend to think about it, but of course I stay. That plea in her voice is new and not a little soul crushing.

We sit down at the kitchen table again, and I put the list between us. "So?" I ask.

She reaches out and runs her finger along the edge of the paper. "What do you want to know?"

My mother stays until the sun starts setting, and this is what I learn: one, she has quite a few regrets; two, she's lost her marbles; three, that's it.

No, I jest.

In fact, as she's telling me about an undisclosed fear of heights, how she wishes she'd gone to Paris when she was younger, and about the girls who taunted her throughout middle school because she couldn't do a handstand, the 2D, child-approved version of her gradually expands and crystallizes into a real human being. I don't know why I've never truly asked about her life before, but if nothing else comes of this list, at least it's giving me a few stories to pass on to the baby-grain when he or she gets older.

The only item she refuses to discuss is Bart—whoever he is.

I try one more time when we're standing by her car and she's getting ready to leave. "Can you at least tell me what you need to apologize for?"

"You really want to know?" Mom opens the car door, but doesn't get in.

I pull my cardigan tighter around me. It's May 14, but summer is still a long time coming. The thermometer topped out at forty-eight degrees today. "I do."

"Tell you what." She pauses with her mouth half open as if about to let the words spill out, the crinkles by her eyes deepening. "You agree to do this for me, and I'll tell you everything." She pats the roof of her car twice then gets in the seat and pulls the door shut. Seconds later, she's speeding down the street.

I've been had. Again. Only this time, I don't mind. I haven't obsessed about Patrick in several hours. Perhaps helping Mom wouldn't be the worst decision I could make.

She's certainly given me something to think about.

CHAPTER 7

I get home from my Sunday-morning grocery run around noon the following day, my heart lighter than it's been in several days. I had a good night's sleep, the sun is shining, madeleine cookies were on sale, and for once Patrick and I have a whole afternoon home together.

"Pat?" I call toward the interior after I shed my jacket and shoes.

"In here," is his instant response from the living room.

I set the groceries away and go to find him. He's on the couch, and I place a kiss on his forehead from behind, to which he responds by patting me on the side of my head. A book is open in his lap, and a folder with papers spilling out of it sits on the table.

"What'cha doin'?" I ask, and plop down next to him.

"Oh, some business stuff," he says in a tone that usually means *nothing you need to worry about.*

The thing is, I really want to know.

Patrick and I met when he installed the new software for my school's computers almost two years ago, and after we shared a few laughs about our outdated system, he asked me out. I'd been single a long time and was tired of my daily after-work routine consisting of feeding the cat, feeding myself, watching TV, and going to bed. I said yes, we dated, then his lease was up, and it made sense that he move in with me. Maybe there were never fireworks and glitter, but we were pretty good. Solid. At least my daily after-work routine improved to include an exchange of words between humans and, despite what he said at Mom's birthday barbecue, the occasional horizontal samba. We used to have fun. We used to talk to each other. If I can get us back to doing that again, I *know* I can make it work.

"Tell me," I press on. "I feel like I haven't seen you since last weekend."

Patrick looks up, an amused squint in his eyes. "You're in a good mood today." He puts the book aside and grabs the folder. "Okay," he says. "I was going to surprise you, and it's still in the planning stages, but..." He holds up the front of the folder, which has a logo made up of a black square with what looks like a diving swallow cutting across it. "Jared is doing a start-up, and I'm thinking of joining him."

I lean in for a closer look. A business statement typed underneath the logo reads *Swallow's Nest Investment—Put Your Eggs in Our Basket*. I almost laugh out loud at the cheesy tagline but catch myself.

"I thought you had a full plate consulting. Will you have time for this too?"

He squirms a bit under my gaze. "Well," he says, putting the folder away. "If I do this, it will be instead of the firm."

My jaw drops. "Quit your job? But you like it there. And aren't you up for a promotion in the fall?"

He shrugs, and my good mood vanishes.

"You didn't think this was something we needed to talk about?"

"We're talking about it now, aren't we?"

"You know what I mean." I get up and pace a few steps away before turning. "Look, I know how close you and Jared are, but I read somewhere recently that ninety percent of start-ups fail within the first year."

"Gee, thanks for your support."

"All I ask is that you think this through."

"It's a solid plan."

"Still—"

"Like I said, nothing's for certain yet." His tone has a bite to it now, letting me know that as far as he is concerned, the conversation is over.

I put as much snark in my voice as I can. "Well, keep me posted then, I guess." I stalk off toward the kitchen, but a sudden urge forces me back. Perhaps it's hormones or maybe that I actually felt good today, ready to tell him my big news, and he managed to ruin it in all of five minutes. Whatever the reason, I can't keep my feelings contained. "You know what?" I snap. "It's always the same with you. We live together. We share expenses. Yet when it comes to major decisions like buying a new car, booking last-minute golf weekends, or, apparently, changing jobs, I'm always the last one to know." I catch my breath, adrenaline coursing through my system, and ignore both Patrick's widened eyes and the sting of my own hypocrisy in light of my still-secret belly boarder. "How about you include me in the decision-making process from time to time? I don't think that's too much to ask when what you're doing affects the both of us."

Patrick doesn't say a word. I raise my eyebrows to prompt a response and still get nothing but a deer in headlights. With a frustrated groan, I head back to the kitchen and start slamming pans around. A few minutes later, I hear the front door close.

I collapse at the table, my head in my hands. To say this day didn't go as planned is an understatement. *So much for reconnecting.* At that thought, my chest tightens further, and the sun disappears behind the clouds as if in agreement that things have taken a turn.

The expression on Patrick's face haunts me. He looked at me like he has no idea who I am anymore, like we're strangers to each other. What happened to breakfast in bed, mini-golf outings, and double features at the movies?

If all those things are truly lost, Aimee might be right.

To force my thoughts away from Pat, I spend the rest of the day submerged in grading and lesson plans. But later that night, when

I'm halfway into a dream, he comes home and curls up behind me in bed, his breath spiced with the tang of alcohol.

"I'm sorry," he whispers, wrapping an arm around me. "Let's talk tomorrow. I'll make it an early day."

And the shadow retreats a little to allow sleep to take over.

Monday afternoon I'm in the small office adjacent to the girls' locker room with Aimee after swim practice has ended. The swimmers have packed up and left, but a meet is coming up with two other high schools, and we still have to coordinate logistics and starts. Aimee has her feet up on a low filing cabinet and her hands at the back of her head. Her eyes are closed.

"So tired," she murmurs. "Just. Want. To. Sleep."

"Come on," I say. "We'll be done in ten minutes, then you can sleep."

She fakes a sob. "You don't get it. There *is* no sleep. Jack has another ear infection, and Lily just learned about the tooth fairy from this brat at preschool and is now terrified some little weirdo is going to fly through her window at night and steal her teeth."

"Sorry." I toss her a Starburst from my stash.

She straightens. "Oh, my hero." She chews the candy, stretches, then returns to her computer.

I watch her for a while, debating whether to tell her what I learned about the bucket list this past weekend. I've been dying to talk to someone about it all day since I didn't get a chance to with Patrick yesterday, but if she's too busy—

"What is it?" she asks, interrupting my thoughts. "I can hear your cogs turning. Pregnancy questions again?"

I *have* had a lot of those. "No, I saw my mom this weekend." I tell her about the list, Mom's request, and how nutty the whole thing is.

"You're thinking about it, though," she says when I finish talking.

"What? No."

She considers me and lets out an ambiguous "Hmm."

Instead of walking into that trap, I ask, "Do you have a bucket list?"

"Of course. Don't you?"

"No."

"Not that it's laminated or anything, but..." She starts counting off items on her fingers. "I want to see the Colosseum in Rome, I want to swim with dolphins, stay at a Catskills resort like in *Dirty Dancing*. Yes, I know it's not real and Patrick Swayze is no more, but still. Umm... Have sex in an elevator, eat lobster off the boat in Maine, and do a safari."

"Wow. You've clearly got that figured out."

"I have two kids under three. Lots of long nights breastfeeding the past few years, dreaming of a different life." She makes a face.

"You truly are a walking commercial for motherhood."

"Oh please. You know it's the best thing I've ever done. Two things can be true at once." She yawns. "So there's nothing you want to do?"

I consider this. "I'm sure there is. I just haven't thought about it."

"Maybe you should." She directs a pointed glance toward my belly.

"You're suggesting my life is about to end?"

"No. Only the current version of it."

"Killjoy." I throw a wadded-up paper at her. "What's wrong with my life now? Is it so hard to believe this"—I make a sweeping motion around me—"could be what I want?"

She squints at me. "This is your dream? Teaching high school, marrying Patrick, and having 2.3 kids and a dog, like your sister? Buying a house with a yard in the right suburb?"

"What if it is?"

"Have you talked to him yet?" she counters. She knows I haven't.

"I will." A vague flicker of guilt makes itself known in the most self-aware parts of my brain. "Tonight," I add when she opens her mouth as if to argue.

"If you say so." She gets up. "I've got to go. Will you call and confirm the bus? And turn off the lights when you leave?"

I tell her it's as good as done, and we say goodbye.

I stay in my seat a while longer, twirling a pen around my finger, thinking about her words. She's right. My life is about to change. I can't do anything about that. The life growing inside me is beyond my control. Is that the only change I'm capable of—passive and slow? Patrick certainly thinks so. Probably Mom and Shannon too.

For the umpteenth time since yesterday, I unfold the list and read through it, bullet point by bullet point. When I get to the end, I go back to the top. And that's when I have what will later be categorized as the Worst Idea Ever.

After confirming the bus, I grab my things and leave the office and the locker room behind. To get to the parking lot, I have to go through the gym, but today I stop in the huge open space, drop my things on the floor and take stock of the wall, my hands on my hips.

1. Learn to do a handstand

How hard can it be?

CHAPTER 8

Turns out even if you knew how to do handstands as an eight-year-old, chances are your thirty-five-year-old body won't respond to that move quite the way you once took for granted. If I had stopped to think, I might have realized there's a difference between resting fifty-five pounds on your hands and one hundred forty-five pounds, but did I stop? No. The first two kicks went all right, mainly because I couldn't quite get vertical, but on the third attempt I did and here I am, on my face in a pathetic heap on the floor. Pain shoots up my arm from where my wrist gave out, and I clasp it with my good hand. The room spins, and my skin goes clammy. *Useless*, a voice screams in my head. *You're useless, Kristin!*

When I'm confident I won't faint, I make my way out to the car and manage, somehow, to get home using only my right hand since the left wrist is now twice its normal size and an impressive ultramarine color.

Does it count as a handstand if it only lasts for two seconds? A pang of pure agony settles that question. Yes. I stood. On my hands. Hence, handstand.

I shuffle into the house with the sole focus of getting ice on my wrist, so I don't notice Pat's bag on the floor in the kitchen and almost fall flat on my face for the second time in an hour. I catch myself on a chair before reaching the floor but not without emitting a loud cry of pain. Within seconds, Patrick is there, a look of alarm on his face.

"What's going on? You okay?"

I still haven't managed to get to the ice and am getting increasingly aggravated by this turn of events. "Do I look okay?" I snarl, holding up my arm.

"Oh my God." Patrick rushes to my side and hovers, not sure where to touch me. "What can I do?"

"Ice. I need ice."

"Ice." He goes into project mode. It's a guy thing—something to do with clear objectives, target within reach, and immediate satisfaction upon completion. I can tell his brain is telling him to optimize his task because he rummages through the drawers for Ziploc bags and towels and asks me where the gauze is.

Not in the mood to be patient, I yell a little louder, "A fucking bag of peas will do!"

He takes a moment to pause what he's doing and looks at me. "I thought you wanted ice?"

I groan internally and clench my jaws together. "All I need is something cold to stem the swelling." Then I add, "Please."

I sink into a chair at the table, and, finally, he brings me what looks like an old bag of mixed stir-fry veggies. With a moan of relief, I wrap it around my wrist as best as I can. It's taken on an uncanny resemblance to an oversized plum.

"That does *not* look good," Pat says, stating the obvious. "What happened?"

"I tripped," I say, not looking up.

"I think it might be broken."

I don't disagree with him but close my eyes and let the cold seep into my throbbing skin.

"Urgent care is still open," he says. "Let's go."

Three people are ahead of us in line, but we don't have to wait long. The nurse is soft-spoken and efficient and takes my vitals with detached politeness before leaving us to get the doctor.

"Does it hurt?" Pat asks.

"Yup," I say, trying not to focus on the fact that I can feel my heartbeat in my hand.

"I bet it's a break," he says with too much enthusiasm for my taste, and I send him a murderous glance that goes unnoticed as the doctor enters.

She grins when she sees us as if we're old friends come to visit.

"I hear you had a fall." She sits down on a swiveling stool that she pulls close to my chair.

"Ahem, yes. At school. Work. I'm a teacher." As if that explains everything.

"Let's have a look, then." She reaches for my arm, prods the discolored flesh, and turns it back and forth a few times. To my relief the examination is swift, and before I can voice my agony, she announces, "Yep, we're going to need pictures."

I cradle my arm against my chest as we walk down the hall to the X-ray technician. Patrick puts his hand at the small of my back while we wait for the doctor to give the tech instructions. They huddle over a form with a drawing of an arm, and she marks what area she's most interested in. Then she signs the form and turns to me.

"We'll need you to fill out these." She hands me the form with the arm first, indicating where she needs my signature, then gives me the other. "And this one has the procedural information and your consent. Is there any chance you might be pregnant?"

Her question reverberates through my head. Everything stills around me, and a sort of sputtered breath struggles up my chest.

"No, we're not married," Patrick says. I suppose he thinks doing it out of wedlock is a handy prophylactic.

The doctor faces me, eyebrows raised in question, still with the form in hand, waiting for me to take it.

"Well," I say in an unsteady voice. I turn to meet Patrick's gaze. "Actually, I am."

Pat stares at me uncomprehendingly.

"What?" he asks, a low sound of amusement accentuating how ridiculous my words are.

"I've been meaning to tell you." I place my hand on his arm. "There hasn't been a good time."

"What?" he asks again, voice now completely devoid of humor. He shakes his head as if shrugging off water.

The doctor clears her throat and mumbles, "I think I'll give you two a moment." She and the tech retreat into an adjacent office.

"Surprise!" I say, trying to add some mirth to the weighty air around us.

"You're pregnant?" Two deep creases between Pat's brows suggest the cogs are still working hard behind his eyes. "When? How?"

"Well, I know you learned the *how* part a long time ago, but when—I'm thinking that last weekend in March. Remember, you had been out, you liked the red shirt I was wearing when you came home..."

"And now you're pregnant?" Finally, he unfreezes, both hands flying to his forehead, where they rub the spot above his eyebrows so hard I'm worried he's going to bruise himself. "I just—" He paces away from me then back again.

The doctor appears in the doorway, an apologetic grimace on her face. "I'm so sorry, but there are people in line. We need to get the X-ray done now."

My gaze lingers on Patrick's face before turning to her. "Of course." I jot down my signature on the two forms. "I'm ready."

"I'll be outside," Pat says, grim faced. Then he stalks off.

Pat opens the door to the car for me without a word. My tongue is dry and too thick, and I can't get a word out until we've driven several blocks.

"Pat," I start, but he silences me by holding his palm up like a stop sign. As if we're in elementary school. Or he's part of the Supremes.

He keeps his eyes fixed on the road straight ahead.

"Okay." My throat tightens further, and I look down at the bandaged appendage in my lap. My wrist has a bad sprain, and I'll need a brace for four weeks, but all in all not a worst-case scenario.

Patrick lets out a snort. "Of all the things," he mutters.

"I didn't mean for you to find out like that."

"Did you mean for me to find out at all?"

"Of course. Pat, come on."

Finally, he awards me a glance. "How long have you known?"

"Only a week." I place a hand on his shoulder. "You were gone with work, and then Mom, and— " *Ugh, I'm a terrible person.* "I'm really sorry."

He doesn't respond, but at least he doesn't dodge my hand.

We drive the rest of the way without speaking, and when we come to a stop in our driveway, he stays seated.

"I'm going out. Don't wait up," he says.

"Where to? Shouldn't we talk about this?"

"Just out. Not in the mood."

I wait a beat for more to follow, but when it doesn't, I close the passenger door, and he backs away.

As he disappears down the street, I fumble for my keys and head inside. I know I'm to blame, but I'm starting to add anger to the guilt and sadness I'm already feeling. No "How are you doing" or "Let me help you." A simple acknowledgment that we're in it together would have been nice. I'm willing to bet he's headed to Jared's for some beers and football, and I won't see him until tomorrow after work.

Crap, crap, crap.

After struggling to get my jacket off, I pour myself a glass of water in the kitchen before I settle in on the couch under a blanket. Morrison surveys me from across the room but makes no move to approach even though I call for him in my nicest kitty voice. I swear, sometimes I think he's been sent here to observe and report back. I imagine his superiors, whoever they are, would be less than riveted by what he has to say, though, so I stick my tongue out at him, just to give the poor feline something to record. *"Yes, Master, it was most peculiar. Yes, the tongue. In my general direction."* Morrison speaks with a British accent, as do most cats.

To my immense satisfaction, I win our little staring contest, and when Morrison sneaks away, I pick up my phone and scroll through my emails. There's nothing of interest. On impulse, I pull up a blank message to Pat and contemplate the screen. Maybe it's digital courage, but I am suddenly overcome with resentfulness at his reaction. Before good judgment can prevail, I type: *Are you not happy about it at all?* It goes through, and I wait for the rippling dots to appear that would indicate he's responding. They don't.

Dammit! I toss my phone to the other end of the couch.

I let out a yelp when Morrison jumps down from the shelf behind the couch and lands next to me. He pushes up against me and meows loudly, butting his head into my armpit.

"Aw, hi, kitty," I coo. "That's a good cat." Finally, he's decided to do what pets are supposed to do and offer some comfort in a time of need. I scratch under his chin and wait for the purr any normal cat would let out at such treatment. Instead, he slaps my hand with his paw, claws out, hisses, and jumps off the couch in one swift motion. He runs to the opening to the kitchen, where he stops to watch me, meowing again. I groan at the ceiling. Of course! I've forgotten to feed him. He doesn't care about me. The poor thing is hungry.

Yeah, I'll make a great mother.

CHAPTER 9

"Wow, you've got it bad," Aimee says when she finds me dabbing at my eyes during lunch at school. "You guys still not talking?"

I squelch a sob. I've tried, but both Tuesday and Wednesday, Pat has come home past my bedtime, pretending the couch is his bed of choice, and this morning he wouldn't even look at me in the kitchen. "I'm talking, only he's not responding. And these mood swings... It's like an emotional ghoul has possessed my body. Which, I guess, isn't that far from the truth."

Aimee smirks. "How many weeks are you now?"

"Dr. Sanders says nine."

"And still no morning sickness?" She pouts in mock disgust. "You bitch. You have no idea how lucky you are. If you complain about crying one more time, I will not answer for my actions."

She's right. Aside from that one barfing episode, which I now think was unrelated to the baby-grain, I've felt fine this whole time.

"I'm ridiculously tired, though. This morning I bent down to pick up a paper I dropped, and I swear I woke up three hours later on the floor."

"Right... Which is why you were on time for work?"

"Slight exaggeration, so sue me." I know I'm lucky despite this ridiculous emotional roller coaster. I've heard the horror stories others go through—thanks, Mom. "Don't worry, I promise to balloon to twice my size once I start showing."

"One can hope." Aimee tosses a grape into her mouth and winks at me.

My phone chimes with a message, and I click it. "It's from Pat." I skim the words—*We need 2 talk. Dinner tomorrow night. Rosebud @ 6*—then hold it up for Aimee to see.

"Finally," she says. "He probably needed a few days. It must have been quite the surprise."

I award her a glare. "Don't you take his side. I'm well aware." I read the message again, warmth I recognize as hope spreading through my belly. I'm sure Aimee is right, and these past few days of silence have been his way of gaining some perspective. The more I think about it, the more certain I get, and even allow myself a flicker of anticipation at sharing this experience with him. Maybe things will change—we'll find our way back to each other, be a family.

Cue the waterworks.

When I approach the restaurant the following evening, I'm no longer as confident. The text message he sent is still the only communication we've had, and since he's coming straight from work, I don't even know if he's actually going to show. Considering how long we've been together, I'm sweating a ridiculous amount at the prospect of sitting across from him for an entire meal.

I pull my car into the parking lot at Rosebud at five minutes to six. I turn off the engine but leave the keys in the ignition while I check my hair and teeth, fluff my newly acquired cleavage, then change my mind and pull my top a little higher. What if he's still mad? I tap my fingers in a furious rhythm against the steering wheel. What if *he* wants to break up?

A family exits the restaurant—mom, dad, a toddler, and a little one in a car seat. The dad holds the door for them before taking the baby from the mom. She thanks him, and he leans in to kiss her cheek while the toddler skips up and down behind them.

My throat constricts. *Not now.*

Before my mutinous emotions can take over, I inhale on a count of four then head inside. The hostess greets me when I enter and efficiently guides me to a table in the back when I give her Patrick's name.

He stands up when I approach, which is something he never does—not even when we were first dating. He kisses my cheek and helps me with my chair, and the whole thing feels as if we're in a play. It's a struggle not to compare it to the easy interaction between the parking lot family.

"I wasn't sure what you wanted to drink, so I didn't order yet," he says.

The server comes, and I ask for a mineral water. Lord knows I could use something stronger, but I'm being good. Pat gets a glass of pinot noir.

While we wait for service, we busy ourselves with the focaccia and olive oil on the table while exchanging quick smiles between bites. To avoid eye contact, I glance around the room, taking in the warm neo-Italian atmosphere. The restaurant is packed, but heavy drapes and plentiful decor ensure the sound level remains a pleasant murmur bar the occasional clink of a glass and clatter of plates.

"How is your mom?" Pat asks, after tasting his wine.

It's the first time he's asked about her since we got the news, and for a moment, I'm stumped. "Good, all things considered. No change."

"Oh." He bobs his head twice, picks up another piece of bread.

I clear my throat. "How was your day?"

"Good, good. Peters landed that account I told you about last month, so we'll be busy come the end of the year."

End of the year. Christmas. That's when the baby is due. I'm about to tell him when the server comes to take our orders. I get the ravioli, and Pat orders the lasagna.

"Can I get a small Caesar, too, please," I add. The server scurries off, and we are alone again. "Eating for two," I joke, patting myself on the stomach. "The end of the year will be busy in more ways than one."

Something akin to panic enters Patrick's eyes, and he takes a deep gulp of his drink.

My good humor fades. He's not there yet.

"How's work?" he asks, fiddling with his napkin. "The old schoolhouse."

I stare at him. "Work's good." I launch into a detailed account of the many acts of kindness bestowed upon me since the wrist injury. Patrick hums and nods as I talk but doesn't speak except to order another glass of wine.

Finally, our food arrives, and we both dig in. I'm pleased he's chewing with his mouth closed, but with each bite, each minute gone by, the muscles along my spine bunch tighter and tighter. Didn't he ask me here to talk? This is like waiting outside the principal's office when you know someone has tattled on you but you're not sure what about.

Patrick is on his third glass of wine by the time the server clears our empty plates. I've resorted to picking my cuticles for lack of something else to do and expect him to ask for the check when instead he requests the dessert menu.

"Listen," he says after ordering a coffee, "I know I shouldn't have reacted the way I did on Monday. I guess I was in shock."

My hands still on the table. "I should have told you as soon as I found out."

"Yeah, you should have. To find out like that..." He reaches across the table for me. This is so out of character I almost giggle.

"Kristin," he says, leaning in. "I know we've been together a long time. And I'm not blind. I know things haven't been great lately. We're still good, though, right?"

My gaze locks on our entwined hands while I scramble for a response. He squeezes my fingers so tightly my knuckles press into each other. "I..." I look up at his face to find earnest expectation plastered across his features. Hope. He hasn't looked at me this way since we first moved in together and he bought me that secretary desk I'd had my eye on. But this is all wrong. "I'm not sure—"

Before I can finish my sentence, he reaches into his pocket with his free hand and puts a small box on the table. My heart somersaults. What the...?

"Kris, I think we should get married."

I have lost All The Words. The box sits there, miniscule yet imploring, and I expect it to pop open any second and reveal the whole thing as a practical joke. When it doesn't, I shift my gaze to Patrick, who looks more like he wants to run away than have a Kodak moment. He's still holding my hand, but his grip has faltered, and his palm is clammy.

"Will you?" he says, squinting. "Marry me?"

I come alive enough to blink. Not a regular, moisten-your-eyeballs kind of blink but a rapid, crazy-person flutter that doesn't stop. Eventually, I have to pull my hand from his and press my fingers to my eyelids. He's done it. He's really done it. Mom is going to be beside herself. Maybe this is exactly what she needs to reconsider treatment—something to look forward to.

Gradually, the sounds of the restaurant come back to me, and I look up. Patrick has moved the box closer to me and opened the lid to display a golden band with a single red stone. I recognize my birthstone—the garnet. *He remembered.* The red stone gleams in the candlelight as I reach for it. I'll have what Shannon has. Surely we can make it work.

"If you want a diamond instead, we can get a diamond."

I shake my head and pick it up. It's heavier than I expected but perfect all the same, and the magic weight aids my resolve. *I can do this.* "Pat, I think—"

"Look, I know this is a little out of the blue," he says, scrubbing a hand across his face, "but I guess I didn't realize this was what you wanted. We've never really talked about it, and I thought we were good, and then this whole... baby business." He gives a shaky laugh. "It was like, 'Ahhh, what are you doing, Pat? Can't you see your girl wants more?' So I figured, let's make it official. I mean we already live together, so it's not that big of a change, but at least it's moving forward. That's what you want, right?"

"Well, yeah—" I start, but he's not done.

"And so I told myself, let's get married. Let's 'put a ring on it,' as they say. Everyone will be happy, everything will be settled, and we can move on from this. Forge ahead." He does a whole-hand point toward me. "Then in the future, if we feel like, *yes*, let's add some little bundles of, eh, joy, you know, to the mix, we can talk about it. The point is, we'll have all this time. Lots of time. We've got a nice thing going here. It's certainly the best relationship I've ever been in, and I think maybe you too." He sinks back in his seat, chest puffed out, clearly satisfied with a job well done, and drains what's left in his glass.

I frown, my mind racing. It's the longest relationship I've had, for sure. But I rub at my sternum to get rid of the heartburn that manifests at the thought of it being 'the best.' After a beat I set the ring back in the box on the table and look at him, head cocked slightly. "Patrick," I say in a tentative voice. "There's not that much time. You do understand I'm pregnant now, right?"

He leans forward. "Yes, but that's what I'm trying to say. *Instead* of that, let's get married. We're not ready for kids." He says it as if I'm a little daft for suggesting otherwise.

"Hmm." My forehead furrows further. "That's not quite how this works, you know. It's not like I can tell the baby to stay in there longer. It will come out in December regardless of whether or not we're ready."

He looks away, rubs his neck. "Not necessarily."

Just then the busboy comes to clear the table, and we both sit back while we wait for him to finish.

"Not necessarily?" I ask when we're alone again, a heavy chill having settled in my core. "And you'd better not be suggesting what I think you are."

Patrick's expression hardens at my challenge. "I'm not ready to be a dad," he says. "Hell, I don't even know if I want kids."

"A little late for that, don't you think?"

"Now you're being unreasonable."

I gape at him. "*I* am?"

"Keep your voice down." He glances around to make sure we don't have an audience. "I think we should talk about this."

"What's there to talk about? I'm pregnant. We're having a baby. Yes, it wasn't planned, and I should have told you right away, but that doesn't change the fact that—"

"I want you to get rid of it."

The air leaves me in a rush. He says it so fast and so quietly, for a moment I think—hope—I misheard him.

"You what?" Tears spring to my eyes.

"Look, I'm not saying never. You want kids in the future, I'll compromise. But not now. I'm about to change careers. It's not the right time."

I take him in fully, the man I've spent the past two years with, and his features make no sense to me. All things previously familiar about him dissolve and scatter, leaving a stranger in his place, and not a nice one at that.

"How can you ask that of me?" I gasp. "I'm not getting younger, and I want this baby."

"How can you ask *that* of me?"

I run the back of my hand across my wet cheek before I scoot my chair back. Arms and legs leaden, it takes every ounce of energy I have to rise from my seat. The velvet box taunts me from the middle of the table.

"I guess I can't," I say, my lip quivering. "We're over. Don't bother coming home tonight."

Patrick looks as if I've slapped him, but I couldn't care less. Without looking back, I walk out of the restaurant and away from life as I know it.

I somehow make it home in one piece and stumble into the house, eyes blurry with smeared eyeliner. At the sight of Pat's golf shoes by the door, another round of tears breaks forth, and I sink to the floor, clutching my purse to my chest. I've done it now. I'm all alone.

No, not all alone. I dig through my purse for my phone and speed dial Aimee.

"Come on, come on," I sniffle. "Pick up!"

"Hey, Kris!" comes her chipper tone on the line.

My greeting is a sputtered wail.

In the twenty minutes it takes her to get to me, I don't move. She finds me leaning against the hallway closet door, still in my shoes and jacket, and her first order of business is to take those off and get me onto the couch.

"What happened?" she asks after wrapping me in a blanket.

"Patrick... baby..." I stutter. Then I take a long, shuddering breath. "He wants me to get rid of it."

Aimee's expression comforts me more than words. I'm not overreacting, then.

"I broke up with him."

"Oh, hon." Aimee scoots closer and wraps an arm around my shoulders. "I'm sorry, I really am. That must have been so hard."

"He proposed," I say, the absurdity of the evening hitting me full force. "I was about to say yes."

Aimee's mouth opens, but nothing comes out.

"I know," I say with a bitter laugh. "I thought I knew him. Better than this at least. I thought we could maybe make it work." I hang my head. "You were right."

"No," Aimee starts. "I didn't mean—"

"It's okay. *Clearly* we are not on the same page, and I know things weren't great anymore." My face contorts anew. "But to think someone I've shared so much with could suggest we get rid of our baby because the timing is inconvenient for him. He carried a 'her body, her choice' sign when we went to the Women's March, for God's sake."

Aimee pats my arm until I've settled again then asks, "Do you want me to beat him up for you? I have a toddler with a mean karate kick I can sic on him."

A laugh forces its way from my chest, releasing the constriction therein. "That's okay. Thanks, though."

"No corporal punishment. Got it. Is there anything else I can do?"

I let my head loll back against the cushions and draw in a shaky breath. "Can you get the two big suitcases from the garage?"

"I like the way you're thinking." She jumps up and disappears out the door.

Together Aimee and I move through the house, stuffing Patrick's things in the suitcases willy-nilly—his suits, his work books, his stupid trophies, his shoes. My hands are shaking, and I'm out of breath, but it feels good to be doing something. As if my sorrow has turned into a beast with a purpose. When the bags are full, we set them in a corner of the hallway, out of the way.

It's close to midnight when Aimee leaves. I'm tired but not eager to go to bed, so I grab a can of pop and a bag of chocolate-covered raisins and sink into a chair at the kitchen table. The wind has picked up outside, and I wouldn't be surprised if it rains before morning. The edge of one of the suitcases is visible from the table, and I glare at it with open hostility. The storm that raged inside me before may have settled into churning waters, but dangers still lurk in their depth.

Mom was right; Patrick must not understand I'm thirty-five.

"The timing is perfect," I say out loud then add in a mumble, "Maybe even a tad late."

I push off the chair and grab a grocery bag for a final sweep of the place to take down all the pictures of us scattered around the house, except the one from his cousin's wedding where I was in super shape. He's an idiot, that's the only explanation. A selfish douchebag who doesn't deserve me. How could he?

The question is still echoing in my mind when I make my way to the bedroom a little later. I'm exhausted from all the emotions and at the same time wired from my sugary snack, so I turn the water on in the shower and set it to hot. I sit on the toilet lid while I wait for the water to heat up. Peel off my socks and pants. Pull my top over my head. The soft wads of my stomach rest on top of the elastic in my underwear, not quite welling over, not quite contained. I press my fingers into it, probing.

"Are you in there?" I whisper. Then I stand up and look at myself in the mirror. I'm still not showing, but my breasts have definitely received an upgrade. "Sorry for messing things up," I say, rubbing slow circles around my belly button. "Don't worry. Even if it's just you and me, we'll be fine."

If I say it enough times, it must be true.

CHAPTER 10

I wake up early the next morning, tears streaking my face. Morrison has taken over Patrick's side of the bed as if he knows the spot is now vacant, and the thought makes the events of the previous evening come rushing back.

"No," I say, loud enough to startle the cat. I shove the comforter aside and swing my legs over the side of the bed. I'm not wallowing today. I need to get out of here.

The clock on the nightstand shows a quarter to six in the morning—too early for anything to be open—but I get ready all the same and have some cereal. At the sight of Patrick's suitcases in the hallway, I chew a little faster.

Two hours later I find myself in Rockford or, more specifically, in Mom's driveway. She lives in a small ranch-style home in a neighborhood of identical little boxes built sometime in the sixties. Hers is yellow with white trim and a cobalt-blue front door. The flowerbeds are bursting with azaleas and tulips, and her collection of glass orbs, ceramic dragonflies, and painted rocks glisten in the sunlight. Not quite the kind of curb appeal I'd look for in a house, but it suits my mother, for sure.

Before I can knock, she pushes the door ajar, eyes wide. "Kris? What are you doing here?" She has two cats in her arms and holds the third back with her foot. Dressed in jeans and a white button-down shirt, she looks almost like a normal mom.

"I broke up with Patrick," I blurt.

"You...?" She hesitates but then opens the door wider to let me pass.

"How are you feeling?" I ask, walking deeper into the house. I'm done beating around the bush. Early sunlight beams through the floor-to-ceiling windows in the living room, illuminating the vibrant green of her junglelike gathering of houseplants, courtesy of her greener-than-green thumbs. An eclectic collection of paintings covers most of the walls, but as usual my attention is drawn to the one on prime display above the mantel. Mom painted this homage to Van Gogh's *Sunflowers* when Shannon and I were in elementary school, and it's striking not only for its bright palette but also for its size and the memory of how long it took her to complete it to satisfaction. The way I remember it, we barely saw her that summer. After all these years, I'm still not sure if I love it or hate it.

I enter the kitchen and am engulfed by the smell of some kind of flowery tea and the vague muskier scent of cooked cauliflower that forever seems to permeate this house. Sitting down at the kitchen table, I take off my jean jacket and wait for her to answer.

"What happened?" she asks instead.

I brush a few imaginary crumbs off the table. It's not like I can lie about this, can I? What will she say when I tell her I turned down the proposal she's been waiting for forever?

"If you get me some coffee, I'll tell you. And you didn't answer my question."

"I only have tea. And I'm fine. Dr. Brink is pleased."

"Okay." My brows furrow. "But you're still, you know...?"

"Dying? Yes. Unfortunately." She directs her gaze to the cat that's jumped in her lap and coos, "But don't you worry, Miss Claudine. Patti will give you a good home."

Patti is Mom's best friend in the Gladiolas, a local art club for spunky retirees who take accessorizing very seriously. The two share a love of both all things sparkly and everything feline.

I take her up on the tea offering and make myself a cup. It's chamomile and tastes exactly like hay. Or so I imagine.

"Okay," I say, steeling myself. "Just promise not to get mad. I can't deal with mad right now."

"All right."

"Pat found out I'm pregnant and asked me to marry him."

A light turns on in Mom's eyes, so I hurry to clarify. "He wants us to get married *instead* of having a baby. He wants me to have an abortion." Saying the words out loud breaks my defenses once more, and the vise in my chest tightens further.

Mom must see what's coming for she hands me a paint-spattered tissue from her pocket and waits until I've calmed down before she asks, "He'd marry you to make you get rid of my grandbaby?" Her lips press together into a taut white line, and she shakes her head.

I blow my nose again and wipe my eyes. "He says he's not ready."

Mom falls quiet. "You know," she says eventually, "he had me fooled. All this time. Sure, I thought he was a bit soft and undefined perhaps, but then again, so are most men—office workers in particular. I had no idea he was completely spineless." She locks me in her gaze. "Good riddance, is what I say. And good for you."

I hiccup in surprise.

"Now go clean yourself up, and I'll fix us some waffles."

After powdering my nose, I join Mom in the kitchen. Mom is seated next to the steaming waffle grid, waiting for the light to turn green. She already has a plate with a short stack ready next to her, and she's found butter, syrup, and cinnamon to complete the feast.

"Thanks, Mom," I say, sitting down.

Her eyes flicker to mine but return to the grid right away. She releases a golden waffle from it, plops it onto the stack, and pours new batter onto the hot plates.

"Here, dig in." She pushes the plate toward me. "Do you need help?" She nods at my brace-adorned arm.

I give up trying to spread butter with one hand and put the knife down. "Sure, that would be good."

She pours syrup onto the bottom of the plate, places the waffle on top, flips it, and sprinkles it with cinnamon. The sight nudges a memory loose. I think she used to do that for us when we were very little. Before we started kindergarten and she declared us self-sufficient enough to justify disappearing into her studio at all hours.

"I did a handstand," I blurt as she's cutting it up.

Her head jerks up, her hand pausing in the air. "You did what?"

I shake my head. "Don't read too much into it. I just wanted to know if I could still do it."

Amusement blooms on her face. "And?"

"Does two seconds count?"

"It's two seconds more than I ever managed," she says. "Is that how you hurt your arm?"

I confirm her suspicion, and she starts laughing.

"Oh, Kris," she says, eyes crinkled. "Leave it to you... Though I must say I *am* impressed by the effort."

Against my will, her glee rubs off on me, and I grin back at her.

And perhaps it's this unexpected camaraderie that we—a dying woman and a newly single, pregnant one—have found this morning over waffles and a laugh, or the fact that life as of last night is upside down anyway, but suddenly I have no idea why I *wouldn't* help her fulfill her last wish.

Without a word, I get up to grab my purse, rummage around in it, and produce the bucket list, which I smooth out on the table between us. "I have some concerns."

Mom seems to be holding her breath. She watches me with cautious eyes. "Um, yeah, of course."

"The handstand counts. There is no way I'm subjecting my wrist to that kind of strain again, and neither should you. I'm not getting any smaller, and you're not getting any younger."

She agrees, and I cross it off.

"And no tattoo. I'm not a 1930s sailor."

"But you—"

"Nope. I have no wish to be permanently marked."

She considers this, and I can tell she wants to argue. "Fine," she says at last. "You'll have to come with me when I get mine, though."

"Deal." I make a note of it.

"Anything else?"

I read through the list even though by now I know it by heart. "Well, obviously I can't promise I'll fall in love."

"Yes, it's perhaps a bit soon."

I snort. "A bit? Could be I'm not made for love."

Mom tuts and rolls her eyes. "Fine, no tattoo and no promise of love. Is that it?"

"You have to tell me who Bart is. That was the deal."

She considers me for a long while over the brim of her mug. Then she puts it down, licks the spoon, and places it just so beside the mug on the table. I wait, hanging on her every movement.

"He's the man I left when I got pregnant by your father," she says, finally. It could be the early-morning light playing tricks on my vision, but it looks like her cheeks are flushing. "He's also the only man I've ever truly loved."

I frown. "Then why were you with my dad?"

"Why do we do anything? For adventure, for desire, for vanity. Because I could."

"But why not call him up and apologize yourself? Why is it on your list?"

"You don't know how it was." She moves the spoon an inch to the left.

"So tell me."

"He asked me to marry him." Mom's gaze is faraway again, lost somewhere in a past before my time. "We'd been going out for quite a while, but the second year he was stationed in Texas for six months—he was an army man—and, well, let's just say I knew you girls weren't his." She swallows audibly a couple of times. "I wanted to say yes. I *would* have said yes." She looks at me. "Unfortunately, I'd recently realized my *blessed state*, and even if I'd been so tempted, which I wasn't, I couldn't have passed you off as his." She must see the question on my face for she adds, "He's Black."

"Okay, so he proposes, you decline, then what? Did he get mad?"

"I never gave him an answer." She says it so quietly my ears strain to hear.

"You never—"

"No. He proposed, I asked to think about it, and the next day, instead of going to our agreed-upon meeting place, I went with your dad to New York. And you know how that panned out." She gives a self-deprecating half smile. "I tried looking him up a few years later, but he had moved. In a way it was a relief at the time—I was mortified—but now I've found him. He lives in Seattle."

I consider this a long time. "Jesus, Mom," I say eventually. "That's pretty cold even for you."

She hums in agreement.

"So he didn't know you were pregnant?"

She shakes her head. "I could have been kidnapped or dead for all he knew. Oh, what I must have put him through." She rests her forehead against the fingertips on her left hand. "Will you help me do it?"

"Apologize to him?"

"Yes. In person. I don't think I'll go through with it on my own. And I would so like to see him. One last time."

As far as regrets go, I have a feeling this one tops all the others on the list. Plus, I must admit I am rather curious about this man who was her one true love.

I take a deep breath and exhale until my lungs are empty.

"I'll do it, Mom. I'll do your bucket list with you."

CHAPTER 11

Two weeks later, I'm on the floor in my mother's living room, googling *knitting for beginners* in a frenzy. Several balls of yarn are scattered about, and Mom stands over me, needles in hand slightly too close to my face for comfort.

"Can't you find anything?" she asks, impatience tinting her voice. "Stop, what's that one?"

I bite my tongue. *I'm a great teacher. It's what I do best.* And teachers don't yell at their students.

Because I'll be in a brace for another week, I had the brilliant idea to learn to knit theoretically and teach Mom to do it in practice. Did I say "brilliant"? I mean "terrible." It turns out the old adage is true—it's impossible to teach old dogs new tricks. Or at least to remain sane while doing so. Especially if the dog is your mom and has a black belt in stubbornness.

"Mom, I told you, this is the one we want." I pull up a website that shows step-by-step instructions how to cast on and get started.

"I don't like her hands," Mom says, pointing to the photos on my screen. "It looks like she bites her nails."

"How is that important?"

"Would you rather have a handsome professor or an ugly one?" She leans even closer, and I have to push her hands aside to avoid being impaled on the needles.

"Okay, how about this? You pick out a yarn you'd like, and I'll look at the ugly hands. I mean, instructions." I make a sweet face and turn the laptop away from her.

Mom puts her hands up in surrender and surveys the yarn. "What are we making?" she asks. "A sweater?"

"Try a scarf, maybe. Let's start small and work up to clothing."

"No need for snark. I was just asking." She picks up a dual-tone pink-and-purple bundle. "This one."

"Okay, good." I scramble to get through the basic instructions, cursing myself for not doing this in the privacy of my home. I've had no time. The last day of school for my students was yesterday, and as always it was a mad dash to the finish line.

"How do you hold these things?" comes Mom's voice from the couch. "Do you point them up or down?"

"Hold on a minute." I finish reading and scroll back up to the top. Right. Slipknot, working yarn, tail yarn, loop.

"I'm so excited," Mom says.

At least that's something. I steel myself, trying to remember why I'm doing this in the first place, and move the laptop to the coffee table.

"First, you're going to make a slipknot around one needle." I use my good hand to drape the yarn in a loop on the table. "Use your fingers to pick up that string and pull it through."

"Which string?"

"The long one."

"What happens if I use the other one?"

I close my eyes on an exhale. "The world ends. Please, pick up the long one."

"Okay, okay." She does and squeals in delight when, lo and behold, a slipknot forms and she can slide it onto her needle. "Now what?"

"Now you make some more loops." My eyes flicker to the screen as I try to explain how to do this—yarn across palm, needle under, loop around, yarn across, needle under, loop around.

After three failed attempts, Mom puts the needles down and announces she needs a break.

"Already?"

"My hands are tired. How about a little walk?" she asks.

"I thought you wanted to learn?"

"I do. But right now I want some fresh air. And to be honest, you could stand to tilt your face to the sun now and then now that you're single again."

This is true since Patrick has officially moved out.

Mom grabs her sunglasses off the side table. "We can pick this up later."

I think I'm beginning to understand why none of the things on the bucket list are crossed off.

"How did it go?"

Before I can answer Shannon's question, a small voice interrupts her on the other end, to which she responds, "No you can't have a snack, it's almost lunchtime."

"Sorry," she says to me. "I had yoga this morning, so the kids were home with Thomas, and now they seem to think our house rules are dispensable." Her voice has an edge that's not usually there, but as if catching herself, she retracts, "Sorry, I'm just tired. The kids are fine. Everything is fine."

And here I was picturing her life as an idyllic 1950s commercial. But that's on me. After all, I'm pretty sure Thomas neither smokes at the breakfast table nor calls my sister Dollface when he comes home from a long day of doctoring, fedora in hand.

"Knitting, huh? Is she driving you crazy yet?" Shannon asks, breaking my trail of thought.

It's Sunday, and I'm on my way back to Chicago to meet Patrick for a coffee. He's been calling. A lot. I figure if I give him thirty minutes of my time, he might back off.

My brain hurts after staring at knitting tutorials all weekend, but I'm not telling her that. "We got thirty cast-ons done, and several rows of decent knit stitches. All things considered, a fair accomplishment. It's all good."

"I can take over if you want. I'm planning on driving down next weekend. Maybe I can help her out?"

Interesting. When she first found out I'd agreed to help with the list, she went on and on about the lunacy of the dying and the pregnant and how she for once would like not to be the only rational person in the family. The tune has certainly changed.

"That's not necessary," I say in my nicest voice. I can only imagine what bringing Shannon into this mix would do, and it's not a pretty picture. *Why don't you have Shannon help you out?* That was pretty much the tagline to any request Mom made of me growing up. Not this time.

"You sure? I feel so sorry you have to do this with your bad wrist. It's not like you're the handiest person on an average day, and now you've got that brace to deal with too."

My grip on the phone tightens. Shannon always was the master of innocuous stabs tucked into otherwise benign conversations when you least expect them. I call them cuddle-slaps. She hasn't lost the ability. "We're managing fine. Like I said."

"Oh, don't get all—you know what I mean."

"Yeah, I know it real well," I grumble.

"Let me know if you change your mind. It might be nice to spend some time together."

I suppress a laugh. I can think of nothing less nice right about now considering my ego is smarting. No wonder she chose to be a nurse. That's all they do—sweet-talk you until you're distracted then jab a needle into your flesh. Yeah, I'm on to her.

"I think I'm losing you," I say, tapping the phone against my chest. "Shannon? Hello?" I hang up.

Patrick greets me with a stiff hug when I arrive at our favorite cafe, Coffee Grounds. He looks drawn, and his T-shirt is wrinkled.

We order our beverages and take a seat by the window.

"How've you been?" Patrick's gaze runs over me and stops in the middle for a beat too long before returning to my face. I'm still not showing, so I'm thankful he doesn't comment on my belly.

"Good. Great. You?"

"Fine." He sips his coffee, and I can tell he scalds his tongue because his face flares red and he sucks in his lower lip while pushing the cup away.

"Need some water?"

He declines and leans forward in his chair. "I've missed you." When I don't respond, he probes, "Have you missed me?"

I'm not prepared for a direct question and try to buy some time by folding a leg under me in the chair. I've missed him less than I thought I would.

"Come on, Pat. Don't do this."

"Not at all?" He runs a palm across his chin. "We were together for almost two years. I asked you to marry me."

"To get me to agree to an abortion!" It comes out louder than I intended, and a few other patrons glance our way. "Not because you love me," I say in a lower voice.

Patrick shakes his head but doesn't contradict me out loud. For a long while, we stir our drinks, sip, and focus on the table, the wall decorations, the view out the window—anything but each other.

Patrick breaks the silence. "We were good together. I know we were."

I nod. "Once maybe, but then, I don't know, it's like we stopped talking. I don't think either one of us were happy. We kept going because it was convenient. You'll see that, too, with time. It's better this way."

"How can you just end it?"

"How can you ask your long-term girlfriend to get rid of your baby?"

He lets out an exasperated huff. "That's not the point."

"It is the point." I lean in. "At a fundamental level, we want different things, I see that now. We have different values, different priorities. Looking back, I'm surprised we even lasted this long."

Pat scowls.

"Do you suddenly want to be a dad then? Should we stay together for the baby?"

He doesn't respond.

"To avoid loneliness? For the stability of two incomes?" I cross my arms. "We hardly saw each other the last six months, and you're quitting your job." I take a calming breath and expend some effort letting the tension go before I continue. "You know I'm right." Then because I'm still feeling less than charitable, I add, "You don't have to like it. You just have to accept it." He hates it when I say that.

If glares could kill.

"That's it then?" he asks. "What about the baby?"

One of my hands instinctively goes to my belly. "What about it?"

"It's mine, isn't it?"

"Of course it's yours."

"What happens with it?"

"What hap—" I try to temper my returning irritation, with limited success. "It grows in my belly for nine months, then it comes out, and it will have at least one loving parent to help it grow up to be a decent human being."

My sarcasm doesn't seem to register. "And if I want to see it?"

I'm momentarily stunned into silence. "Do you?"

Patrick shrugs. "I don't know. Maybe. What if it looks like me, you know."

I slump back in my chair and watch him, tired of this back-and-forth. "Look, we're not together anymore, and I think it's as it should be. That said, I would never keep your kid away from you. I want her, or him, to have a relationship with their dad. But I'm not going to chase you for it. And you can't come and go as you please. It's a person, not a fad. You're either a present father or not there at all. You have a few months to decide."

"But we're over for sure?"

"We are."

His lips turn down. "I guess I kind of figured."

We both have another sip of our drinks, which by now are on the cool side.

"Any plans for the summer?" he asks as we walk out into the sunlight.

I flinch. "Some plans." I grunt.

California. In two weeks. With Mom. At the thought, cold sweat breaks out at the nape of my neck. *What have I done?*

CHAPTER 12

"I can't do this," I say for the umpteenth time. "I change my mind."

Aimee is driving Mom and me to the airport on what I'm sure is the last day of my life. My will is on my desk at home, as is the contact information for my lawyer. All bills have been paid, and Morrison is at Aimee's house. At least in practice, I'm ready to die.

Mentally, not so much.

My gaze is locked straight ahead as the road rushes by, blessedly brace-free hands in a firm grip on the seat, and my heart hammering its way out of my chest.

Aimee and Mom exchange a glance in the rearview.

"I'm pregnant," I try. "I'm allowed to change my mind as often as I'd like."

Aimee snorts. "The pregnancy card only flies with significant others who have a stake in the baby. I'm *impervious* to your.*guiles*."

"You do crossword puzzles?" Mom asks from the back seat.

"Yeah, pretty good, huh?"

"Guys, focus. I want to go home," I whine. "I'm telling you I don't feel good."

Mom leans forward between the seats. "It's not the baby, is it?"

"No, the baby is fine. It's your list. It's not agreeing with me."

Aimee snorts and flashes me a grin. "Oh, don't get your maternity panties in a bundle. You're going to California! What's not to like?"

"Don't you think it's time?" Mom adds. "You've gone your whole life without getting on a plane. Imagine what the second half could be like."

The hairs on my arms rise. "That's the problem. In my imagination, a plane ride equals there not *being* a second half."

She snickers and pats my shoulder. "Pishposh. You'll be fine."

"Let's have some music." Aimee turns the volume on the radio up. She has on a classic rock station, and the speakers start blasting "Stairway to Heaven."

Seeing my look of panic, she hurries to turn it off. "Don't worry. It's not a sign."

I am not convinced.

Aimee accompanies us into the departure hall, where we print boarding passes and get our bags checked. I'm not sure if she's here for moral support or to make sure I don't escape, but I appreciate her presence either way.

"This is it," she announces as we approach the security check. "End of the line for me."

Sweat breaks out on my neck. "Um..."

"Kris." She takes me by the shoulders. "You'll be fine. Your mom is here, and people fly every day."

"Mm-hmm." I ogle the large scanners I have to go through.

She pulls me into tight hug. "Don't worry. You can do this." She releases me and turns to Mom. "Good luck."

Mom thanks her, takes me by the arm, and starts dragging me into the corral. Aimee trails along on the other side of the rope.

"Follow the line, find your gate—it's H6—and wait until they call boarding. Then all you have to do is find your seat, sit back, and relax. There's nothing to it. Oh, and call me when you land."

"We've got it," Mom says.

My lip quivers, but I hoist my bag higher on my shoulder and turn away from Aimee. *Don't look back, don't look back, don't look back.* Tears well in my eyes by the time I reach the conveyor belt, but if I was expecting sympathy, I don't get it.

"Put your things in this," Mom says, handing me a tray.

I'm about to ask what she means when she disappears into the scanner, leaving me behind, so I stuff my carry-on into the tray only to have the TSA worker promptly take it out.

"Sweaters, shoes, belts, and phones, ma'am. Any electronics in your bag?" he drones.

I shake my head and hurry to rearrange my belongings with trembling hands. He pushes it through.

The scanner is like a closet, open on two sides, and I have to stand with my arms up while it buzzes around me. Too late, I remember I'm pregnant and should have asked if it's safe for the baby, and I add that worry to the pile. If the baby-grain comes out with an extra arm, at least I'll know why.

By the time I grab my things on the other side, my hands are shaking enough to make zipping up my sweater a task, but I continue on toward Mom, knowing there is no turning back.

A few steps along, a voice calls out behind me, "Ma'am! Excuse me, ma'am."

I turn and start at the sight of the TSA worker coming after me. My mouth goes dry. They found something, and they need to bring me to an interview room like they do in movies. Visions of dark chambers with a lone spotlight shining in my face come before me. Surely they'll let a female agent do the strip search?

"Your shoes, ma'am," the TSA agent says.

I gape at him. "I'm sorry?"

"Your shoes." He looks down at my feet.

I follow his prompt. Nothing but white cotton is covering my toes. "Shoes would help," I say, thinking an old blanket would also be good, as in something to throw over myself. "Thanks," I squeak and take them from him.

He gives me an odd look but doesn't linger.

Great, now I'm probably on their watch list.

We make it to the gate with plenty of time to spare. Thankful to be out of the worst crowds, I find us two seats near a window and collapse into mine without pause, my nerves frayed from the sensory overload brought on by this gateway to hell. We have forty minutes until boarding, so Mom decides to check out the shops.

"Are you sure you don't want to come with?" she asks. "You could get a book."

In response, I hold up the novel I brought.

"Suit yourself."

Reading works as a distraction for about three minutes, until an earsplitting roar overhead interrupts the peace. Certain the building is about to collapse, I whip my head around to try to determine the cause of the noise and spot a giant plane through the windows right in front of me. Its belly is dark silver, smooth and hard, and it's getting closer and closer to the ground. *Too* close. Why is everyone around me so calm? *They're crashing!* I want to scream. *We're all going to die!* Only the plane lands, gracefully for such a big bird, and I'm left with my mouth open, eyes wide in terror.

I grab my bag and rush to the nearest bathroom, where my stomach empties itself until nothing is left of that morning's breakfast. I really can't do this. I don't want to die. I don't want my baby to die. If Mom survives the crash, I don't want her to have to bury me, filled with guilt that it was her list that sent me to an early demise. How will she live with herself, knowing she was the one who booked us on this certain deathtrap? Yeah, I *saw* our plane sitting at the gate, and it most *certainly* does not look sturdy enough to carry us all the way to Los Angeles. Plus, there are a lot of workers surrounding it, clearly indicating faults that need fixing—not exactly a great vote of confidence.

After rinsing off my face, I return to the gate, where my seat has been taken by a man in canvas shoes and a ponytail. I find another one, farther away from the window, and pull out my phone to call Aimee. She'll have to turn around and come get me. There's nothing else to it. I don't care what she says. I don't care what Mom says. I will not be going to Santa Barbara to paint the sunset now or at any other time. Change of plans.

The call rings and rings and eventually goes to voicemail. "Hi, this is Aimee. Please leave a message at the beep." I gear up to start pleading, but her voice continues, "If this is Kristin calling, *don't* leave a message. Take a deep breath and have some candy. You will be fine, and I am not picking you up. Call me when you land. Bye."

There's a tone then silence, and I hang up, phone clasped in my hand. It would appear I have no choice.

"There you are." Mom sits down in the chair next to mine, a newsstand bag full of goodies in her lap. "Here." She hands me a Twix bar and a bottle of water. "You look like you need it."

I hold the foreign objects, confused for a moment as to what they are. Mom's voice is far away when she says something about two magazines for the price of one. I'm having a hard time understanding her.

"Kris," she says. Then closer to me, "Kristin."

"Huh?"

"Eat the chocolate."

When I don't move, she takes it from my hand and opens it for me. "Always so melodramatic," she mutters.

Mechanically, I take a bite, and as the sugary treat melts on my tongue, the world comes into focus again. Mom is still talking about the shops. Her face is animated, her eyes alight with excitement.

It's her last wish, a voice in my head says. I recognize it as the white angel on my right shoulder. *Don't disappoint her.* I glance from Mom to the plane outside and wait patiently for the angel's more entertaining counterpart to show up, to no avail. Not a big surprise. She is the devil, after all. So this is how it's going to be.

My thoughts are interrupted by a tinny voice over the PA system, announcing boarding is about to start.

Mom stands and hands me my boarding pass. "I'm boarding before you since I'm in first class."

I take the document and frown at her. "What?"

"I figured there's no point in saving my money, so I got an upgrade. You understand, don't you?"

"Um..." The Twix turns to stone in my stomach. "I guess..."

"Great! See you inside." Mom waltzes off to join the throng of people gathered in front of the gate. Some are intent on their phones while others chatter in good humor. Mom does neither. She looks straight ahead, focused only on the art of queuing up.

It's an oddly comforting sight. Predictable and therefore proof the illness has not yet gained the upper hand. It is possible, I suppose, the plane won't crash, and all these people will land safely in LA to get on with whatever adventures they have planned. I could join them.

But then the queue starts moving faster, and the flash of comfort disappears. Fresh sweat breaks out on my brow, and my hands start going numb. *I'm doing this for Mom*, I remind myself. I should get ready, but still I remain in my seat, watching the line get shorter and shorter. *One, two, three, go.* I clench my teeth and try to get up, but it's as if the chair holds me in a magnetized grip. My legs aren't strong enough to get leverage.

My eyes begin to sting in that all-too-familiar way. As usual, Mom will wish she had asked Shannon instead. This time was supposed to be different. I wanted to make her happy, to offer something. Instead, this.

Tears stream down my cheeks as the last few people in line disappear into the jet bridge. I've failed. I'm going to miss the flight.

CHAPTER 13

I bury my face in my hands and let it all out. My mom is dying and I'm about to become a single mother, yet I can't even muster up enough guts to get on a damn plane.

"Are you okay?" a voice asks next to me.

No! I want to scream. *I am very, very far from okay.*

"Are you supposed to be on the plane?"

I wipe my face with the back of my hand and peer to my left. A woman about my age with a concerned expression surrounded by a cloud of dark curls is seated next to me.

"They called for a Kristin Caine a moment ago. Figured I should check."

"Oh." I sniffle and hiccup one more time. "Yeah, that's me."

She waves to the gate attendant then digs through her tote for a packet of wet wipes. "Here. You've got some—" She gestures to my eyes, and I realize my mascara must have escaped. Again.

"Thanks." I clean up as best as I can without a mirror, and then before I can stop myself, hand her the tissue back. I cringe at my stupidity, but she doesn't bat an eye. She simply disposes of it in the nearest garbage can.

"Sorry," I say sheepishly.

She waves off the apology and sits back down. "You sure you're all right?"

And something about how she looks at me when she asks makes me want to tell her everything. "I..." I start. "I can't get on the plane." My throat tightens anew.

She hands me a bottle of water. "You're afraid of flying?"

I open it and take a deep swig, feeling the cool liquid rush all the way down into the emptiness of my stomach. "Yeah."

"But you still want to go?"

I exhale with force. "I have to. It's a long story."

The woman exchanges another wave with the gate attendant, who's looking at his watch. "You know what I think?" she asks. "I think you can do it."

My gaze flicks to hers.

"The trick is to take it one step at a time. For example, can you stand up?"

I take a tight hold of my bag and push off the chair.

She smiles at me in encouragement. "Good. Now, let's go talk to that guy over there." She gestures toward the attendant. "Can we do that?"

I follow her to the counter like an obedient puppy, and when the man holds out his hand for my boarding pass, I give it to him.

"Welcome, Ms. Caine," he says. "Let's get you to your seat."

I freeze. *No, I can't.*

"We're going to walk down the jet bridge now," the woman says, guiding me through the doors.

I follow her with rigid movements, the carpeted floor muting all sound. I drag my feet, yet we reach our destination too fast, the airplane doorway looming like a dragon's jaws in front of me.

"You holding up okay?" she asks at my side.

I give a jerky nod. If I do what she says without thinking, maybe it'll be all right.

We enter the plane, and she exchanges a few whispered words with the two flight attendants at the front. She seems to know everyone.

Mom is in the third row as we pass. She's engulfed in one of her magazines and doesn't look up. *Just as well.* I slink by as fast as I can, face burning.

"Okay, you're in 14A, so a little farther back. It's a great window seat, right in front of the wing. You'll have an awesome view."

A cold trickle of sweat pools between my breasts and finds its way to my waist as we move farther into the belly of the plane. As far as I'm concerned, it doesn't matter where I sit. It's not like Death will descend and spare me because "Oh, only middle and aisle seats today, you lucky window dweller." It's a plane. There are No. Good. Seats.

"Do you want your bag in the overhead or under the seat?" my helper asks in my ear.

I give her a confused glance. I'm supposed to know that?

She answers for me. "Let's put it under the seat. It'll be easier to get to."

I find row fourteen, and after shuffling the already-seated passengers around, I sit down.

"You're doing great," my helper says. "I'm five rows back if you need anything."

"Thank you," I manage, my hands struggling with the seat belt.

The old lady in the middle seat studies me, lips pursed. She looks from me to my helper. "You two know each other? I don't mind switching."

The male steward approaches with an expression that screams *service industry.* "Is there an issue?"

"Do you mind if we switch, Alex?" my helper asks.

I am present enough to notice she knows his name but not to make sense of the silent back-and-forth that ensues between them.

"Really," the old lady chimes in. "It's no problem. Maybe it would make *everybody* more comfortable."

"Kristin?" my helper asks.

"Yes, please," I squeak. And it's settled.

Once everyone is in their seats, my helper turns to me and offers a formal handshake. "Lily Landon," she says. "Your personal air travel guide."

"Kristin Caine." The first smile in hours breaks out on my lips. "Sorry to ruin your trip."

"Meh." Lily's face pulls into a sideways frown. "I prefer company. Don't worry about it."

She futzes with her seat belt and tray table for a bit then chats with the elderly man to her right, and all I can think is how weird the air smells and that perhaps this is my fault.

Finally, Lily leans back in her chair and turns to me. "Have you ever flown before?"

"Nope."

Her blue eyes widen. "I see. Okay, well, in a minute they'll do a security demonstration, and then they'll back away from the gate and taxi to the runway."

She goes on to explain step-by-step what I can expect, but I can't hear her. I stopped listening at "security demonstration." *I knew it!* Even the people who work here know this is dangerous. Yes, I've heard the statistics that driving a car is far more dangerous, yada yada yada. But is it, though? Because not once have I gotten into my Toyota and had a voice explain to me what to do in case of a water landing. For the record, I would roll down my window before becoming submerged, cut my seat belt with the cutter I keep in the console, and swim to the surface as far from the car as possible.

"Kristin?" Lily puts her hand on my right one, which is gripping the armrest so hard the knuckles have turned white. Her palm is warm and dry and startling to my icy digits.

"Huh?"

"They're starting." She points to Alex the steward in the aisle two rows ahead of us. He's smiling and making some joke to his colleague, and then a voice comes over the speaker welcoming us on-board. In spite of myself, I'm fascinated by his fluid hand movements during the demonstration, his calm, self-assured handling of the life vest and oxygen mask, and his ability to retain that poise while the speaker voice paints such horrifying scenarios.

"Here, you can read what they said if you want." Lily hands me a safety card from the seat pocket.

I take it and scan through the instructions, but it serves no other purpose than to give me tunnel vision. I set the card away and close my eyes. For the next few minutes, I focus on my breathing, in and out, steady and even.

I am as close to relaxed as I can be when the lights flicker and a loud hiss fills the cabin. I yelp and bolt upright, but Lily is right there, her calm voice explaining, "It's the AC. They restarted it. Nothing to worry about."

Ugh, I'm going to be sick again. The seat is too small, the air too thick, the lights too bright. My skin crawls.

"I need water," I gasp. "And a bag."

Without responding, Lily hands me what I requested, and I lean my head against the seat in front of me, the bag at the ready. I can feel her hand on my back, and I try to focus on matching my breathing to its rhythmical strokes. It helps the nausea pass.

"Thanks," I say as I try and fail to open the water bottle.

She takes it from me and twists the cap off. "Of course. Need anything else?"

"Maybe," I say between swigs. "Maybe talk to me. Keep me distracted."

"I can do that. What do you want to talk about?"

"Anything. How do you know everyone here? What do you do for a living? Where are you from?"

"Okay, okay. Calm, now. My mom used to work for Delta, so I fly on buddy passes, and as a freelance photographer, I fly a lot. Let's just say it doesn't hurt to be on a first-name basis with the service staff. Plus, it makes traveling more fun."

I make a spinning motion with my hand, prompting her to continue.

"Um... Okay, I'm from Portland originally, but right now I don't really have a home. I broke up with my partner, Max, a while back, and I've been on the road so much since then, I haven't had a reason to get a place."

"Why photography?" I ask, the constriction in my chest easing.

"Well"—Lily leans back in her seat—"my dad is a filmmaker—documentaries—and I used to love coming with him to shoots. He got me my first camera when I was ten, and that was it."

She goes on to describe a fairly traditional upbringing where school took a back burner to her budding craft even early on. She got in trouble with her mom for cutting school, while her dad celebrated her every win in local photo contests. They eventually divorced, and she stayed with her mom, who was the steadier parental unit.

"At the time, I would have loved to live with Dad, but it didn't work out that way." The way she wrinkles her nose makes me suspect there's more to that story, but I don't press.

I'm about to launch into another set of questions when the engines roar to life, and we are pushed back in our seats.

"Here, take my hand," Lily says. "It's liftoff time."

I squeeze my eyes shut and hold my breath. This is it. The end of the line. The whole craft is shaking, and all I'm doing is waiting for the bang, followed by screams of hysteria as we plummet back to where we should have stayed if we'd known what was good for us.

To my surprise, soon there's a shift in the air, a release of pressure, and then the sound recedes. I look out the window, and... we're flying. Far below, the grid of roads and houses gets smaller and smaller, forests and cornfields turning into abstract shapes of green and gold.

We fly through a thin cloud, and the wisps of it soften the image further.

"Um." Lily's voice interrupts my newfound reverie, making me aware I'm still clutching her hand, which I may or may not have crushed in the process of getting airborne.

"Oh gosh, I'm so sorry," I say, releasing her.

"No worries." She rubs her fingers discreetly. "So? What do you think?"

"It's pretty cool," I concede. "And, you know, I'm alive. Which is a plus."

"Well, for what it's worth, I'm proud of you." She awards me with a heartfelt beam that jolts something in the back of my mind. "To be honest, I didn't think you'd go through with it. I was totally improvising."

I gape at her. "And here I thought I was in good hands."

"And now you don't?" Her eyes twinkle.

"We shall see. Still four hours to go. Don't let this new calm me fool you."

"Wouldn't dream of it." She giggles. "So, what's your story? What made you do this?"

Now that's a question. "For my mom," I say. That's the simplest answer. "She has terminal cancer, and I've agreed to help do her bucket list."

"Wow." Lily's eyebrows go up. "Are you very close then?"

A loud "Ha!" escapes me, and I clasp a hand to my mouth. "Did you see the lady in first class with the magazine and the purple reading glasses? That's her."

Her jaw drops. "She's here, and she left you alone?"

"She thinks I'm being dramatic."

"Unbelievable. You're a bigger person than me."

"I couldn't say no. Plus, I'm newly single and a teacher, so yay, lots of free time this summer."

"Still. And sorry about you and..."

"Pat. Yeah, it's okay. We wanted different things. It's, um... complicated."

I leave it at that.

I'm returning from the bathroom when the first turbulence hits. It's little more than a jostle, but I'm already wary of walking around in a machine thousands of miles up in the air. My hands are shaking when I return to my seat, and Lily notices.

"It's nothing to worry about. It feels scary, but it's just shifts in air pressure outside."

"Oh, *just*," I say, tightening my seat belt as far as it can go.

"The flight attendants are still moving about. If they expect something worse, they ask them to sit down."

The captain's southern drawl comes over the speaker. "Good evening, folks. Quick update from your captain. We're currently cruising at an altitude of thirty-four thousand feet and making good time to our final destination of Los Angeles. Headwinds have us there approximately twenty minutes ahead of schedule. We are expecting some turbulence over the next fifteen minutes or so. Nothing to worry about, but please remain in your seats with your seat belts on until the sign is turned off. Thank you."

Lily looks at me with an expression that says "what did I tell you." Then the captain comes on again. "Flight attendants, please take your seats," he says, and her face drops. She regains her composure fast enough, but the damage is already done. I'm light-headed again, clinging to my armrests, and seeing my life flash before my eyes before she can say she's sorry.

"Tell me about Portland," I say, desperate for anything to keep my mind off what will surely be our imminent plummet.

"Okay, Portland." Lily dives headfirst into accounts of neighborhoods, schools, demographics, favorite hangouts, favorite places to shoot pictures, etc. She talks and talks, and I hang on to every word, breathing as evenly as I can, and to my surprise, when she finishes talking, our ride is smooth once again.

I let out a sigh of relief and tilt my head back.

"That was good," Lily says. "You didn't freak out as much as I thought you would."

"On the outside." I glance at her then close my eyes again. "Ugh, I'm exhausted. I can't believe anyone willingly does this regularly."

"Something to drink?" Alex the steward's voice rouses me, and I look up to find him leaning into our row.

"I'll have a rum and cola, thanks," Lily says without preamble. "So will she." She nods to me.

"Uh, no, I—"

"You need it. Trust me." Lily takes our cups and mini bottles from him and sets them down in front of me.

"But I—"

"It will help you sleep if nothing else." Lily accepts two packets of pretzels too. "As much as I enjoy your company, I'd also like to try to get some rest." She flashes her teeth at me, teasing.

Blood rushes to my face as she holds up her plastic cup for a toast.

"I'm pregnant," I blurt. "So I really shouldn't drink."

She gapes at me for a long moment before setting her cup down. "You're pregnant?"

"Thirteen weeks."

She gives a low whistle. "Wow. And now you're single. That's hard-core." The crease above her nose deepens. "How did you guys swing it? Donor?"

My chin retracts. "Donor? What do you—"

"Max and I looked into it a few years back," she continues, "but it wasn't the right time. Is it yours or Pat's?"

It's like she's talking in riddles, and I squint at her, my brain churning. What am I not getting?

"It's both of ours. I didn't cheat or anything." Somehow, I'm aware this doesn't quite answer her questions because how could the baby be Pat's but not mine?

Lily's face flushes. "No, of course you didn't. I didn't mean—I'm sure however you conceived it was a joint decision."

"However I con—" I give a slight shake of my head. "The regular way. And sure, we may have been a bit drunk, but he most definitely consented."

Lily's eyes flicker all around as if she's physically scanning her brain for words, and her mouth opens and closes several times before settling into a troubled pucker. "Hmm," she says. "So Pat is short for..."

"Patrick."

Her expression cracks, and I more sense than see the laughter traveling from her belly up to her face before it bursts out of her mouth in a sharp bark. She clamps a hand down on my forearm as another chuckle sputters past her lips. "So... Hmm... I'm..."

I open my mouth to speak, but she holds up a finger to stop me. All I can do is wait for her to explain on her own what has her so discombobulated. It takes a while, but eventually her expression settles, and she faces me again.

"I'm sorry," she says, humor still flickering across her lips. "Normally, I'm not this off. I thought Pat was Patricia or something."

I'm smiling, too, though I'm still not quite caught up. "You thought— But why?"

"Max is short for Maxine. I assumed."

Finally, the coin drops. "Oh. So you're..."

"Yup."

"And you thought I was..."

"Mm-hmm."

I let that sink in. "I'm not, though."

"Not even bi?"

Somewhere in the back of my mind, memories of drawing hearts in my journal around my best friend's name call for attention, but I shove them back. That's not the same thing. I was a kid, and I've only ever been with guys. Heck, I'm pregnant by one. "Um... no..."

"Gotcha." Lily's teeth dig into a corner of her lower lip as she nods. "My mistake. No hard feelings?"

"No, of course not."

She chuckles again as she settles in her seat and opens her snack pack. I'm still reeling from the confusion but do the same, thoughts swirling. Lily is gay. I'm not sure why this surprises me so much. Although I suppose if her ex had been called Mary or Amanda, things would have been clearer from the beginning.

For the next hour or so, we don't talk. Lily reads her book, and I read mine. Or I try to. My thoughts keep returning to what she told me of herself and intermix with a feeling reminiscent of how square I felt in college when I finally encountered people passionate about politics, minority rights, and feminism for the first time, and people with lifestyles different than mine. I wanted desperately to be like them but had no idea how, so I never lingered in their company unless there was a party. And lots of liquid courage.

Annoyed at this echo of inadequacy, I force myself past the sentence in my book I've now reread five times. Suddenly, a specific memory of something Lily said earlier comes to mind.

"Is that why you couldn't live with your dad? Did he not approve?" As soon as the questions cross my lips, I wish I could take them back. Thankfully, Lily doesn't appear to take offense. She puts her book down and considers me for a moment.

"What makes you think there was a reason?"

"The way you said it before. I'm probably wrong, though. Sorry. I didn't mean to pry."

"No." She moves to better face me, her left shoulder against the backrest. "I don't mind. And you're not wrong." She looks down at her hand, concentrating on the thumb spinning a wide silver ring on her left index finger. Several emotions flicker underneath her skin across rounded cheekbones. Anger? Sadness? Determination? Her eyelashes are dark and long against her cheeks even without any makeup.

"Dad didn't mind," she says. "Still doesn't. But he remarried pretty fast. It—she, Cynthia—may even have been one of the reasons they divorced in the first place. I don't know."

"And she has a problem with you?"

"I think the problem is she's a conservative moron." She says it conversationally, without emotion, but I can tell from the set of her mouth she cares more than she lets on. "I didn't want to make Dad choose, so I see them on holidays and never more than a day or two at a time." A smug grin blooms on her lips. "I brought Max with me one time, and Cynthia almost had a stroke. Not one but two dykes in the house. Holy smokes." She mimes someone's head exploding, and I let out a hushed laugh.

The cabin is quiet, the lights dimmed. Most of the passengers are either asleep or engrossed in a book or movie, and as we huddle together in our little corner of the plane, I'm reminded of childhood blanket forts, flashlights, and whispered secrets. The hum of the engine drones meditatively, and finally, I settle in body and mind.

"Sorry about Cynthia. That must suck."

"It is what it is."

Our eyes meet as I nod in agreement. Her pupils are huge in the muted glow of multiple screens. I look away first, lean my head into the headrest. It's getting heavier by the minute, as if I've not slept in days.

"Do you think I'm boring?" I ask when the silence stretches too long.

Lily's mouth quirks up. "*Boring* is not the word that comes to mind."

"No?"

"No."

"Good." I yawn.

"You should try to get some sleep. You've had a long day."

In response, I yawn again.

"Here, you can use my neck pillow." She hands it to me, and I tuck it into the corner by the window and settle in.

I'm still asleep when we land.

CHAPTER 14

It's evening local time when we step off the plane and into LAX. I am barely functioning, having just woken up, so Lily steers me to the gate area, a gentle hand on my elbow.

Mom is waiting for me and raises a sharp eyebrow when she sees my companion.

"What happened to you? Are you sick?"

Before I can respond, Lily sticks her hand out. "Hi, I'm Lily."

Mom takes her hand. "Jane. I'm Kristin's mother."

"So I hear."

"The flight was a bit stressful," I say. "Lily helped."

"Stressful?" Mom's lips flatten. "It was right on time."

"You know what I mean," I mumble.

Mom is quiet for a beat. "Well, you made it, didn't you? Let's get the bags. I can't wait to get to the hotel and clean up."

Lily and I follow her to baggage claim at a safe ten-yard distance.

"So, that's Mom," I say.

"I see. At least you're driving to Santa Barbara. I assume you're okay in cars?"

"Better, at least."

"Is it all modes of transportation then?"

"Airplanes are the worst, but yes. And being away from home, among strangers." I look around us. "Lots of strangers."

"Well, you're here now, and you're in one piece. Got to give your mom that." She winks.

We claim our bags without mishap and make our way to the shuttle pickup. Lily is heading downtown for a job and calls a car to take her to her friend's house.

"I guess this is it," I say when we reach the curb where she'll await her ride. The evening is mild and calm, but I'm so tired I'm shivering despite my sweater.

"I guess so." Lily sets her bag down and pulls out her phone. "We'll stay in touch, though, right? You have to keep me posted on this adventure of yours."

She asks for my number, and I give it to her.

"There, I sent you a text so now you have mine too."

"Which shuttle line is it?" Mom asks. "I hope we didn't miss it."

"They run every ten minutes," Lily says, to which Mom offers a curt "Thanks."

The clock is ticking, and I know I don't have a lot of time before Lily's car comes, so I say the first thing that comes to mind, as cliché as it may sound. "I couldn't have done it without you. I really, really appreciate it. More than you know."

"Aw, come on." She pulls me into a hug. "No need. I had a good time."

I struggle for something else to say, but by then it's too late. A blue sedan pulls up, and Lily announces it's her ride.

"You got this." She squeezes my hand. "Text me."

I raise a hand in goodbye when they pull away from the curb, and then she's gone.

After sleeping like a child, I wake up to bright sunlight, having forgotten to close the blinds in our hotel room. The shower is a glorious waterfall of bliss, and the breakfast buffet the best meal I've had in a while even with Mom's nonstop commentary on fellow patrons. If I could only put off the two-hour drive north a little longer, I would be a happy camper, though to Lily's point, driving seems rather benign in light of my recent induction into the world of air travel.

Getting the rental car is a seamless experience, and I remind myself to thank Aimee for helping Mom coordinate these plans. As soon as she heard I'd agreed to do the list, she begged to be part of it, already painting vivid pictures of me falling in love with a French artist over cappuccinos on a cobblestone Parisian sidewalk. Not entirely helpful, perhaps, but at the very least, supportive. Making any practical arrangements while also being in the midst of it all would not work well for me. Tagging along is quite enough.

I send her a quick text update on where we are and to give her the kudos she's due. While I have my phone out, I also send Lily a wish of a good morning. I add a smiley face first but then delete it, second-guessing myself about seeming too familiar.

She texts back right away. *Happy driving. Wish I could come. Love St. Barb, hate dt LA.* Frowny face, sunset emoji.

Grinning, I tuck my phone back in my purse.

"What are you smiling about?" Mom asks from the driver's seat.

"Nothing." I reach for the GPS, plug in the address of the hotel, and roll down my window. As soon as Mom's lead foot hits the gas pedal, the wind tousles my hair, and I inhale the California air. The sun is hot on my arm but the breeze soothing, and for once, I'm not at the edge of my seat.

The hotel is right on Butterfly Beach.

The day has turned overcast with only glimpses of the sun now and then, so we're not in a hurry to get to the beach. Once our luggage is deposited in our shared room, I suggest we find someplace to eat.

"I'm tired," Mom says. "I think I'll lie down for a bit. You go." She sinks onto her bed to kick off her shoes. "Can you find my pills in the bag over there? The yellow tube."

I pull out a small canister labeled *hydromorphone*. The warning triangles on it give me pause. "Are you in pain?"

Mom looks at me from beneath heavy lids. "I have stage four cancer." She leaves it at that.

The canister is deceptively light in my hand as I hand it over. "Why haven't you said something?"

"What's the point? Complaining won't make it go away."

She pops a pill in her mouth and rinses it down with water. Her neck is so thin I can follow the movement from across the room.

"What?" she asks when she sees me staring.

I sit down at the foot of her bed. "Help me understand. Why doesn't this bother you more? Why aren't you fighting it?"

Her lips press together. "I thought we were done talking about this."

My hands fly out in exasperation. "We never started!"

"I told you I don't want to die like that—have it dragged out, the pain prolonged. If I must die, so be it, but it will be on my terms."

"What about me and Shannon? Zach and Hayley? My baby?" My voice breaks. "You'll never even meet it. If you had more time..."

Mom's stern expression cracks, and her eyes turn glossy. She takes a while to answer. "I'm sorry, but it's too late."

"But Mom—"

"I want to rest for a bit." She looks at me, eyes pleading. "Bring me back some lunch?"

I swallow hard. *No, I don't want to bring you lunch. I want to bring a magical cure, if not for the illness then for your stubbornness.* "Fine."

"Thank you," she says, voice steadier. "For doing this. I don't think I said so before."

Her words knock the air out of me like the fall I took from the monkey bars in third grade. I can't remember Mom ever thanking me for anything before, at least not in such a heartfelt manner.

"You're welcome," I say once I manage to suck in enough air to produce speech again. I force a smile onto my lips. "I'll be back in a bit."

I've never dipped my toes in the ocean before. With the surf rinsing my ankles and my toes sinking into the damp sand at the water's edge, there's a matching swell in my chest rocking me between despair over Mom and awe at the wonder before me.

I pick up a smooth stone and roll it between my fingers to focus my mind elsewhere. My stomach helps by reminding me finding food is becoming a priority. Most of the developments at this part of the coastline are private homes, but eventually I spot a cluster of small shops and eateries a ways away and set my course in their direction.

Before long, my server, surfer-dude Hank, brings me a plate of Santa Barbara's best sliders with a side of waffle fries to accompany the spectacular view. I throw a fry in my mouth and pick up my phone.

Aimee answers on the second ring. "You caught me at the perfect time. I'm finally alone. It's only the second day of break, and the kids are already driving me bananas."

"Hello to you too." I chuckle. "You should be here, then. Beach, food, solitude."

"I hate you."

"Is it that bad?"

"Not really. I just like complaining. So how is it? How's your mom? Have you painted your masterpiece yet?"

I laugh. "We got here an hour ago. We might try later if it clears up. And if a masterpiece is what you're expecting, don't hold your breath."

"You have a few days."

I dip a fry into the ketchup but drop it onto the plate. "Yeah, I wanted to talk to you about that. Any chance you can cancel the Seattle flight and get us a car instead?"

"That's a long drive."

"But a *drive* nonetheless."

There's a break on the line, some static, and then Aimee comes back, clearer. "Sorry, had to take you off speaker. I'm in the grocery store parking lot."

"The flight?" I prompt.

"Um... sure. I can change it until the day before. It will extend your trip, though. Are you sure your mom is up for that?"

The question echoes into nothingness.

"I should ask her," I say eventually. "Don't do anything until I do." Then another thought strikes. "Would you be okay keeping Morrison longer?"

"Of course."

"Are the kids nice to him?"

Aimee hesitates then says, "Uh, sure. No worries." Maybe sensing my skepticism, she adds, "He'll be—he's fine."

I'm afraid to probe further.

"You know, this is actually good," she says, changing topics. "If you're gone longer, it gives me more time to plan for Europe."

The hairs on my arms stand at the thought. Why couldn't the Eiffel Tower in Vegas count?

"And I'm still looking into *La Bohème*. It doesn't seem to be in with the opera houses this season, but I'll figure something out."

While she talks, I look out across the ocean where the waves swell and shatter, never-ending. Like them, I've been set in motion, and all I can do is roll with it. My instinct is to fight it, but even I know that would be futile.

"Got it. I'll let you know what Mom says."

"Flying to Seattle would be faster."

"Not listening."

She lets out a characteristic guffaw.

We talk a few minutes more about her plans for the next couple weeks and what they're doing for the Fourth of July, and then we hang up.

The wind is picking up, conjuring impressive breakers twenty yards away, so I ask for my check and brace myself for the walk back. I need to check on Mom and get our supplies ready. The clouds race low across the sky, but in the distance a blue patch grows larger with each gust, promising decent painting conditions later on.

It's unfortunate I don't have an artistic bone in my body.

Mom is sleeping when I return to the hotel. The afternoon light softens the contours of her face, and she looks so peaceful in easy repose, I'm hard-pressed to wake her up. For a while I busy myself with checking email and unpacking what few clothes I brought, but eventually I can't delay any longer.

"Mom." I sit down next to her and wait for a reaction.

Her breathing catches in the middle of a long inhale, but she doesn't stir.

"Mom, time to wake up."

"Huh?" She opens one eye and peers at me.

It feels wrong to be hovering above her—presumptuous—so I move to my bed to give her space.

"I wasn't sleeping. Just resting."

"Right. How are you feeling?"

She seems to take stock and opens the other eye. "Just what I needed." She stretches. "What time is it?"

"About five o'clock. Sun's breaking through the clouds finally. We have about three hours until sunset."

"Mm." Her eyes drift closed again, and within less than a minute, her breathing has slowed. A chill creeps up my spine that I do everything I can to suppress. *She's fine.*

"Mom," I say a little louder.

"I'm up," she mumbles. "Give us a hand, will you?" She reaches for me, and I help pull her to sitting. "It's the pills. They make me groggy." She yawns as if to emphasize this statement.

I eye the yellow canister. "Can I get you some water?"

"Please."

I do, and she drinks in big gulps. She also eats a few cold fries and a slider I brought back for her, which seem to do her good. The color gradually returns to her cheeks.

"So," she says when she's done. "Ready to paint?"

Ready as I'll ever be.

CHAPTER 15

This must be what it feels like to show up to a party in costume, only to realize you read the invitation wrong. Because of my poor packing skills, I'm wearing all black amidst beachwear-clad, sunburned families, cuddly couples in summer pastels, and Mom in a perfect oversized cotton shirtdress with the sleeves rolled up. Everyone stares at my pudgy ninja self as we make our way across the beach, dragging our paint supplies behind in a cart.

I pretend to fit in as we set up our gear next to one of the lifeguard towers, and it's going all right until I get to the borrowed easel. The hotel concierge got excited when he found out we were there to paint and lent us both the easel and the wheelie cart for our outing. The cart helped a lot in the sand, but the easel is another story. It's made of wood and, folded up, fits in a pouch the size of a small briefcase. The trouble is, in order for it to be a helpful sidekick, I have to do a series of *easy* maneuvers that will transform it into a canvas-supporting stand. It reminds me of a Rubik's Cube but without the colors to guide you. Mom is no help. As soon as we stopped, she opened her lap easel and got to work, and now she is absorbed in her own world. I know better than to disturb her.

After ten minutes, my shirt is soaked. The stupid easel won't cooperate. I let out a particularly profuse litany of curses, upon which a man leans over the tower railing above me and shields his eyes against the sun.

"Everything okay there, ma'am?"

I squint up at him, but the low sun makes it hard to make out any features.

"Do you happen to know anything about these?" I ask, gesturing to the easel. "I can't get it up."

"Hold on." He grabs a lifeguard buoy off the hook and comes down the stairs. Up close, he looks barely older than my students, and I'm glad I'm not in the water actually relying on him to save me. However, regardless of whether he does or does not live up to *Baywatch* standards, he has my easel up and ready in less than two minutes.

"It's this lever here," he says. "You need to push it down while you pull this up. That way it locks in place."

I bob my head up and down as if that makes perfect sense and holler a "thanks" after his tan backside as he returns to his post.

The sun still has a while to go before it will touch the water at the horizon, but if I want to do any painting at all, I'd better get cranking. Mom has made good progress, her landscape sketch already resembling our view, so I pull out my palette, squirt a few paints on it to mimic hers, and get ready with my brush. Outlining schmoutlining. I figure I'll wing it. Sun, horizon, water, sand—it's not rocket science.

A few strokes of ultramarine and it's clear I've underestimated what it takes to paint water. I know, I know—the tutorials I watched back home talked about paying attention to the values of color when mixing paints, but it seems so unnecessary. Isn't water always blue?

"Mom, what am I doing wrong?" I ask, glaring at my canvas, disheartened.

She starts out of her trance and observes me over the top of her glasses.

"Looks like pretty much everything," she says with a smirk and returns to her palette. "Try, try again."

I groan inwardly but forge on, determined not to give up. A little bit of Scarlet Lake red, a little bit of Windsor Lemon yellow, a dab here, a dab there—pretty soon I, too, am lost in the minute movements of brush to canvas.

"It's beautiful," Mom says, jolting me back to my conscious mind some time later.

I squint at my painting. I did mix a great orange, but there's still work to be done. "I don't know about that."

"I meant the sunset," she says dryly.

"Oh. Right."

Mom has put her brush down and sits, chin tilted up, basking in the gilded rays of a day nearly gone. Her skin takes on the glowing color of fall foliage before decay sets in. If I were an artist, now would be the time to capture *her*.

Forcing my attention back to my canvas, I'm struck by its woeful inadequacy. Mom has made clear she requires something at least resembling the natural world, and if I'm to achieve that, I can't delay. I sneak a glance at Mom's painting in the hope of a helpful hint. *I can do this.*

The sun sets.

It's like that feeling when someone snags your candy the very instant you're about to put it in your mouth. My canvas has a sun, a few pink clouds, and an area of assorted horizontal blue lines. Together, they make me want to cry.

Just then a seagull takes off from the lifeguard tower, and—*splat*—my sun is no longer orange but a chalky white. All I can do is glower after it, and when I look back down, Mom is scrutinizing my work.

"If you're being honest, don't you think it sort of deserves being pooped on?"

And she's right. It is, by far, the worst sunset picture anyone has ever painted. Despite it all, I start cracking up. She does the same.

"Yours is great," I say, admiring it over her shoulder.

"I've had a lot of practice. You should put it on your bucket list." She winks then returns her attention to her painting and adds a couple details I would never have thought of—the breakers adorning the shallows, a lone seagull in flight. It's mesmerizing to watch.

The sky transforms, a slow progression through the color spectrum that we watch in silence. Before it gets too dark, I fish out my phone and snap a picture of my failure that I send to Lily. I have a feeling I know exactly what she'll say.

First comes *ROFL* and then *It's so bad it's good.*

Mom glances my way when I giggle but doesn't say anything. I'm about to text back when my phone rings, and Lily's number pops up on screen.

"Hey," I say, getting up from my chair.

"Oh my gosh, you're killing me." She sounds like she is actually rolling on the floor, and it makes me laugh too.

The sand is still warm beneath my feet as I pace a few steps away from our setup. "I know, right?"

"I mean, I got the water part and the clouds, yes, but why a white sun?"

I explain about the bird, and then she's literally howling.

"Ah, I can't breathe," she sputters between giggles. "My cheeks hurt."

"I don't know how anyone can do this," I say when she's calmed down. "Mom's looks amazing, but I don't know, it was over so fast."

"Take a photo next time. Then you can finish up afterward in the comfort of your home." She says it in a singsong voice, like a commercial.

I definitely should have thought of that on my own. "At least I'll have a second chance tomorrow."

"Oh please, please, *please* send me a photo. This job is the pits—nothing but stuck-up models and designers with overinflated egos. I could use the laugh."

"Thanks for the vote of confidence."

She backtracks in good humor. "What I mean is, I'm sure tomorrow's painting will be worthy of the Smithsonian."

I laugh again. "Yeah, yeah. Not everyone is blessed with artistic abilities, you know. As I believe I've thoroughly demonstrated."

"You have other strengths. And I still think it's cool you're doing this with your mom. Even if she doesn't appreciate you," she adds in a lower voice.

I glance back at my mother, who's packing up the supplies. Her gratitude earlier echoes in my mind. "I think maybe she does, in her own way."

In the silence that follows, I have two thoughts—that talking to Lily is my favorite part of today so far and that the light is fading awfully quickly around me. I want to keep talking to her, but I also need to help Mom and get back to the hotel before it gets dark. Reluctantly, I tell her I'd better get going.

"Let me know how it goes tomorrow. Good or bad. I want to know."

I tell her I will, and we hang up.

"Lily?" Mom asks, one brow raised when I return to our things. "You two certainly became fast friends. What was so funny?"

"My painting."

"Ah. Yes, I see."

I consider her a moment. "Hey, Mom, why *didn't* you wait for me at the airport? You knew how scared I was."

Her gaze is inscrutable in the fading light, and she continues packing up brushes, though her movements slow. "You're an adult. You shouldn't need my help."

"I almost missed the flight."

Her eyes flicker to mine. "But you didn't."

I want to object, but in a way she's right. I did make it here, if not completely on my own. At least she didn't argue when I said we'll be driving to Seattle, so there's that.

We finish stacking the cart, and I dump my ruined canvas in the nearest trashcan. Tomorrow I'll be better prepared, I vow, walking back across the sand. I'm going to get this painting right, if not for the Smithsonian then to make my mother proud.

"I'm staying here," Mom says the next afternoon by the pool when I suggest we get ready and head down to the beach early. She hasn't moved since eleven this morning, content, it seems, with her book in the shade.

"No. Come on. We're here to paint. It's your bucket list. Now's your chance."

"I did my painting yesterday. Unlike some."

It's true I still have a lot to do before I can check it off the list, but I wasn't picturing doing it alone. "We've traveled all this way. It's Butterfly Beach," I cajole, making a wide sweep with my hand. "Up you go."

Mom removes her sunhat and sunglasses and turns her face to me, startling me into silence. A deep crease mars the space between her brows, and her eyes are red-rimmed—not from tears but from something altogether more menacing.

"You'll have to go without me," she says, forcing her lips up. "I'm not at my best today."

My face goes slack. "Why didn't you say something? We've been out here for hours. Maybe it's too warm for you. Do you need a doctor?"

"Calm down," she says, tone sharp, and puts her sunglasses back on. "I'm... fine." She adjusts her position on the chaise lounge, not without effort. "I simply want to stay here and rest. There's no need to be so"—she wrinkles her nose—"emotional."

"Then I'll stay too."

"Pishposh. You'll do nothing of the sort. You promised you would paint the sunset. It was part of the deal. And you certainly have your work cut out for you."

I ignore the stab at my ability. "But you're unwell, and I don't feel comfortable—"

"Kristin!" Mom growls. "Enough."

I cast my eyes down to allow my runaway heart to settle. "Can I get you anything before I go?" I ask after a while. "Do you need your pills?"

Mom leans her head back against the folded-up towel. "Already took some." She places her sunhat over her forehead, thereby obscuring her whole head.

"All right," I say, deducing the conversation is concluded. "I guess I'll see you when I get back."

I choose a new spot closer to the hotel by a small pier today. It's not as scenic, but I breathe easier knowing Mom is within quick reach, plus the ancient warning signs on the pier's spindly supports are rather interesting. They look to mean birds here turn electrical when fed ice cream, though I suppose that could be a misinterpretation on my part. Rebuses were never my forte.

I set up as close to the water as I can to get some relief from the heat, but soon it's clear the breeze is not enough. I'm sweating bullets within minutes, and I can't even blame it on the easel. I only pinch two of my fingers in the process of setting it up today, which must be considered a victory since I do it on my own. I've brought water and snacks, but my new tourist shop T-shirt clings to me like an annoying date—a no-no for sensitive pregnancy skin. I don't even stop to think before I yank it off. Most of the people in my vicinity are in skimpy bikinis, and I'm wearing a black grandma bra, so I doubt I'll offend anyone.

Oh, glorious relief. I pour some water down my back for good measure, and then finally, I can get to work.

I'm leaning over, rummaging through my bag for a brush, when I become aware of agitated voices nearby. A second later I'm almost stampeded by the crowd pouring off the pier and onto the beach past me. They run so close to where I'm sitting, my canvas walks off its easel with the reverberating footsteps.

"Do you mind?" I yell to whomever might listen, but they all ignore me.

At first, I try to get back to setting up my colors, but the excited shouts cut in, an insistent distraction. The sun is still high enough that the sky is blue, but it won't be long before the colors change. *Time's a-wasting.* And yet, I find my curiosity piqued, because a large crowd has gathered at the water's edge about fifty yards away, with still more joining them. One last glance at my canvas, and I grab the tote with my wallet and phone to go investigate.

The crowd is several heads deep, so I cut around them in the shallows to see what's going on. I pull up short when I spot the school of stranded dolphins. The crowd murmurs with concern, but nobody seems sure what to do until a voice rings out from the other side of the animals.

"We have to get them farther out." It's my server from the slider shack, and he's already wading out to one of the bigger animals writhing in the sand. "Come on, people. Look alive!"

Before I consciously decide to help, I've swung my tote onto my back and am wading toward one of the gleaming gray bodies. The water chills my calves, but the prickling gooseflesh is a distant discomfort the moment I touch the dolphin's smooth skin.

The animals are heavier than I would have expected, but they lie still while we drag and push them into deeper waters as if they know

we're on their side. There are about fifteen of them and enough people helping that we have them freed in less than a half hour. Once the
last dolphin swims away, the crowd cheers, and I know I'm not the
only one who's choked up. There are hugs and pats on backs, and I
have all but forgotten why I'm on the beach in the first place until
the glow from the setting sun reflects off a camera lens next to me.

The colors. I need to get them mixed.

I turn to head back to my spot and nearly run headfirst into a
woman in a crisp white shirt and perfect hair that for some reason
doesn't move in the breeze. Before I can dodge her, she shoves a huge
microphone into my face and introduces herself.

"I'm Laura Coulter with KSBY News. Can you tell us what just
happened here?"

My mind goes blank, then I stutter, "Eh, y-yes. There were dolphins."

"So we hear." Her sparkly whites are blinding in the low sun as
she turns to the camera. "A school of dolphins stranded here at Butterfly Beach today were saved by a group of onlookers who didn't
hesitate to help the unfortunate animals. I'm here with..." She points
the microphone at me again.

"Um. Kristin," I say into it. "Kristin Caine."

"Kristin Caine, one of those heroic helpers. Kristin, can you walk
us through what happened?"

I blink at her a couple times, but when that doesn't make her go
away, I explain as best as I can the sequence of events leading up to
the present moment.

"So all of the animals are safe?" Laura Coulter asks.

"They swam away." I try a smile into the camera.

She beams at me and turns toward the lens. "Well, there you have
it, our sunshine story of the day. Thanks to people like Kristin, our
dolphin friends live to see another day. Back to you in the studio,

Matt." Laura puts the mic down and, with a quick 'thanks' in my general direction, she and the cameraman start walking away.

"Is this TV?" I call after her, regaining my senses.

Laura turns but keeps walking backward in the sand. "Live broadcast," she says. "You did great."

Light at heart from a new sense of accomplishment, I make my way back to my easel, and it's not until I reach it that I spot my T-shirt slung across the stool. I stop abruptly, and even though I know what I'll find when I look down, the sight of my wet black grandma bra sends a wave of heat to my cheeks.

Crap.

I get back to the hotel a little later with a decent start of a painting, considering I was far from in the moment when finally putting brush to canvas. Thank goodness for Lily's suggestion to snap a photo because knowing that, somewhere out there, TV footage of me in my underwear is swirling about is distracting, to say the least. It's probably okay, though. A thirty-second clip at a local TV station no one will ever see? No great damage done.

Mom is no longer poolside, and her empty chair makes me hurry my steps to our room, where the curtains are drawn. The sight of her in bed makes my stomach drop. *We shouldn't be here*, I think. *I need to get her home.* The realization strikes like lightning. What if my indulging her like this is making her worse?

"You look like you need a shower," she says from the depths of her comforter.

I sit down next to her. "Sorry. Did I wake you?"

Her nostrils flare. "And you don't exactly smell like cake."

"Sorry." I get up and move to my side of the room. "How are you feeling?"

"Better."

"Really?"

"Don't start." She reaches for the remote on the nightstand and turns on the TV. "How did it go?"

I hold up the drying canvas for her to see before setting it on top of the dresser.

"Better than yesterday," she says.

High praise indeed.

I'm out of the shower, rubbing stretch-mark-preventing cocoa butter all over my belly per Aimee's instructions, when the sound from the TV cuts through my thoughts.

"Now some good news to brighten our day," the newscaster says. "A school of dolphins saved at Butterfly Beach a few hours ago. Laura has more information."

I run into the room, snatch the remote from the bed, and turn up the volume, breathless as I see again the crowd, the glittering ocean, the last of the dolphins being helped.

Back to the studio, back to the studio, back to the studio.

But no, there I am, staring at the camera like a surprised bog witch. Oh my God, I look even worse than I thought. My face is flushed from exertion and sun exposure, the hair around my face lies plastered against my skin, and, yup, up close you can totally tell it's a bra.

I bury my face in my hands and groan. Because this isn't the local news channel—this one covers all of Orange County.

"You saved dolphins?" comes Mom's incredulous voice from behind. She's staring at me, eyes wide. "You're afraid of water."

"It wasn't deep, and they were stuck." I squirm under her gaze. "Ugh, how embarrassing."

"Why? You should be proud."

I should? I'm too stumped to answer, so when my phone rings, I gratefully pick it up.

"Were you just on TV?" Lily asks.

I groan again and sink into one of the chairs by the window. "Out of all the people on the beach, she chose to interview me, the naked pregnant lady. Who does that?"

Lily lets out a loud cackle. "Remember when you asked me if I thought you were boring? I'm pretty sure you're the dictionary definition of the exact opposite."

"It's mortifying," I say, with the high pitch of exasperation.

"No, it's not. You guys did a great thing. It must have been so exciting."

I take a big gulp of air and allow myself to relax. "Yeah, I guess."

"I'm going to need details."

While I tell her about it, the whole experience finally sinks in. Real, live wild dolphins are safe because of something I helped with today. And, while the interview is beyond cringeworthy, I wouldn't have the last few hours undone for anything. I tell Lily this, and she is quiet for so long I ask if she's still there.

"Yeah, I'm here." Her voice is tentative, dreamy almost. "I'm just—I worked at a kibbutz in Israel one summer years ago, obviously not with dolphins, but I had forgotten that feeling of community you get from a joint cause. Thanks for reminding me. I needed that." She lets out a surprised snort. "You cut right through all the noise, don't you?"

The compliment sends a prickle of satisfaction through me where I sit, phone pressed to my cheek. "I do my best," I say, tone intentionally light. She doesn't respond, and for a long time there's nothing but silence on the line.

"Hey, Lily."

"Yeah?"

I venture a quick glance at Mom. She has her eyes on the screen, but her ears are practically flapping. I bite my lip. "Um... how is work going?"

"Oh. Well, only one more day, then I'm done. Finally. I wish I could say I was through with model jobs, but they pay the bills."

"So where to next? Are you staying in LA?"

"Ugh, never. I'm going home for a bit. Mom needs help decluttering her attic, and I've offered my services. You? Flying up to Seattle, right?"

"No, actually. Opted out of the deathtrap, so we're driving instead." I lower my voice. "Unless we end up going home."

"Home?" Mom's voice hits like a whiplash. "What do you mean, *home*?"

"Hold on," I say to Lily and put my hand over the phone. "I'm worried about you, okay? I want to make sure you're... strong enough."

"Of course I am," she spits out. "We're going home over my dead body!" Her jaw is set when she returns her gaze to the TV.

"Did you hear that?" I grumble to Lily, a chill lingering along my spine from Mom's choice of words.

"Sounds like you're driving," she says, matter-of-fact. "Wait, when are you going?" Her voice grows louder, excitement tingeing it.

"Wednesday is the plan. Why?"

"I'm going to my mom's. In Portland."

"So you said." I have no idea what she's getting at. Are they mutually exclusive or something? If I go to Seattle, she can't go to Portland? I mean, I know they're close, but they're not even in the same state.

Oh! Light bulb moment. "Are you driving too?"

"Yes!" Lily laughs. "We can carpool! If you want to, that is. And if you can stay another day. I can't pick you up until Thursday."

Of course I want to. With Mom not feeling well, I would have no choice but to do the driving, so I can think of nothing more tempting right about now. A huge weight lifts off my shoulders. I'll have backup for Mom, I won't have to drive, and heck, Lily might even know the way.

"Hold on, let me check with the boss lady."

I briefly explain the situation to Mom and why I think it's a good idea.

"Fine, if it'll make you stop babbling about going back home," she says.

I beam, returning to my phone. "Thursday, it is."

"Excellent," Lily says, audibly smiling. "I should be there by noon."

CHAPTER 16

Mom and I spend the remainder of our time at Butterfly Beach lounging by the pool and going for walks on the beach. She's doing better, and I don't bring up going home again. Bart is next on our list, and I know how important finding him is to her.

Lily picks us up midday on Thursday.

I've had time to regret my decision multiple times since our call—we don't really know each other, after all—but when I see her, relief washes the tension away. Something about her presence is familiar in the way of apple pie, walking barefoot in grass, and a reading nook full of pillows—you know it's altogether good.

"I'm so glad this worked out," she says by way of greeting. "Traveling alone is such a drag."

"I hope you're a better driver than Kris." Mom hands our luggage to Lily, who puts it in her trunk.

"Practically a professional. Don't worry, Jane." Lily winks at her, and I swear a small smile flickers across Mom's face.

We've been on the road for less than an hour when my phone rings. I don't recognize the number but answer all the same.

"Kris?" Patrick's voice sounds far away like it always does when he's in his car.

"Pat, is that you? Where are you calling from?"

"New phone. Where are you?"

Still the king of brusque greetings. "Just left Santa Barbara."

"So it wasn't you," he says, still echoing.

"It wasn't me where? Can you take me off speaker?"

He does. "I thought I saw you last night at the movie theater."

"Okay."

"Yeah."

"That's it?"

"What's going on?" Mom asks from the back seat.

I wave her off.

Patrick clears his voice. "So, how are you doing?"

"Um..." I close my eyes and pinch the bridge of my nose. "You want to know how I am?"

"Well." He pauses as if searching for the right words. "I couldn't help but think about, you know... Ah, I'm so bad at this!"

Another silence stretches out. I have a vague idea where he's going, but I'm done helping him communicate.

"I mean, you're pregnant."

"Mm-hmm."

"How, you know, how does it feel?"

I roll my eyes, more at how hard it is for him to get the words out than at the actual question.

"My pants are tight, but I don't feel it moving yet, if that's what you mean."

"Oh, okay."

"Yeah, I'm only fourteen weeks. It's too early."

"I see." He pauses. "When will you be home? Can we meet?"

I tell him about my plans for the immediate future, and he sounds so genuinely disappointed that, despite everything that has transpired between us, I feel sorry for him.

"I'll let you know when I'm back. I should go now."

Patrick makes no move to actually end the call, so I do, and I sit with my phone in my hand for a while after the line goes dead.

"What did he want?" Mom asks.

"Not sure," I mumble.

"Maybe he's warming up to the idea of being a dad?" Lily takes her eyes off the road to glance at me.

"I'm not going to make assumptions, considering." I fill her in on the more jarring details of how Patrick and I ended and everything that's happened since. "He might come around and want to be a present father, or he might still want nothing to do with it. I'll be okay either way. Once the baby is born, he'll have to make a decision, of course, but there's still time."

Mom pats my shoulder but doesn't say anything.

"Wow." Lily looks at me again. She has one of her hands draped across the steering wheel, the other resting by the open window. The wind makes her dark hair even bigger, and she is engaged in an eternal struggle to keep it out of her eyes. "I don't know how you can be so calm about this."

I shrug. "We weren't right for each other. Hindsight is twenty-twenty. Whatever. This baby is wanted, no matter what."

"And you don't miss him?"

I look within as I have so many times in the last month, searching every corner of my heart. "I really don't."

"You're lucky." Lily speeds up as she overtakes an RV. Once she's back in our lane, she continues. "Max cheated on me. With a mutual friend of ours."

"Yikes."

"Who's Max?" Mom asks.

"My ex-girlfriend."

"Oh," Mom says. Then another "Oh," this time tinged with a deeper current of understanding.

I glance back at her in silent admonition not to comment further.

Lily doesn't appear to notice our exchange. "Yeah. Looking back, I know things weren't great, but we were together for over five years.

I thought we'd get married, start a family. You'd think she'd have the decency—"

She doesn't finish her sentence. When she resumes speaking, her voice quivers slightly. "Anyway," she says, smiling half-heartedly at the road. "Water under the bridge, right?"

"How long ago was it?" I ask.

"Ah, I don't want to say."

"Why not?"

"I don't want you to think I'm completely pathetic."

"She said to the single, pregnant lady."

She chuckles. "That's different."

"Come on. I told you my stuff."

She seems to contemplate this. "Fine. I found out New Year's Eve before last, so a year and a half. And, despite appearances, I'm over it. Still makes me mad on occasion, though."

"Understandable."

"Are you mad at Patrick?"

"Of course. He's a total idiot. But..." I tilt my head in Mom's direction. "I have other things to think about right now."

Lily glances in the rearview at Mom, a knowing smile blooming on her lips. "How convenient."

I'm not sure what she means by that, but I don't press on.

Soon I'm lulled into a half sleep by the road noise and the blur of the passing landscape. We have several hours to go until we reach San Francisco, where Lily has friends who don't mind houseguests for an overnight stop. For once, last-minute plans don't stress me out. In fact, I think in my dreamy state, neither do this road trip, my mother's expectations, or the thought of being a single parent. The last thing I remember thinking is how calming Lily's company is and how it's a shame we only have such a short time together.

CHAPTER 17

"I've decided to add something to the list," Mom announces from her seat by a kitchen window overlooking Golden Gate Park when Lily and I clean up our takeout that evening. Lily's friend isn't home, but his nanny was here to let us in. She's made herself scarce to the kids' room now.

"Oh yeah? What's that?" Lily asks, sitting down again.

Mom shows her something on her phone screen.

"It's a good spot for it," Lily agrees. "What do you say, Kris? Want to do some whale watching tomorrow?"

I close the dishwasher and join them. "Some what?"

"We're going whale watching," Mom says. "The boat leaves at nine."

"Um..." I let out a sputtered huff. "Nope."

"What do you mean 'nope'?" Mom tries to mimic my tone.

"I'm most definitely not going whale watching."

"But it's on the list."

"Nice try, but additions don't count. That's like amending a contract after someone signs it and not telling them. No. Besides, that would mean an extra night here, and I *strongly* feel we'd be overstaying our welcome."

"You strongly feel..." Mom stares at me.

"Actually, I don't think Jon would mind," Lily says before I cut her off with a look. "Which is not the point," she mumbles.

"I'm already doing a lot, Mom," I say, trying for a softer tone. "But open water wasn't part of the deal."

Mom taps her phone and puts it aside. Disappointment pinches her mouth, and as much as I'm decided in this, I feel bad. "Maybe you two can go," I say.

Lily looks up. "But you'd be on your own for the day."

I put my hands up as if weighing the two options. "Alone time or being pulled to my watery grave by the kraken. Yes, it is a tough choice."

She elbows me with a grin. "Weirdo."

Mom's eyes cut between us, but then she picks her phone back up. "I'm game if you are," she tells Lily.

They're gone by the time I wake up the following morning. I am to meet them at the docks when they return this afternoon, and until then, I'm free to do as I please.

I get dressed then sit back down on the bed, and I'm surfing my phone when out of the corner of my eye, I see the door handle turn and the door opening a crack. A white-blond toddler peers in at me, shows me a plastic octopus, then retreats. Ten seconds later, his small hand reappears, this time holding a shark. I like this kid. It's as though he's been sent here to reaffirm that I made the right choice not to go on a boat today.

"Nate?" a man's voice calls from somewhere in the house.

Two fish appear. Plush replicas of Nemo and Dory.

"I like that movie," I say.

The boy—who I assume to be Nate—giggles. He pushes the door open wider and drags a basket of toys over the threshold. I'm his audience now, and what follows is a rapid introduction to all his inanimate friends.

"There you are." A man appears in the doorway, carrying an infant. "I'm so sorry," he says to me. "Emma had a blowout, so I took my eyes off this one for a moment." He places a hand on Nate's head. "Let's pick these up and leave our guest alone. Okay, bud?"

"I don't mind," I say, scooting off the bed. "I'm Kristin, by the way. You must be Jon."

"I'm Nate," Nate says.

Jon chuckles. "He's got better manners than me, it seems. Yes. Jon. Sorry. It's been a busy morning, and I still have to warm up her bottle." He nods at the bundle in his arms.

"No worries. And thanks for letting us stay the night. Maybe Nate wants to show me the rest of his toys while you do that."

Nate gives an exaggerated nod and looks up at his dad.

"Thanks," Jon says. "I'll make some coffee too. It'll be ready in ten." He backs away.

Nate has already started lining up his friends, so I join him on the floor.

"You're very patient," Jon says when I enter the kitchen. "Do you have kids of your own?"

"Not yet." I pat my unassuming belly and accept the mug he's offering me.

"Ah." His eyes brighten. "When are you due?"

"December."

"Still some time to go."

I bob my head in acknowledgment.

"Milk and sugar are on the table."

"Thanks."

Jon remains standing, swaying slightly with Emma in a harness on his front. I study him on the sly as he adjusts the straps. *Is he a single dad with two kids?*

"We're normally better organized in the mornings," he says as if he senses my question. "But my wife had to go out of town for work last minute, so, you know... You improvise."

"You both work, then?"

"I'm part-time until Emma turns one, but yes. Busy days. Takes teamwork."

The thought is there before I can stop it. *I won't have a team.* If Patrick decides he wants nothing to do with his child, will I be enough? Will I be able to do all the midnight feedings, dirty diapers, and tantrum taming? I will love him or her, that's a given, but will he or she love me back or find me lacking? The only single mother I know is *my* mother, and that is not a history that needs repeating.

Jon butters a slice of toast and hands it to Nate. Nate, in turn, shoves it into the rubber jaws of a smiling frog.

Jon looks on, an air of affectionate indulgence on his features. "So, no whale watching for you today?" he asks me as I put my mug away.

"Nope, not for me."

"Nate here wants to be a marine biologist when he grows up," Jon says.

That would explain all the ocean-related toys.

Nate beams up at me. "So I can swim with the *dorks*."

"He means orcas," Jon clarifies.

"Wow, you must be a brave kid," I say to Nate. "Water gives me the heebie-jeebies."

He giggles. "But you're a grown-up."

I shrug. He doesn't need to know this grown-up has more hang-ups than a whole preschool full of children.

"Any other plans?" Jon asks.

I look out the window at the blue sky. I may not be on that boat, but maybe I can push myself a little bit. After all, I've never been to San Francisco before. "Some sightseeing," I say. "I want to ride one of those trolleys that you see in the movies."

By the time I'm due to meet up with Mom and Lily again, I've braved some of San Francisco's steepest hills, bought a seal keychain for Nate and a sweatshirt for me in a souvenir shop, refueled at In-N-

Out Burger, marveled at the size of the sea lions in the harbor, and done enough people watching to tide me over for the next year. I've documented each activity with selfies that I've sent to Aimee, whose only response was, "Who are you and where's Kristin?", but I can't wait to also show Mom and Lily.

"How was it?" I ask when they step off the boat.

"Just extraordinary," Mom exclaims. Her hair is windblown, and her cheeks red. *Hearty* is the word that comes to mind. Surely the doctors must have gotten her diagnosis wrong. She pulls out her phone on approach. "A whole school of orcas," she says. "Just look at this."

I "ooh" and "aah" for an appropriate amount of time before turning to a smiling Lily. "A success then?" I ask.

"It was very cool."

"I hope she wasn't too much," I say in a lower voice.

"Not at all. She's a neat lady."

I laugh at that. "That's one way to put it."

My adventures don't elicit quite as big a response in Mom as I'd hoped, but she does raise an eyebrow when I tell her I rode the trolleys alone, which I choose to interpret as mission accomplished. I'll take the scraps if I have to. Plus, I've impressed myself, and that's not nothing.

"So, what now?" Lily asks. "I'm kind of hungry."

"I need a nap," Mom says, contradicting my earlier assessment. "You girls go ahead. I'll take a taxi back."

After putting Mom in a car, Lily and I set off strolling along the water. The sun has brought out her freckles after a day on the water, and her curls are, if possible, even more unruly than I've seen them before. The vibrancy she exudes makes me feel ordinary next to her. Like maybe I should have gone with them and not been so *me*.

"There's a fish-and-chip shop up ahead. Hole in the wall. Let's grab some to go and eat by the water." Lily steers me across the street and up a block.

"What did you mean when you said my mom was 'neat'?" I ask while we wait for our food.

Lily shrugs. "I don't know. I appreciate people who are straight shooters." She gestures forward with her hand. "She asked me how old I was when I came out. When I knew."

I groan. "Jeez, Mom."

"No, I didn't mind. We talked about all sorts of things. My point is she's a go-getter."

"Because she asks questions?"

"That and, you know, she wanted to see whales, so she saw whales."

"Checking off all the things on her list," I fill in. "Kind of the point of this trip."

"Mm." Lily nods then squints at me. "It's never struck you as curious that her bucket list basically forces you to do pretty much everything you're scared of?"

I consider her question. "Not really. She and I have always had different interests." It's a coincidence, that's all. And yet... The question percolates a few more turns. "No," I say again, more firmly this time. "It's her list. It has painting and Bart. The handstand..." I nod to myself.

"If you say so."

Our number is called, and Lily gets the bag. We find a bench overlooking the bay and dig in in silence.

"She speaks pretty highly of you, you know?" Lily says before plopping the last bite of fried fish into her mouth.

"Oh, I doubt it." I take a swig of my water.

"No, I'm serious."

"You don't have to do that."

"Do what?"

"Try to make me feel better about skipping out today."

She turns more fully toward me. "Kris, I'm really not. I didn't know you were teacher of the year two years in a row, for example. Or that you make the best fudge."

"She told you that?"

"Among other things."

A smile tugs at my cheeks. "I had a booth at the farmers market one year and sold out in an hour. I'm surprised she remembers."

"I think she just wants you to be happy."

I wrinkle my nose and look out across the water. I'm about to say that Mom has a strange way of showing it if that's the case, but I swallow the bitter sentiment down. It doesn't fit here. "I'm happy right now," I say instead, and I mean it. I'm always happy when I'm with Lily, it seems.

"Good." Lily beams, and it hits me square in the chest. "Me too. But you know what would make me even happier?"

Her excitement is contagious. "No, but I'm all ears."

"Ice cream," she says. Her eyes twinkle as if she's just shared a great secret.

"I second that."

"And I also need to pick up some cheese for my mom," Lily says. "She's obsessed with trying new cheeses, and it just so happens there's a market a few blocks away that has both. You game?"

I stand and hold out my hand for her garbage. "For you, anything."

Something curious flickers behind her blue gaze as it meets mine. An odd beat. But it's gone before I can swallow down the new sensation it leaves in my chest.

"Dairy coma, here we come," she says, giving me the balled-up paper bag and getting to her feet. "Prepare yourself for a treat of the most spectacular kind."

And I'm not sure that I can. Prepare myself, that is.

The next day we hit the road again, heading north into the redwood forests, when Lily says, "Don't be mad, but we have a surprise for you."

She and Mom snicker in silent collusion.

I've been talked into driving today, so I can't take my eyes off the road to see their expressions, but I can hear the glee in Lily's voice.

"What is it?"

"We'll tell you in a bit," Mom says.

Great. Did she add something else to the list? Mountain climbing? Snake charming?

"It's on the way," Lily adds, settling my misgivings somewhat. Could be yet another sight Mom wants me to see. San Francisco was more than fun—don't get me wrong—but I'm done playing tourist for a while. My knees still ache from all the walking.

Eventually, we come upon a sign for Mossbrae Falls, and Lily shouts, "That's our exit!"

I manage to make the ramp, and I'm getting excited because there are certainly no waterfalls in Chicago. The road gets more and more narrow as we make our way into the forest. It's midday so the sun seeps through the leafy canopy, tinting everything in lime and jade, and then, there it is—a parking sign and, through the growth, water glistening in the distance. I start to pull over, but Lily stops me.

"No, keep going straight."

"But the falls?"

"Oh." She turns and looks out the window. "Sorry, not where we're going."

I can't help but pout, and I'm sure she can hear it in my voice when I demand to know where, then, we are going.

"I showed Lily the list." Mom sounds as though she can barely contain herself. "And she booked you a ropes course!"

It takes every ounce of self-control not to slam the brakes. "You what?" I risk a quick glance at Lily, who's beaming next to me.

"A ropes course. I happened to know there's one up here."

"Yes, but—" The skin on my neck prickles. "But I—"

"What?" Mom's question has an edge to it.

"I..." *Don't want to. Am not a monkey. Will fall and die.* "I'm pregnant."

Lily laughs. "It's totally safe. You wear a harness hooked on to the ropes at all times. It'll be fun, I promise."

"I—" My voice fails me. What's the point? They're not going to let me say no to this one since it was on the original list. Mom grins at me in the mirror, satisfied, it seems, with this turn of events. I curse her under my breath but then take it back, feeling guilty.

"It should be around the next bend," Lily says.

And that is how I end up perched in a tree twenty feet in the air on this fine Saturday afternoon.

CHAPTER 18

There it is again, that recurring question. *What have I done?* The small platform I'm standing on is built around a large tree right beneath its canopy, and all I want to do is cry and climb back down the ladder that brought me up here. Mom and Lily are still on the ground with the instructor because the platform can only fit one person at a time.

"You can do this," Lily hollers up to me.

"I very much doubt it," I whisper under my breath.

The first obstacle of eight is a rickety suspension bridge that I'm supposed to cross without holding on to anything. I can cheat and cling to the line tethering me to the overhead wire, but such behavior is for chickens, or so I've been told.

"Arms straight out and walk," the instructor calls to me.

"No cheating," Mom chimes in, in a singsong voice. "I'm doing this vicariously, remember."

She's agreed to stay on the ground, which took little convincing, come to think of it.

"I can't," I call back. "It moves."

"It's supposed to." Lily laughs, and I venture a look over the edge. *Whoa.* Bad idea.

"Then you do it," I yell.

"I'm right behind you."

I will the swaying bridge to solidify. Oh, fuck it. At least if I fall and die, I won't have to do the other obstacles. The first tentative step has me teetering like a bad mime feigning tightrope walking. The second is better.

"Yeah," Lily shouts. "There you go."

Emboldened by her enthusiasm, I take another couple of steps—tiny ant steps, but still—but then I stop. Now that I've reached the point of no return, the ground seems even farther away, the air around me even more volatile. A choked croak escapes my lips when a hole appears in front of my stiff toes. The next rung is missing, and I have to step over the gap to continue.

"I'm coming up," Lily announces. "Keep going."

"Easy for you to say." My gaze is fixed on the hole I need to pass, and my heart is hammering as if it, too, wishes nothing more than to escape.

"Do you have a choice?"

I know I don't, but that doesn't make it any easier. "Fine," I say, and in pure defiance I grab my tether for support and step forward. The bridge rocks, but I'm still standing.

"No hands," the instructor calls up to me.

"Fuck you," I mutter, proceeding slowly but surely to the next platform, still holding on. When I reach it, I grasp the trunk of the tree with both arms and lean my helmet against it. This is ridiculous. Why would anyone voluntarily subject themselves to something like this?

"Here I go," Lily calls as she steps onto the bridge, arms stretched wide, her tongue poking out of the corner of her mouth. Her eyes are big and bright, and the way the sun hits her through the leaves makes it seem like she's floating. I'm utterly captivated until she reaches me. This platform is bigger, so there's room for both of us.

"Wow! That was awesome." She's panting, cheeks flushed. "Don't you just love the adrenaline rush?"

Despite my precarious perch, I smile at her gusto. "Not the word I'd use, but I'm glad you're having fun," I say, somewhat drily.

"Oh, come on." She gives me a little push—enough for my grip on the tree trunk to tighten. "Let's go. Onward and upward."

I give her an icy glare, which only seems to make her happier, and then I turn to obstacle number two. My tethers refastened to the next line, all I have to do is climb like a spider through the horizontal net strung between the trees. *Piece of cake.* I crack my knuckles, and then I'm off. To my surprise, I reach the next tree with no mishap, and for a brief moment, my confidence is boosted. This lasts for about thirty seconds until the instructor shouts for us to proceed forward, and I'm faced with a ten-foot gap I have to traverse using a vine as if I'm freaking Tarzan. Do I hesitate? Why yes—yes, of course. But then mind over matter kicks in, and I grind my jaws together. The only way down is through, after all.

Somehow, I'm still alive when the final zip line brings me down to the ground. I have a red rope burn on one shoulder, and my shins are bruised from crawling on all fours across two parallel wires—I know!—but other than that I'm unscathed.

"Nicely done, ladies," says the instructor, who I've come to view more as a personal nemesis in the past hour. "If you'd like to sign up for another go, come see me at the front desk."

I almost laugh in his face. Never have I ever wanted anything less. Except for maybe flying.

"I wish we could, but we're not staying in the area," Lily says.

The instructor-slash-nemesis waves us off as if to say he already knew that and sets course toward the tourist center, where I assume he hides out when not taunting people stupid enough to perform death-defying stunts for fun in his trees. Lily follows him to return our equipment.

"You did it." Mom beams at me. She touches my shoulder tentatively at first then pulls me to her in a quick hug. It's so unexpected, I don't have time to react. "How are you feeling?"

"A little shaky," I admit. "And—" I stop midthought, noting as if from outside myself the blood draining from my face. "Dizzy, actually." Tiny dots emerge in my field of vision, and her voice saying my name reaches me from far away. I try to respond but can't make my lips form the words.

"Oh my goodness. Kris?" Mom grabs my arm and lowers me to the ground then pushes my head between my knees. "Take a deep breath."

"What's going on?" I hear Lily call.

"She's about to faint. Get some water."

I focus on my breathing, and little by little the ground comes into focus. A tiny ant busies itself among the blades of grass between my feet. "I'm okay. Really."

"I'll be the judge of that." Mom strokes my back as if trying to rub warmth back into my skin. "I'll not have you pass out in your condition. Oh, this is my fault. I shouldn't have made you—"

I raise a hand to silence her and try a reassuring "I'm fine."

"Here's the water." Lily hands Mom a bottle, which she opens and shoves in my hand.

"Drink up."

I let the cool water run down my throat and refresh me. Before long, I'm restored enough to walk over to a bench by one of the buildings. Lily sits down next to me.

"Do you need anything else?" Mom asks, hovering. "A cold rag? Some ice? Something to eat?"

"They have food here?"

"I'm sure there's something." Her voice suggests no establishment with concern for their safety would deny her whatever she requests, and having assured herself I'm no longer at risk for a tumble, she excuses herself to go in search of sustenance.

"All better?" Lily asks.

"Adrenaline shock, I suppose. Not used to it."

She laughs softly. "Aside from that, what did you think?"

"It was awful." The corner of my mouth twitches. "Terrible."

"But you did it."

"I did."

"I love it. It's a high for me—you know that unreal feeling where you want to laugh and cry all at once. Like all your emotions are right beneath the surface."

"Maybe you're pregnant too," I say, rubbing at a kink in my neck.

"Very funny." Lily is quiet for a long while, then she bumps my arm with her shoulder. "Hey, you're not mad about this, are you?"

"Why do you ask?"

"You don't exactly seem happy."

"I didn't realize that was a requirement." It comes out a bit snarkier than necessary.

"I'll take that as a yes, then."

"No, I... Just because..." I take a deep breath that fails to calm me down, instead releasing my carefully contained inner chaos. "Climbing around in trees is not something I'd choose for myself, okay? *I* have a sense of self-preservation like a normal person, so spending over an hour pushing myself past any logical limits, completely terrified, and sweating like a pig..." My breathing sputters, and that now-so-familiar lump is making my voice thicker and thicker. "Sorry if I'm not ready to break into dance yet."

Lily's eyes widen as I speak, and her cheeks redden.

I give her a final glare for punctuation then turn away. I know she's done nothing to deserve this, but she's here, and I need to direct all this turmoil somewhere.

"Come on, Kris," she says.

I suck in a long, jagged breath. "I'm sorry. I just... I feel so weird."

"It's completely normal. When I did my first bungee jump, I cried for hours after."

"Really?"

"Yeah. I think it's a response to surviving danger."

"No, I mean—you've done more than one bungee jump?"

Lily's eyes crinkle. "If you haven't noticed already, I'm *not* one of those normal, self-preserving people you were talking about."

I rub at my eyes a few times for good measure, and when I look up again, my gaze gets stuck on the ropes high up in the trees. "I can't believe I actually did that," I say, mostly to myself.

"I took a picture," Lily says. "When I was still on the ground. Do you want to see?"

I scowl. "Super attractive, I'm sure, from that angle. The harness accentuating all the juicy bits—"

"Okay, that's enough of the self-deprecating commentary." Lily pulls out her camera. "Yes or no?"

Shamed by her stern gaze, I say, "Yes, please," and she shows me the screen on her humongous camera. In the shot, I'm sort of backlit, which renders me, the bridge, and the framing trees mere silhouettes against the bright-blue sky. I've passed the first gap in the suspended bridge, and at least one of my arms is stretched out in a graceful arc, if I may say so myself. My back is straight and my head up.

I take the camera from Lily to see better. "I look like I know what I'm doing." I smile at the picture. Maybe she's right. Maybe it's the doing that counts. I hand back the camera and look up at her. "I really am sorry for acting like a baby," I say. "And I *am* glad I did it." I lean my shoulder to hers, and she reciprocates by tilting her head to mine. We sit like that for only a short moment before my mother returns, and as if on cue, we straighten and separate, the skin on our arms reluctantly unsticking.

"This was all they had." Mom holds up a packet of gum. "And I don't know about you, but I'm getting hungry. Ready to go?"

I get to my feet and stretch. "Ready," I say and hook my arm through Mom's. "I'm starving."

CHAPTER 19

We arrive in Portland the next evening and are greeted by a rain shower and sunlight, which turns into a rainbow before we know it. The air smells of pine and earth, and if it wasn't for the hideous metal structures flanking the city center, I would say Portland seems a pretty lovely place. We've agreed to stay the night before continuing on to Seattle since Lily assures us her mom adores guests.

Lily's mom, Barb, lives alone in a little house much like my mom, but that's where the similarities end. She wears her salt-and-pepper hair in a long coiffed bob, used to be a finance manager for Delta Air Lines, and still dons those blouses with a bow at the neck even though she's been retired for years and the eighties are long gone. She's shorter than Lily, her complexion fairer, but when they smile, the resemblance is a gut punch.

"This is Kristin and Jane," Lily says.

Barb embraces us each in turn. "I've heard all about your adventure. Come on in, put your feet up."

"And this is for you." Lily hands her mom the disposable cooler containing various samples of cheddar, asiago, and gorgonzola.

Barb peeks inside. "Oh, you know me so well, hon!" she exclaims. To Mom and me she says, "I'm just *obsessed* with cheese."

Lily winks at me in a "told you so" kind of way. The gesture swirls around my belly.

After Barb puts her gift away in the fridge, she leads us through the house to the deck out back, where we sit for a while in pleasant conversation.

Lily wasn't exaggerating when she said her mom likes guests.

"I know it's been twenty years, but once you kids move out, it gets so quiet," she says. From the look on Lily's face, I take it this is something she hears every time she visits. "Don't you agree, Jane?"

Mom seems to struggle to find a response, so I chime in. "We had a small place. I spent more time at my friends' houses. Plus, I moved out when I was seventeen."

"You did?" Lily frowns at me. "You never told me that."

"You've known her a week. There's bound to be things that haven't yet come up," Barb says in a matter-of-fact way, getting up.

Lily and I look at each other in mutual incredulity. Has it really only been a week?

"What kind of pizza do you like, Jane?" Barb asks.

"Mom doesn't cook," Lily stage-whispers to me.

"I heard that."

"That's why I learned how—so I wouldn't starve." She raises her voice on the two last words. I take it this is a private joke between them.

"I have a phone." Barb holds up her cell as proof. "And I live in Portland, where foodies pop up like mushrooms in a marsh."

"I don't mind whipping something together," Mom says. "As a thank you for letting us stay. To be honest, I miss my kitchen."

Barb frowns. "You do?"

"She's a great cook," I assure her.

Barb grins. "Well, twist my arm. The store's three blocks away. I'll drive."

Lily chuckles. "Come on, Kris, I'll give you the grand tour."

I lie awake in what was once Lily's domain, engulfed in the oddness of sleeping in a room that's remained frozen in time for two decades. She's insisted on taking the less comfortable pullout couch in the family room, but with Kurt Cobain's dimpled chin only inches away, I'm regretting agreeing to this. Nothing makes you feel as old as being reminded of your lost youth, and the room is practically a shrine to all things nineties. There's even a non-ironic collection of Beanie Babies taking up the top shelf in one of the bookcases.

I cover my eyes with one arm and listen to the traffic faintly audible through the window. Then I have a sudden impulse and reach for my phone.

What was it about Nirvana? I type and hit Send.

I thought you said you were tired, comes Lily's response.

The music or Kurt's lovely locks?

The locks, of course :)

A quiet laugh trills from my chest.

What time are you leaving tomorrow? Lily asks after a short radio silence.

Probably right after breakfast. Since we'll be knocking on a virtual stranger's door, it will be best to do it during daylight hours. I also have a feeling Mom wants to get it over with. She tucked in early tonight, but the squeaky springs from the guest room next door suggests the kind of restlessness that only comes with uncertain anticipation.

Oh, okay, Lily responds.

Two little words, so many possible connotations. Does she mean "Oh, okay, cool beans," or "Oh, okay, that's a bummer"? Or maybe it's simply "Oh, okay," end of story? It's not like it matters. Our friendship is most likely one of those rare-but-brief chance convergences meant to be for reasons that will become clear after the fact. It's not likely to last, but when I look back at it, I'll be thankful I had the experience. She and I live different lives in different places, and while we might stay in touch via phone or email for a while, I don't want to kid myself that ours will be the shortest-ever real-life meeting to

stand the test of time. When I leave here tomorrow, the most likely
scenario is we'll never see each other again.

As soon as the thought enters my mind, I'm choked up. Because
that sucks. And I know this is an odd feeling to have after only knowing someone for a week, but everything is easier when she's around.
My life is easier. I'm happier. I can ride planes and climb ropes twenty
feet in the air, and—

A knock on the door interrupts my reverie.

"Yeah?" I ask, pushing myself up to sitting.

"It's me. Can I come in?" The door muffles Lily's voice.

"Um, sure." I hurry to wipe a stray tear off my face.

Lily's curly head first appears in the opening then her pajama-
clad self. She closes the door behind her, pads across the floor, and
plops down at the foot of the bed. "You like my decorating, huh?"

"He looks like he wants to eat me." I wrinkle my nose at the Nirvana poster. Thankfully, my voice is steady.

"Which was the whole point, if you get my meaning?" Then she
adds, anticipating my question, "I was a bit confused back then."

A shimmer of a smile skims across her face, and again I'm overcome with the sense of familiarity.

She fiddles with the edge of her T-shirt for a bit then asks, "How
long will you be in Seattle?"

"It depends on how long it takes. Mom's insisting we squeeze in
the hot-air balloon ride, too, and since that has no way of ending
well, I guess it could be forever."

"Ha! You're so morbid. And after that?"

"Back to Chicago for a bit, I think. I miss my house, my bed,
Morrison. Though I doubt he misses me. Stupid cat."

Lily is silent for a long while as if thinking hard about something.
She alternates between pressing her lips closed and biting her cheek,
and it looks so painful that eventually I can't take it any longer.

"What is it? You didn't come in here to talk about your old posters, so what's on your mind? More ways to give me a near-death experience? Parachuting? Deep-sea diving?"

My attempts at joking don't go well. Lily looks at me with big eyes dark as bottomless pools in the murky room.

"Dad texted. I was hoping I could ask you a favor," she says.

"Of course." I lean forward. She sounds so serious I'm starting to worry he's dying too.

"He invited me to their Fourth of July party, and since I'm in town, I can't get out of it."

"Mm-hmm," I say as if I understand completely, though nothing could be further from the truth. "And?"

"And I haven't seen them since last summer."

"Which makes the party... a real serious affair?" I try, grasping for straws.

"No, of course not."

"Then what?"

"I don't want to go." She throws herself backward onto the pillows I've tucked against the wall and glares at the ceiling. "So I was thinking, what would make it tolerable?" She gives me a pointed look that makes me feel completely daft for not having already deciphered this coded message.

"And you've decided?"

"Oh, for God's sake." She lets out a sharp sigh. "Would you come with me?"

A warm flash shoots through my chest. "To the party?"

"Yeah. I haven't told you half of what it's like, and I could use some moral support. I know we haven't known each other long, but—"

"Of course." Inside I'm doing a little happy dance because this means it's not goodbye quite yet. "Count me in."

CHAPTER 20

"So, we'll see you in a few days." Barb kisses Mom's cheek then holds her at arm's length. "You'll have to show me how to use the slow cooker when you get back. With you here, I'll be an ace in the kitchen in no time!"

Mom laughs, and it thrills me to see them click just as quickly as Lily and I have.

"Do you have the address plugged in?" Lily leans closer to the open window of the car I've rented and looks at the dashboard GPS. The bags are in the trunk, I've a bottle of raspberry lemonade in the cup holder, and a nineties mix cued up in the playlist. Kurt got me nostalgic. What can I say?

"Yup. We'll go straight to Bart's and then to the hotel."

"Text me when you get there, okay?"

"I will."

"And we'll see you back for the Fourth?"

"Wouldn't miss it."

I wave to Lily through the open window as we head toward I-5 per the GPS guy's instructions. This one is programmed to a male voice with an Australian accent, and I can tell he and I will get along swimmingly from his very first "G'day, mate."

"That was a good time," Mom says once we've reached the outskirts of the city. "Nice people. But I'm going to bring Barb a nice monstera when we come back. A bit more green in her lovely home would be just the thing." She nods to herself. "You know who Lily

153

reminds me of? That friend you had in high school. What was her name? Ella something or Agnes?"

There's an echo of a flutter in my belly. "Alice?"

"That's the one. They have that same spark. I'm glad we'll see more of them."

She rests her head against the seat and closes her eyes to the sun shining in through the passenger window. A slight smile plays on her lips, and her fingers tap the rhythm to "The Sign" by Ace of Base on her leg. I force her comment out of my mind and do the same on the steering wheel. When the chorus comes, we both chime in singing about the importance of opening one's eyes.

A fist squeezes my heart. *Mom.* I've called her that my whole life, but I've never before *felt* it the way I do in this moment. I turn up the volume to drown out my thoughts and keep them from going dark places. *Not now. Not today.* Today is a good day.

We reach Seattle by early afternoon and are greeted by the glittering expanse of the Puget Sound. Compared to flat Chicagoland, the city looks exotic with its urban sprawl nestled in lush hills, and I have to force my gaze away from its sunbathed charm and back to the road if I want to avoid accidents. It's too early for rush hour, so while it's definitely more congested than I'd prefer on any given day, I am confident enough I'll be able to navigate my way to Kirkland, the Seattle suburb where Bart supposedly lives.

"Do you know what to say if we find him?" I ask once we get closer.

"*When* we find him," Mom corrects but doesn't elaborate further.

She's been quiet the past half hour, thumbing a piece of paper in her lap, giving me time to consider how I would feel in her situation. There's the obvious possibility the address is wrong, and this was a wild-goose chase. Or if Bart is there, he might turn her away, words unsaid. Is she worried he won't recognize her? That she'll break down? Or, perhaps even worse, that she'll still have feelings for him after all these years?

Out of the corner of my eye, I catch her holding the paper up closer to the window. The sheen gives it away as a photo.

"Is that him?" I ask.

She hesitates, but then at the next light, she turns it for me to see. In the picture, Mom is wearing a long floral dress and nude lipstick. Her hair is longer and her face smooth. Bart stands a head taller than her, his multicolored butterfly collar level with her forehead. His arm is around her shoulder, and they are both smiling.

"When was it taken?" I ask.

"Some party."

"He looks nice. You too."

She doesn't respond at first, but after a while she asks, "Do you think he's still mad at me?"

I spot our exit and merge into the right lane with some effort. Construction season has narrowed the expressway to two lanes. When I'm safely where I need to be, I say, "That's a long time to hold a grudge."

"I suppose." She tucks the photo away in her purse. "And he wasn't an angry sort of man."

"Well, there you go."

"I'm just nervous," Mom says, and it's another first. She's the in-control one. The on-top-of-things one. The fearless one. Or so she's let me believe.

As she sinks deeper into her seat, I feel myself straightening in mine. "Don't be. I'll be with you every step of the way."

"I know. Thank you."

As before, I'm not sure what to do with her gratitude, so in response I mumble, "We're almost there" and "It'll be fine." She's not the only one in need of that reassurance.

Bart's house is located at the top of a ridge next to a middle school. It's a skinny two-story about two yards from the next identical building, and so the block goes, but it seems to be a newer development. The surrounding neighborhoods consist of a mishmash of larger and smaller homes, some clearly dating back half a century or more. *Randomness* is the word that comes to mind since it's nothing like the straight grids and conformity of my hometown. I suppose it has its charms.

I park in the street even though there's plenty of room in the shaded driveway.

Mom sucks in a loud breath. "I can't do this." She looks at me with something akin to panic. "This is a bad idea."

"Mom." I unbuckle and turn to her. "We're here *now*, two thousand miles from home."

"You do it. I'll wait here."

"But I'm—"

"Find out if this is his house at least." Her eyes plead with me. "I need another minute."

Her agitation is contagious, and butterflies flutter freely inside me too. I can't very well drag her out of the car, so with a resigned "Be right back," I open the door and close it behind me with a thud.

"Hi, my name is Kristin Caine, Jane's daughter," I mumble to myself as I walk up the few steps to the front door. "Hi, I'm Kristin, Jane Caine's daughter."

I ring the doorbell, but there's no chime, no tune, no ding-dong. Mom follows my every move through the windshield, so I try again, pushing the button a little harder. Nothing. In frustration, I bang on the door with more force than necessary, and this time it only takes a few seconds before it's yanked open, and I'm face-to-face with someone definitely resembling the man in the photo. It's not Bart, though.

This man is younger than me, and he's fairer than the man in the picture.

Momentarily stumped, I clear my throat and clasp the strap of my shoulder bag a little tighter.

"Um, hi. I'm looking for Bart Perkins?"

"And you are?"

"Ah, my name is Jane. No." I shake my head. "I mean Kristin. I'm Kristin. Jane Caine's daughter. Mom is in the car."

The man squints at me as if I'm talking in riddles.

"This *is* Bart's house?" I ask, thinking Mom might have been misinformed, after all.

The man considers me for another moment. "It is. He's not here."

"Oh. When will he be back?"

The man shifts his weight from one foot to the other as if antsy to get away. His grip on the door hasn't faltered.

"Who is it, Mike?" A tall blond woman looking to be in her early sixties appears behind him.

I address her over his shoulder. "I'm Kristin Caine. My mom, Jane, knew Bart a long time ago. She's—we've—come to see him."

"Jane?" The woman stares at me blankly for a moment, but then a light bulb goes off behind her eyes.

"Oh. Jane." She takes Mike's place in the opening. "And you're the daughter?"

"Kristin," I repeat. "I'm sorry, I don't mean to intrude."

"No, no. I'm Donna." She offers her hand. "This is Michael, my son. Bart's son."

Her grip is strong as we shake. "You'll have to forgive my initial confusion. I haven't heard that name in many years." She peers at me with curiosity. "Do you want to come in?"

"Um, sure... Mom's over there," I say, gesturing toward the parked car. "Do you mind if she comes too?"

Donna's chin tilts up with a start as she peers beyond me. Her lips part. "She's here?" Her eyes flicker to mine.

"Mom?" Mike puts a hand on her shoulder. "Who—"

She pats it and gives him a quick smile. "It's okay. You've heard of Jane, remember?" A silent exchange ensues between them before she turns her attention back to me and says, "Of course. If she wants to."

I signal to Mom to join us, and she does, if with some delay in her step. She eyes Donna with caution as she approaches.

"Jane," Donna says, extending her hand past me. "I'm Donna, Bart's *wife*."

They shake, staring at each other as if taking stock, each holding the other's hand and not letting go.

"A pleasure to meet you." Mom's voice sounds strangled.

Donna releases Mom's hand. "Why don't you come inside?"

We step into a large front room divided in half by a Pergo walkway. On one side is the dining room, and on the other a formal seating area. I trail them through the hallway and into the open kitchen and family room.

"Coffee?" Michael asks.

I'm not used to the lack of air conditioning out here, and it's late enough in the day that the sun has hit its stride. The thought of something hot is not appealing. "Do you have anything cold?"

Michael opens the fridge. "Water or apple juice."

"Apple juice would be great."

"Just water for me." Mom looks around the room.

"Sorry for barging in like this," I say in an attempt to break the tension. "We were hoping to speak to Bart, but if this is a bad time, we can come back."

Donna and Michael share a silent look.

"Unfortunately, Bart's not here."

"So we hear. Will he be back soon?"

Donna sinks onto one of the counter stools, and her features drop. "No," she says, voice glum. "No, I'm afraid he won't."

Michael moves to her side. "We put him in hospice last week. It's a matter of days."

And so we learn how fate has sent its pawn cancer for both Bart and my mother at the same time. His started in his lungs. Diagnosis eleven months ago. Aggressive.

"There's not much left of him. Michael coming to stay for a bit has been a great help," Donna says.

We've moved outside to their tiny concrete square of a patio for the breeze, and Donna has her feet up on the only empty chair. Bart's chair, I assume.

"I'm very sorry," Mom says from the edge of her seat. Her movements are still tentative as if she's aware this space is not hers and can be easily disturbed. Her glossy eyes rest on me for a bit before she clears her throat and says with more bravado, "I have cancer too."

Donna's eyebrows dart upward for a split second. "Oh no."

"Yes. Kris is helping me take care of some unfinished business. That's why we're here."

"I *was* wondering." Donna relaxes into the cushion behind her. "I have to admit, there used to be times when I worried we'd see you one day."

It's Mom's turn to look surprised.

"I mean no offense," Donna continues. "I'm not upset you're here or anything. I understand." She pauses to take a sip of her coffee. "That was a long time ago."

Michael offers a refill of the apple juice, which I accept.

"He told you about me, then?" Mom asks.

"He did. It took years before I got him to admit he'd had his heart broken, mind you. Men—they think they can hide things like that from their wives. As if we can't read it in their panicked gazes every time we say goodbye, in the grip on our hands, in how their shoulders relax when we tell them we love them.

"Once it was in the open, I'd like to think the ghost of your memory held no power over him anymore."

"Mom!" Michael snaps.

My mother holds up a hand to settle him. "No, I understand. And nothing makes me happier than to hear he moved on." Her lips turn up, but there's no glint in her eyes, and her lids are heavy. "I want to apologize. If what I did affected you in any way..." She looks from Donna to Michael. "I only wish I had been able to tell him the same thing. I suppose now it's too late." She continues more to herself, "Too late for a lot of things."

Donna seems to consider this for a long time while we sip our drinks and listen to the neighbor's brood of kids playing on an oversized trampoline. I'm about ready to suggest we take our leave when she speaks again.

"Bart does have some lucid moments, still." She looks at Michael, as if for approval. He nods almost imperceptibly. "Why don't you come with us tomorrow? Maybe there is still time to say what you came to say."

CHAPTER 21

In our hotel room that night, Mom leans against her pillows, watching me as I get ready for the night. I walk back and forth between the bathroom and my bags, pulling out toothpaste, pajamas, and hairbrush—returning them when I'm done. I pretend I don't notice her scrutiny.

"It's been almost four decades," she says out of the blue. "And I'm not ready to say goodbye." Her voice breaks on the last syllable, and I freeze in the middle of folding up my jeans. *Bart. She's talking about Bart.*

She buries her face in her hands, and her shoulders start to shake. My gaze flickers around the room, uncertain where to settle, but when her crying doesn't stop, I go to her.

"Shh," I say, placing an awkward hand on her arm. "Shh."

She sniffles but looks up. "I guess he'll be the one waiting for me," she says morosely. "That's not how I pictured it at all."

I hand her a tissue and wait for her to calm down. I don't tell her he may well be waiting for his wife of more than thirty years instead, but the thought comes to mind.

"At least I'll get to see him. I really didn't want to take this with me to the grave." She blows her nose long and hard.

I once read an interview with Astrid Lindgren, the Swedish author of Pippi Longstocking fame, who said that, as she and her friends got older, they used to start every conversation with "Death, death, death," just to strip it of its power. With Mom breathing numbered breaths in front of me, and me unable to get out a single word

161

of comfort as she brings up her impending demise, I can't help but think that's not a bad idea.

"What time do you want to get up tomorrow?" I ask instead, not meeting her gaze.

Mom pats my hand on top of the sheet, gives it a brief squeeze that forces me to face her.

"Eight o'clock is fine." She squeezes my hand again then lets go and turns to fluff her pillows. "I hear the breakfast buffet is supposed to be good."

"Mom."

It's a quarter past eight in the morning, and she hasn't stirred despite the alarm. I'm reluctant to get up, too, knowing what lies before us, but since there's no backing out, I'm at least awake.

"Mom, time to wake up."

The only response I get is light snoring.

I give up and head to the bathroom, where I do my morning toilet, which largely consists of brushing my teeth, rinsing my face in cold water, and checking for belly growth. I'm fifteen weeks along and at that point where I'm both tempted by the maternity sections at the stores and not quite ready to jump off the cliff. *A couple more weeks.* I turn to look at my profile in the mirror. Yup, it won't be long before I can't fit into my current wardrobe.

I rest my hands beneath the slight curve of distended flesh, trying to imagine what it will look like in a month, two months. It still seems so odd to think I'm growing a human inside of me. I know other women may experience it differently, but for me, the intricate engineering going on in there appears a distant happening. Like a tsunami in the Pacific or glacier calving in Antarctica, it's not real to me even though it's... *real.* I have no aches and pains yet, I don't waddle, I'm not sick, and I can still paint my toenails. With everything else going on, I almost forget about the baby-grain at times. To avoid dwelling on whether this makes me a bad mom, I return to our room and pull the drapes apart, bathing the green carpet and rumpled sheets in unforgiving light.

"Mom!" I jostle her bed a bit to get a reaction. Nothing. Her face is half-turned into the pillow, mouth open. My heart skips a beat. *No, she is breathing.*

I'm about to shake her again when I spot the open medicine canister on the nightstand. It's still half-full, but I know for a fact it wasn't there when I went to bed, so she must have been up in the middle of the night. Looking closer, the lines etched on each side of her mouth stand out in sharp relief to her pale skin.

"Mom?" I try again, more insistent this time. Stroke her shoulder. "We have to get ready. You're seeing Bart today, remember? Can you wake up for me?"

Finally, she stirs, her arm moving up and over her head in a slow stretch.

"Did you sleep all right?" I ask, still eyeing the yellow bottle.

She opens one eye. "Shannon, is that you?"

A shiver prickles my neck. "No, it's Kris, Mom. We're in Seattle."

She stretches again and opens her eyes fully. "Oh, Kris. Sorry. I was taking a nap."

The weight I carry in my heart as of late grows heavier still. "It's eight thirty in the morning. We're seeing Bart today. Um... do you remember how many pills you took last night?"

She rubs her forehead and sits up. Looks around. Her gaze is getting clearer by the minute, but her features are still slack and soft like melted and refrozen ice cream.

"I think two." She picks up the bottle and looks inside. "It was keeping me awake."

By *it* I take it she means the pain.

"I feel better now," she says. "Did you eat breakfast?"

"No." I take a moment to study her. "Are you sure you're up for this?" She is about to meet not only the only man she ever loved but a man dying from the same plague also ravaging her body. It would be remiss not to recognize the strain this could bring.

She straightens with ill-hidden effort. "Of course. Some coffee, and I'll be as good as new. Just give me a minute, and we'll go downstairs."

Mom and I wait in the lobby of the hospice facility while Donna and Michael go inside. There's no telling how long it'll be before Bart's awake, so the magazines get my somewhat divided attention while Mom paces between the red armchairs and fake potted plants scattered about. She doesn't want to talk. The set of her lips makes that clear.

When the time comes, Donna sticks her head into the waiting area and calls for us in that hushed voice reserved only for libraries, churches, and places where people come to die.

"He's awake. We've told him you're here."

I glance at Mom, whose face is flushed, agitation palpable around her, then grab my purse and follow them deeper into the building. Donna's heels click a staccato rhythm against the linoleum floor, while Mom moves soundlessly in her mesh mules. There's an odd fluttering in my belly, which I interpret as nerves. *This had better be the right thing to do.*

Michael looks up when we enter the hospice room. He's perched on the edge of the bed, reading a newspaper article aloud for his dad, and when he falls silent, Bart also turns his head.

He is ten years older than my mom, but it might as well be thirty. His dark skin has that yellowish tint of life escaping, and what must have been a once-robust frame seems fused to the bed he's on, leaving only the slightest protrusion underneath the sheet where his body lies. Still, I'm not as shocked as I thought I would be. I'm focusing on his eyes, and they are the same as in the photo—a deep brown and, at least in this moment, filled with clarity.

Mom grasps my hand in a clawlike grip and stiffens at my side. I don't dare look at her.

"Jane," Bart says. "Is it really you?"

I give Mom a reassuring nudge, but she doesn't move.

"Hello," I say in her stead, leading her up to the bed.

His eyes shift to me. "You're her daughter?" he asks in a thin voice that matches his figure. "You're not much alike."

"One of them," I say and take the hand he's lifted toward me. "Kristin."

"Except the eyes." His gaze bores into me. "The eyes are the same."

A slow burn starts in my throat, which I try to clear away. "I'm so glad I finally get a chance to meet you."

"Oh, Bart." Mom's voice is barely a gasp next to me.

I take a step back to allow her to get closer. She draws in a jagged breath but lets go of my hand and approaches the bed.

Bart taps the narrow space next to him on the bed with one finger, and she perches on the edge, seemingly ready for flight.

"Hello, Janey," he wheezes. His eyes close and remain so for long enough that I start to wonder if he's fallen asleep. When he opens them again, it's obvious it takes some effort.

"How are you?" he asks.

Mom wipes escaped tears from her cheek with a tissue. "Never better," she says with a sad smile, taking his hand.

I glance at Donna, who nods at me. We've talked about this, about allowing Mom and Bart to speak in private, and she's given her blessing. She cocks her head to Michael, who gets up from the bed and joins us.

"We'll be right outside," she says.

The ailing two are not listening.

"He had a good life," Mom says in the car back to the hotel. She hasn't cried since she emerged from Bart's room, and an odd calm has settled on her features. "I didn't ruin him."

"Is that what you were worried about?"

"I don't know. Maybe we'd all like to think we matter more to people than we actually do."

"He never forgot you. He talked to his family about you. And if you hadn't left, he wouldn't have met Donna and had Michael. Maybe it was meant to be. If he can forgive you, you should be able to forgive yourself."

"I suppose that's one way to think about it." Mom turns to face me. "Have you forgiven Patrick?"

Patrick. That's a good question.

"I try not to think about him. It's too recent. I will, though." As I say the words, I know they're true. He hurt me, but I won't hold a grudge. I'm in a better place now.

"Good—ow!" Without warning, Mom bends forward, clutching her stomach.

"What? What is it?" I swerve in my lane, my right hand going to her.

She moans, rocking back and forth.

I pull into the first parking lot I see and reach for her. "Mom, what is it? Do you need a hospital?"

"No," she groans. "I left my pills at the hotel. I was supposed to take them an hour ago." She slumps back in her seat, rubbing at her midsection. She's pale, but her breathing is coming more regularly again. "Please keep going."

I do as she asks but cut my eyes between the road and her the whole way back. *I knew this was too much for her. It's my fault for not ending this in California.*

"I may need your help getting out," she says once I've parked.

It's a slow process, but we make it up to the room, where I lead her to the bed, get her a glass of water and her pills. "One?" I ask.

"Better make it two. And one from the box in my toiletry bag."

I find what she's asking for—a new kind I haven't seen her take before. The name suggests something in the morphine family.

"Are you sure these can be taken together?" I ask, handing them to her.

Her jaw is set in a rigid line. "The doctor said I could if it became necessary."

Her hand is steady as she pops one pill at a time into her mouth and chases them with water. She drains the glass and lies down on top of the comforter. "Fifteen minutes," she mumbles to herself.

Necessary. I glance at the digital clock on the DVD player. It's 4:10 in the afternoon. By 4:25 she'll feel better. I will my heart to slow and the sense of impotence to dissolve.

"Do you need anything else?"

"A little rest, that's all. I'll be good as new. Don't worry."

I sit with her until she falls asleep, glancing at her inert form every so often. We're supposed to go up in a hot-air balloon on Thursday and then drive back to Portland to spend more time with Lily and Barb, but all I can think is *We need to go home.* This trip is making her worse, and I refuse to have that on my conscience. It's time to face reality.

All I have to do is figure out how to break it to Mom.

"I'm doing no such thing!" Mom yells at me. "Give up when we're doing so well? I knew you weren't serious about helping me. Never mind your dying mother's wishes, let's let Kristin have her way and Never Leave the House."

I've returned to the room after a short walk to clear my head, determined and prepared for battle, but this barrage is impressive both in vitriol and velocity. I ignore every instinct to defend myself and stay quiet until she's done. It takes a while, but eventually she runs out of steam.

"Mom," I say, pleading. "We're supposed to get on a hot-air balloon in two days. What if something happens?"

"Then we'll land."

"And the pills make you tired. You've said so yourself."

Her jaw grinds invisible pebbles.

"We tried," I say, reiterating my initial statement. "We did good. We've crossed off more list items in the past couple of weeks than you have since you started writing it. That's something."

"It means nothing if we give up," she hisses. "No, we're staying." She crosses her arms across her chest like a stubborn three-year-old.

I pace the room, alternating between glowering at her and holding back tears. I want her to be comfortable *and* excited, pain-free *and* proud of me, safe *and* happy, and—I can't do it all. I'm only me, Kristin, and the cancer is an all-consuming Goliath I have no weapon for. It will win no matter what I do—it *is* winning—but even if Mom refuses to engage in the fight, I will not. I'll be damned if I let it triumph prematurely.

We're at an impasse, her will against mine, and I only have one card left to play. I may not be able to fight her battle like this, one arm shielding her from harm, the other straining forward, but what if I ensure her relative safety first?

"I'll make you a deal," I say, terror and resolve warring inside me. "You get on a plane home tomorrow, and I will finish your list myself."

Mom chokes on the objection I know she was about to launch. Her mouth remains open, but not a sound comes out.

"You need to take care of yourself," I say, tone gentling. "This isn't working. I know it's not the same as you doing the list yourself, but I promise I'll keep you posted throughout. You just can't... I won't let you wear yourself down like this. Who knows? If you take it easy, maybe you'll even... get to meet your new grandbaby."

It's the wrong thing to say. Mom's head jerks up, cheeks flared. "You know that's not going to happen. Why do you keep bringing it up?" She huffs.

"Sorry."

She waves off my apology like it's a fly.

"I'm serious, though. We can go home together, or you can go by yourself. Either way you're not moving on."

"Ha!" Mom croaks. "Those are my two options?"

I watch her watch me, determined to wait her out this time.

"What about your fears? How are you going to get in that balloon on Thursday or the next flight or find your way alone through Paris?"

My stomach somersaults. "I'll find a way."

She looks less than convinced.

I take her hand. "I promise. You go home and let Shannon take care of you, and I'll stay and finish what we started."

"You've made up your mind?"

"I have."

Mom takes my hand in both of hers and runs her fingertips across my knuckles, worrying my skin for a long time.

"Then I suppose there's no use arguing," she says finally, and I have a brief moment to register surprise that she's actually giving in before she adds, "After all, you are *my* daughter."

PART 2

To do before I die in any order:
1. ~~*Learn to do a handstand*~~
2. *See* La Bohème *on stage*
3. ~~*Learn to knit*~~
(4. *Get a tattoo*)
5. *Climb the stairs of the Eiffel Tower*
6. ~~*Do a ropes course*~~
7. ~~*Paint the sunset at Butterfly Beach*~~
8. ~~*Apologize to Bart*~~
9. *Have a painting displayed at the Louvre*
(10. *Fall in love again*)
11. *Ride a hot-air balloon*

CHAPTER 22

With Mom safely on a plane home, Shannon waiting at the other end, I feel better. That is, I feel better until I realize my job isn't done. The strain of seeing Mom in pain temporarily barred my vision, but with her gone, it turns out the commitment I've made is not a simple theoretical one but a very real, high-stakes, I-might-die one right off the bat.

Somewhere in a nearby field, there's a hot-air balloon waiting with my name on it.

I toss and turn all night, finally getting to sleep in the early hours of the morning, but I wake with a start to my phone chiming with a message before seven o'clock. It's from Mom. I expect it to be some cheery "you can do it" rant, but it's the opposite.

Made it home okay. Cancelled the balloon ride. It didn't feel right to put you through that alone. Mom

I stare at the screen in disbelief. But I was ready. Or, well... maybe not *ready* ready, but I was committed. I suppose I should be grateful, but the vision of one unchecked bullet point on the list nags at me while I shower and get ready, while I eat breakfast in the hotel dining room and check my email.

Finally, I call the balloon company to see if I can undo the cancellation, but it's too late. They have a waitlist for each departure, and someone else has already been only too happy to take our spot.

"Not sure what to do with my day instead," I tell Lily when I call to tell her about it.

"Sounds very anticlimactic," she agrees. "But let me get this straight. You're actually upset not to be high up in the air right now?"

"I know, right? Who am I?" I scratch my forehead and stare at my reflection in the hotel room mirror. I look the same on the outside, but something feels different inside.

"Well, if you've got nothing to do, you might as well just head down here early," Lily says. "I'll help you figure it out."

It's a beautiful morning, traffic is light, and Aussie Guy has my back as I drive south back to Portland. It still doesn't sit right with me that Mom's kept up her end of the bargain and I'm getting off scot-free, but short of chasing down another balloon company, there's not much I can do.

I slam on my brakes and pull off to the side as the revelation hits with full force. *I could find another company.* Portland is bound to have touristy stuff like that too.

Before Lily can even say "hi" when I dial her number, the words pour out of me. "I need you to do me a favor. Hot-air balloon companies in Portland. I can go anytime after"—I pull back out into traffic and hit the gas then glance at the clock on the dashboard—"two o'clock today."

"Are you okay?" Lily laughs. "You sound a little frenzied."

"No. Just realized I can still get this done for Mom. I passed Olympia fifteen minutes ago. Can you call around?"

"Of course. I'm on it." She pauses. "Are you sure?"

The memory of the view from the airplane window imposes. "Nope. But do it anyway. And call me back if you find anything."

"Aye aye."

It's a long twenty minutes of inner turmoil and hope before she calls back.

"Found a place with a cancellation for an evening ride tonight."

"Okay. Book it, book it." I check the time again even though I know for a fact I'll be in Portland long before that.

"Already did."

I let out a long breath as her words settle in my stomach. A low laugh bubbles up my throat. "You must think I'm completely nuts," I say.

Lily chuckles. "No more than the rest of us. But Jane is going to lose her shit."

"She won't believe me."

"I'll take lots of pictures. Promise. I've always wanted to get some high-altitude panoramas of my city."

My eyes go wide as a semi overtakes me. "Wait. What? You're coming with?"

"Of course. You didn't think I was going to let you have all the fun?"

"But—"

"Unless you wanted to go by yourself," Lily hurries to say. "Oh jeez. Am I just a presumptuous asshole for inviting myself along?"

She sounds insecure for the first time since I've met her, so I don't waste any time reassuring her. "No, no. I one hundred percent prefer you to do it with me."

"Oh, phew." I can hear her smiling again. "I'll get back to being excited, then. Up in the air, baby!"

"Up in the air!" I holler back, my heart somersaulting with equal parts thrill and dread.

It's such a relief to see Lily's smiling face again, I almost jump out of my car before it's come to a full stop.

"You made it," she exclaims as soon as I open the door. "And without driving off a cliff or getting carjacked. I guess congratulations are in order." She gives me a pointed look.

"Ha ha, very funny." I squint at the sun halo behind her that makes her dark hair sparkle with hidden reds. My stomach does an elevator dip at the sight, but I brush it off. Who wouldn't feel a little unsteady, considering the colorful canvas waiting for us in the distance?

The balloon takes off from an airfield just south of the city at eight fifteen. The good thing about a last-minute booking is that my nerves haven't had long enough to work themselves back into a knot after the other ride was cancelled. The bad thing is, before I know it, I'm high in the sky with nothing but a flimsy basket between me and a deathly plummet.

"Smile," Lily says, aiming her camera at me.

I try to even though my face feels more like a stiff mask of terror than an expression of a jubilant life accomplishment.

She snaps away then puts the camera down. "Looking a little pale there," she says. "How are you holding up?"

I grunt in response and wrap my arms tighter around my waist.

"Really enjoying it then?" She smiles and hooks her arm through mine, prying it off my torso. Then she leans in closer. "Think about Jane's expression when she sees these pictures." She pats the camera. Her soft words send warm puffs of air grazing my skin. "Try to relax. Everything is going to be fine."

I inhale her now-familiar scent of summer and attempt to release my shoulders. That's a little better, but I still cling to her arm as we continue floating through the air. She's solid and reassuring next to me, and I have to fight off an impulse to rest my head on her shoulder.

"Glad you're here," I tell her. It's an understatement.

She looks at me for a moment, but only my own reflection in her sunglasses stares back at me. "Me too," she says, squeezing my arm, and I wish I could see her eyes because it's another beat before she looks away again.

We go up and down with the winds, the only sound that of the propane filling the balloon and the low conversation between the other four passengers.

"That's the Willamette River," the driver says in response to someone's question.

"So gorgeous," Lily sighs, looking around.

As the minutes tick by, the tightness in my chest recedes, and I'm starting to see what she sees. And it is truly breathtaking. With the wind brushing my face, the setting sun casting long shadows on the open landscape below, and Lily at my side, I unexpectedly find a moment of peace. We're so small on this earth, our existence so brief, and yet there is such beauty to be found in fleeting moments that I know there must be some greater meaning to it all. The certainty that this list, these challenges, are altering something fundamental about me floods through my system and drowns out my fear. What was it Lily suggested? That Mom's list might be more than it seems to be? Maybe there's a nugget of truth to that, after all.

The adrenaline rush upon landing is similar to that after the ropes course but not as overwhelming. I'm at once filled with gratitude to have survived and sad that it's over.

"I can't believe I did that too," I tell Lily as we head toward the parking lot.

"I can." She pauses by the front of my car and grins at me as I open my door. "You can do anything you set your mind to. How do you still not see that?"

But I think maybe I do. Or at least, maybe I'm finally learning.

CHAPTER 23

Mom calls me as soon as I send her the pictures of me in the balloon.

"You did not," she says, full of disbelief. "Bet there'll be a blue moon tonight. That's just... I'm very proud of you, Kris."

My chest expands not only because of her words but because her voice sounds stronger. Perhaps our adventures didn't do permanent damage, after all.

"I had to do it," I say, slowing down to keep the distance between my car and Lily's as I'm following her. "It's part of the list."

"But I gave you an out, and you didn't take it. That's... impressive, frankly."

"Thanks, Mom." I tap the steering wheel to fill the brief silence that follows. "How are you feeling? Is Shannon with you?"

"She's doing my laundry." She giggles as if this is hilarious. "And she's made me dinners to freeze that would tide a whole regiment over for a month."

"She's worried. As am I."

Mom tsks. "There's no need. I'm fine." She yawns. "Though it *is* nice to be home again, I must admit. Claudine missed me so, and my ferns were not happy to have been neglected."

"No doubt. How long is Shannon staying?"

"Only until tomorrow. She's working Saturday."

I thought she was going to be able to stay longer. That's not good. "Maybe I should try to find a flight back sooner. I don't like the idea of you being on your own." I also don't like the idea of leaving Lily in a bind, no matter how sure I am she would understand.

Mom is quiet for a beat. "I thought you were going to a party with Lily?"

"Well, yeah. But that was decided before all this. She'd get it."

There's a dissenting meow on the line, and I picture Mom lifting Claudine off her lap. When she speaks again, her voice is closer to the microphone. "No, you promised you'd help her out. And besides, I don't want you here."

I huff. "Thanks."

"That's not what I mean." She pauses. "There's no need for you to rush home. I'm doing fine, Shannon is near enough, and you don't want to let your friend down."

"Well, yeah, but—"

Her voice softens. "I'll still be here when you get home. You've done good, Kris. Go have some fun."

"Live a little?"

"Took the words right out of my mouth." Her smile is audible.

I do want to spend the holiday with Lily. A lot. And I did promise. After everything she's done for me, it would be nice to reciprocate.

"But are you sure?"

She cackles. "You heard me the first time. I'll see you in a few days."

Barb comes out through the garage, gardening gloves on, to meet us when we pull into the driveway. "Welcome back," she says to me. "So sorry to hear Jane had to go home."

My expression slips with her commiserating tone. "She wanted to be here. But it's for the best."

"Are you sure she doesn't mind? I don't want her to feel like I'm keeping you away," Lily says.

I tell them about my conversation with Mom on the way here.

"Glad she's feeling better, but it must have been hard," Barb says. "It made things real." *Too real.*

As if sensing this is treacherous ground, Lily takes my bag and leads the way into the house. "I imagine you're pretty tired, and I've had a full day of work, so how about we call it a night, and I'll show you around town tomorrow?"

I tell her that's a good idea, so after saying good night to Barb, we head upstairs, where Lily sets down my bag outside her old room. "Let me know if you need anything. I'll see you in the morning."

I'm pretty sure I'm asleep before my head hits the pillow.

When I wake up, the light outside is brighter with the honeyed glow of sunrise. The house smells of bacon, and laughter rises from the small deck below my window. I allow myself to do nothing but lie there staring at the ceiling while letting my senses wake up fully. As the minutes pass, layers to my first observations rise to my conscious mind one by one. Behind the bacon, there's also a scent of something floral—fabric softener perhaps—and beyond Lily's and Barb's voices, the distant grumble of traffic and lawn mowers. Kurt Cobain's chin is aglow with a pink hue as is the rest of the wall opposite the window, shadows fading minute by minute.

I inhale deeply and close my eyes, reveling in the total release of tension. Then I feel it, a quickening of little wings in my belly—only this time I know it's not nerves but something else altogether more miraculous. My hands instantly go to the center of that stirring, fingers forming a triangle around it. I will it to happen again, and within a minute it does.

"Hello, little grain," I whisper, a grin spreading across my lips. And suddenly it's real in a way it wasn't only hours ago. *I'm going to be a mother.* I think of Hayley and Zach, Nate, Aimee's kids. They like me. Why wouldn't my own kid feel the same way?

At that thought, the darker angel appears on my left shoulder, filing her nails. *Of course it will like you—exactly the way you've always liked your mom,* she whispers. The moment of contentment is over. *That's different,* I argue in my head. I will always choose my child first, Mom didn't. I know I can't fault her for working long hours, but when she was home, she often chose her art over board games and bedtime stories and left anything school related up to us.

What about when you *have to work? Or if the kid doesn't want what you want?* The shadow creature smirks at me. *What if it's not like you at all?*

A bigger rolling sensation starts churning inside me, my subconscious ready to fight. I wasn't aware this was something that was nagging at me, yet here it is.

I let my hands fall to my sides and inhale on a count of four, drawing from the strength of two I now bear within.

"I love you," I say out loud, looking down at my belly. "I love you, I love you, I love you."

The words work like a magic spell, banishing evil, and when I listen again, the voice inside is silent. The dark angel has dissolved.

I lie there, smiling, intent only on what's within for a long time.

That afternoon, over a waffle cone filled with pear-and-gorgonzola ice cream—because Portland—Lily and I take a break from sightseeing. The multicolored tote I found at a vintage shop nearby rests at my feet, a stark contrast to my old navy-blue shoulder bag. Every time I look at its bright weave, a thrill rushes through me in recognition of that something at my core waking up—something more effervescent, more alive that's been asleep for a long time.

"What are you smiling about?" Lily asks.

"This tote doesn't match anything I own." I lick the side of my cone to prevent it from dripping.

"Well, I love it."

I grin. "Me too. I didn't say it was a bad thing."

She picks up her camera and aims it at me. I'm used to it by now. She had me posing on bridges in the Japanese Garden earlier to the point where I almost fell in the water.

"Cheese," I say.

The camera goes *click, click, click.*

It's been one of those days you remember years later as one where you wished time stood still. Some of it comes from spending hours in the biggest bookstore I've ever seen and browsing storefronts of quirky artisanal bakeries, marijuana dispensaries, and tattoo parlors, but mostly it's due to Lily. With her at my side, I go from being the only grayscale person in a Technicolor film to fully hued, much like my tote. She has no preconceived notions, she doesn't judge, and being with her demands no effort. Here, away from home and with no one holding me to *being Kristin,* for the first time in my adult life I dare to explore *being me.* It's vain, perhaps, but that's okay. I'm about to be a mom, and when summer break is over, I'll be teaching again. For this limited time, I *want* to have fun. Preferably with Lily.

I'm about to ask where we're going next when two guys rush up to Lily and lift her off her feet in rowdy celebration.

"Lei-lei," the taller of the two says with a wide grin, placing her back on the ground. "It's been too long."

"Grizz." Lily fits herself into his arms, and they stay like that for a long time, at least by my standards.

"Don't mind them," the shorter guy says, stepping around to my side of the hugging statue. He extends a hand. "I'm Beau, Grizz's husband."

"Kristin." We shake. "Old friends, I take it?"

Before he can answer, Lily remembers me. "Kris, this is Grizzly." She frees herself from the guy's embrace, and now they're only holding hands. "You met Beau."

"Nice to meet you, Grizzly," I say with a small wave. That's a curious name. He's tall, yes, but nothing about his frame forces the mental leap to a great bear. A giraffe, possibly, or a moose, but definitely not a bear.

The two men join us at our table, and soon they are far down memory lane. Lily and Grizzly go way back. He's the brother she never had, she whispers to me at one point, and I believe it. If Shannon was anywhere near as likable as him, I'm sure we would also hug and hold hands while reminiscing about our interlinked pasts.

The two of them are hilarious together, but no one can get a word in edgewise, and when minutes turn to an hour, my insecurities find the lull they've waited for to come traipsing back.

Yes, I can't be anyone but myself with Lily, but what if, set against the backdrop of her past, I fall short? I'm a mousy suburban schoolteacher with anxiety issues. She's traveled the world and knows people in every corner of it. With everything she's seen and done in her life, there's no way I can compare.

I'm aware these thoughts are pathetic. I'm an adult who, as part of her job, has told countless teenagers over the years to worry less about what others think of them. I know Lily's opinion here shouldn't matter to me, and yet it does. I want her to like me because I like her a lot. Maybe more than I'm ready to admit because, if I do, it might change things. Complicate things. And right now, I have so many other complicated things going on in my life.

No, it's fine if I don't fit in with the rest of her life, I think, laughing along to a joke I don't get. *It is what it is.*

But I'm not sure I find myself convincing when there's such relief in her pulling me back into the conversation with a touch to my arm and a warm "You guys, wait until I tell you what Kris is doing for her mom."

On the morning of July fourth, Lily trudges into the kitchen still in her pajamas at nine o'clock. Barb and I have already finished our breakfast, and I'm engulfed in an old Judy Bloom book I pulled out of Lily's bookcase. I remember reading it as a kid with a flashlight underneath the covers, cheeks heating, but now it at most gets a chuckle out of me every now and then.

"Good morning," I say.

Lily grunts something inaudible and goes straight for the coffee machine, pours herself a cup, and leans against the counter, radiating sullenness.

"Then don't go," Barb says as if Lily has just spoken.

I look from one to the other, waiting for Lily's response. It doesn't come. She drinks her coffee in silence, her heel tapping against the lower cabinets.

After a minute of this passes, Barb huffs and takes off her glasses. "Seriously, hon. There's no law that says you can't change your mind."

Lily puts her mug down with a clang. "No, I said I'd go, so I'll go."

"Are you talking about the party?" I ask.

"Every time." Barb raises an eyebrow in a pointed arch.

Lily leaves us with a dispirited growl.

"Don't mind her," Barb says to me. "She'll shake it off."

I look toward the stairs and hike my thumb that way. "Do you think maybe I should?"

"Sure. Talk to her. Maybe it'll help. These visits are never easy, but I know she's happy you're going with her."

Her words send little tendrils of warmth through me.

Once on the second floor, I knock on the guest room door and get a flat "come in" in response. Lily has her back to me, pulling on a pair of jeans, when I enter. That's also all she's wearing.

"Oh gosh, sorry," I say, retreating with haste.

"What?" She turns before I can close the door, leaving me stuck in the opening, not sure which way to go. Lily walks across the room to the dresser, picks up an earring, leans toward the mirror, and puts it in. She does the same with the other ear. And her breasts are right there.

"Um, I can come back when you're ready."

"No, come in. I'm almost done." She disappears into the adjacent bathroom but returns a second later with a hairbrush in hand.

"Um, I..." I step into the room. I need to stop looking at her breasts. I don't know why that's so challenging. It's not like I've never seen a pair before. Though if anyone's comparing, she does have a very nice set. Ample but perky. I swallow hard.

"Sorry I'm in such a bad mood." Lily sits down on the bed and starts brushing through her curls. "Going to my dad's—it takes it out of me, you know."

I hum a vague response and force my gaze out the window. That's better. I'm still aware of her naked torso in the periphery, but I'm not looking straight at it. Thankfully, my hands are always cold, so I place the fingers of my right hand over the pulse point on my neck to cool the blood. It's the only way to bring down the kind of blush I know I'm sporting right now. Maybe if she wasn't so brazen about it. Then again, we're friends, and this shouldn't be a big deal.

I steal another look at Lily, who's moved on to rummaging through her bag. Her breasts swing lightly with the movement, and the sight does something to me I'm both wholly unprepared for and haven't put words to in a long time. Not since Alice. I mean, there's tingling. In places.

"Um, I need to brush my teeth," I say and leave before she has a chance to reply. It takes some effort not to run to my room, and once there, I close the door and lean against it as if expecting her to follow and demand entry. My mouth is completely dry, and there's something distorted about the furniture in front of me. The bed grows and shrinks, the desktop is a rolling wave, and Kurt's eyes follow me as I make my way toward the desk chair.

It must be hormonal. I haven't been with anyone since, well, since the baby was conceived. *Wow. That's a long time.* And before that, Patrick and I weren't exactly chasing each other down either. I sit on the edge of the seat and rub my growing belly. I know it's not the first time, but I always thought Alice was a one-off. I've only been interested in guys since then. Besides, everyone says pregnancy does things to you. I've heard the stories—thanks, Mom. So I felt something. Below the belt. But that doesn't mean I would put our friendship at risk. It's not like I want to do anything about it. Yes, her breasts looked soft and smooth like the rounded mounds of risen dough—

What in the holy hell?

I shake my head as if to clear the image by force.

"Get a grip, Kris," I mumble as I push myself up. "Brush teeth, pack a bag, let your *friend* know you're ready to go."

I march into the bathroom and get on with the task. Teeth, bag, ready. Teeth, bag, ready. Teeth, bag—

"Kris?" Lily's voice comes from the other side of the door.

"Yeah?" I say, mouth full of toothpaste.

She opens the door and sticks her head in. "You feeling okay?"

I spit and run the faucet without looking at her. "Sure, why?"

"You ran off so fast I thought maybe you felt sick."

I risk a glance, and to my relief she's finally fully dressed. "No. I, um, had to pee."

"Oh, good." She comes all the way in and sits down on the bed.

"What time do you want to leave?"

"Want to? Never." She pouts.

"Come on. Is it that bad?"

"It's worse. And before you say anything, I know I'm an adult. I live my life the way I want to, I don't hurt anyone, and I don't make excuses. But Cynthia?" She chews the inside of her cheek. "You'll see."

"Then focus on your dad," I say, cajoling. "You said you haven't seen him in over a year."

Lily gives me half a smile. "Yeah, you're right."

I grin, most of the awkwardness forgotten. "Well, how about that? For once I get to be the wise one while you freak out."

She throws a pillow at me and gets up. "Yeah, yeah. Don't get used to it. Meet you out front in twenty."

CHAPTER 24

Lily's dad, Hank Landon, lives in Arlington Heights—one of the city's more prominent neighborhoods. It perches high above the city up in the West Hills, and as we make our ascent, I can't help but hang my head out the car like a dog, taking it all in. Portland sprawls out before us with Mount Hood and the Cascades as a superimposed backdrop, making me suspect Chicago will seem flatter than ever when I go back home.

As befits a film producer with a mistress-turned-wife, the house itself is an enormous contemporary mansion tucked neatly into the green hills. It blends into its surroundings about as well as an albino moose would, but then I have a feeling this is intentional. Who wants to spend millions on a house only to hide it from view?

"Isn't it awful?" Lily grumbles next to me after she parks outside the four-car garage next to a posh BMW and two Mercedes. She's been quiet the whole drive except for pointing out places of interest like a mechanical tour guide. If she were a cartoon there would be a storm cloud attached to her like a personal halo.

"A little gaudy, maybe," I concede.

"My dad would never have bought it if it wasn't for Cynthia. It's not at all his style."

"Well, you know what they say—happy wife, happy life."

Lily glares at me as if I've offended her, and I put my hands up in surrender. "Hey, I'm not the enemy here."

She scrubs a hand across her face. "I know. Sorry."

"It'll be okay. You already know Cynthia will be obnoxious, but you can choose not to listen."

"Ha! Is that what you tell your students?"

"If you knew the drama they bring to my classroom..."

Lily pauses. "Cynthia's sons will be here too. They're cut from the same cloth, if you know what I mean."

"Lovely."

"Nothing like the arrogance of white male privilege."

"You forgot *straight* in that lineup."

She pauses for a moment. "That too."

"I'll consider myself warned." I move to open the door, but Lily stays still. "Are you coming? No point in dragging it out."

"Yeah," she says, but she still doesn't move.

I get out and walk around to the driver's side, and then I open her door. "Milady." I screw up my face and do a silly curtsey, hoping to sway her mood.

"Avoid Charlie," Lily says, turning to me. "He's the one with the comb-over, Cynthia's oldest. He's an ass." She jumps out before I get a chance to respond.

If the outside of the mansion is opulent, to say the least, the inside is downright garish. Even the side entry where we make our approach sports an enormous crystal chandelier, mirrored demilune tables, and a wide staircase that disappears up to the second floor. The place smells rich, too, like expensive perfume—not overwhelming like the department store cosmetics area but as if one of those classic celebrities, Grace Kelly or Greta Garbo perhaps, recently strode through the room.

"Ms. Landon," says a pleasant voice from the depths of the room. "Welcome home."

A middle-aged male figure approaches, a wide grin on his face.

"Joe!" Lily throws her arms around him. "I thought you retired?"

"You know your dad," Joe says. "He needed help, wouldn't take no for an answer." He leans in conspiratorially. "Plus I heard you were making an appearance."

Lily swats at his arms, her face beaming like a kid at Christmas. I clear my throat behind them.

"Oh," Lily says, turning to me. "Joe, this is my friend Kris. She's here for moral support."

We shake hands.

"Joe was Dad's PA until a few years ago," Lily explains. "He did everything from party planning and travel arrangements to Christmas presents and homework help, so I think of him more as my honorary uncle."

"Or partner in crime," he says with a twinkle in his eye and turns to me. "Boy, do I have stories."

"Yeah, yeah." Lily laughs. "Where are the others?"

Joe's bushy brows bunch together in an apologetic scowl. "Party's in full swing on the deck. I take it you were told it would start later." His eyes flicker over our casual getups. "You'll want to change posthaste. Should I bring your bags up?"

"Fuck." Lily shoots a nervous glance toward the back of the house and hoists her duffel higher on her shoulder. "No, I've got it, but if you can find me a drink, I wouldn't say no."

"Consider it done. You want anything, Kris? Beer? Wine?"

Before Lily can reveal my condition, I ask for a glass of wine. I won't drink it, but I have a feeling this is the kind of party where a glass in the hand makes a good prop while a pregnant belly on a single woman doesn't. Thank goodness for whatever foresight made me choose a flowy blouse this morning.

"Drinks will be waiting in the kitchen," Joe says, backing away. "I'll leave you to it."

"I like him," I tell Lily as we climb the stairs.

"He's the only reason this house didn't drive me completely nuts whenever I came to stay growing up. Well, Dad, too, of course, but he wasn't home much."

The upstairs hallway splits into two wings, and Lily leads me down the right one. At the far end, she pushes open a door and steps aside so I can peek in. "This is my room," she says with a sneer. "Need I tell you I wasn't part of the decorating crew?"

She doesn't. The walls are pink and the curtains white frilly lace. A miniature version of the hallway chandelier adorns the tray ceiling, and a rose-patterned quilt covers the bed. Unlike the room at her mom's house, this one bears no trace of Lily.

"Like a unicorn threw up in here," she says, closing the door again as if she can't bear to look at the offensive dwelling. "You can stay in here," she says and opens the door across from hers to let me in. "It's one of three guest suites."

In contrast to Lily's room, this one is all muted colors and wood accents with a panoramic window sporting the kind of view you only see in travel magazines.

"I'm going to go freshen up," Lily says. "See you in fifteen?"

"Sounds good." I set my bags down on the ottoman at the foot of the king-sized bed.

She closes the door behind her, and I'm alone. In the silence, faint voices drift in from outside, and I go to the window to investigate. The sprawling, tiered patio stretches out before me with a lap pool to the left and three barbecues blazing to the right under the supervision of hired staff. The deck is filled with mingling people in expensive-looking casuals, and I can't help but look over at the new skirt I brought lying splayed on the bed. Have these people even heard of H&M? I brush a stray piece of lint off the fabric then cock my head and scrutinize a seam as if that could make the garment worth more than fifteen dollars. At least I brought a pair of heeled sandals.

I open the window to let in a breeze that smells of pine and burning charcoal. Inhale all the way to my toes. I'm about to go fix my hair when a female voice rises above the rest, not because it's louder but because it's directly below my window. I would have ignored it, if not for the familiar name spoken in an unfamiliar way.

"Lily is late again," it says with an edge. "I swear I asked Hank three times to make sure she was *punctual*."

A different female voice whose words I can't make out responds, and then the first woman speaks again. "You'd think she'd show a little more urgency now that we've gone through the trouble."

I'm standing as close to the open window as I can without risking being spotted by the guests, but I can only barely make out the top of some blond hair. It must be Cynthia and one of her friends, I speculate, while waiting for her to speak again. She doesn't disappoint.

"I know, I know. But think of how it looks. The whole family is here. Sometimes I don't know why I even bother."

The friend says something else.

"Oh, I'll be good," probably-Cynthia responds. "At least she's not bringing the other *queer* one this time." High-pitched laughter, and they disappear into the house.

I'm frozen in place. Not because of what she said but because of how she said it—that restrained quiver of loathing. The gloating cackle. In that moment I realize this is not merely a family barbecue, this is a hostile encounter in enemy territory where Lily is the target.

I pull both hands through my hair. My first instinct is to tell Lily to forget all about this. She can see her dad some other time when Cynthia and her ignoramus cohorts are elsewhere. But then a pang of anger shoots through me because why shouldn't she be able to be here with him, celebrating a national holiday like anybody else?

Just then Lily opens the door and steps in, a self-conscious expression on her face. My insides drop as I take her in. She's wearing a dress. And makeup. Her dark curls are pulled back in a tight ponytail that makes her look like one of them. She's beautiful, of course, but seeing her like this, in this costume, makes my throat ache.

"You're staring," she says, pulling at the fabric of the dress. "Does it look weird?"

Yes! I want to yell. *Yes, it looks really weird!*

"No, you look great." I force my gaze away so she won't see the fury and sadness behind it. Under the pretense of needing the bathroom, I leave the room. These fucking idiots! Lily is awesome. She's smart, and funny, and caring. She's found a job she loves that she's great at, she's curious about the world, always open to it and its people. All people. Yet here, in her home and among family, she can't be herself lest she be reduced to whom she falls in love with. How is that all they see when they see her?

I yank the brush through my tresses with a little more force than is necessary then slam it down on the counter.

Fuck!

For a stretched-out minute I stand there huffing, palms on the counter, staring at my reflection. If only there was a way for me to make them see how wrong they are. To show her they're the ones who should change.

The thought is still swirling in my head when we descend the stairs together.

Cynthia pounces on us the second we set foot on the deck.

"Where have you been?" she whispers sharply to Lily, taking a firm hold of her arm and steering her toward the pool area as if she's a fifteen-year-old who's broken curfew.

I follow behind even though my presence is not acknowledged.

"We brought our bags upstairs and changed. We weren't informed it was a luncheon. How are you, Cynthia?" Lily says her stepmother's name with a bit of a bite. "This is my friend Kristin. Kristin, Cynthia."

Cynthia's features momentarily go rigid, but then she adjusts them and offers me her hand. "Pleased to meet you," she says, though I can tell she's anything but. A lofty laugh escapes her as she turns back to Lily. "Funny, your father didn't mention you were bringing guests. Well, not to worry. There's plenty of food, plenty of, ehm, room." Something catches her eye at the other end of the deck, and without so much as a backward glance, she rushes off.

"So that's Cynthia," Lily says, the smirk on her lips poorly hidden behind her wineglass as she drinks several mouthfuls.

"She seems like a lovely woman." I try to keep a straight face. We look at each other and smile, and for the briefest of moments, I'm tricked to believe this is a happy place.

The moment over, Lily suggests we find her dad, and I put in a plug for adding some food to the quest.

"Eating for two?" she asks, a pointed glance at my belly.

"Sure, let's say that."

And we set off through the crowd, taking care not to step on the Louboutin sandals and Gucci loafers currently treading lightly on the concrete.

Lily's dad is exactly as I pictured him, tall and tan with vibrant blue eyes, like he was cut from a sailboat ad, except his light linen jacket has the crumpled look of an artist hiding inside. He greets Lily with a long hug that seems to leave them both a little *verklempt*, and when Lily introduces us, he hugs me, too, with a warm "Call me Hank."

"It's been too long, Lills," he says, eyeing her.

"I know. Sorry, Dad." She takes his hand. "How are you?"

"Same as always," he says with a huff. "More importantly, how are you?"

"Same. Same." The hands they're holding swing back and forth between them.

My goodness, these two are bad at communicating.

"Have you tried the kabobs?" Hank says eventually. "They're delish."

"We're heading there next," I chime in, my stomach rumbling.

"Good." Hank looks at Lily again. "So good to see you, sweetheart. I have a phone call to make, but I'll find you later. You're staying, right? Until morning?"

Lily lets go of his hand, her good mood seeming to falter ever so slightly. "We'll be here," she says.

"Perfect." He grins and starts turning away. "I won't be long."

My stomach makes another gurgling noise, louder this time so even Lily hears. She looks so forlorn, her eyes still on the door through which her dad disappeared, but with what seems like a conscious effort, she adjusts her features at the sound.

"Come on then," she says. "Let's feed the baby."

Hank was right. The kabobs are amazing, and so are the burgers and the sirloin tips. Lily's eyes get wider and wider each time I return to our seat on a ledge by the pool with my plate refilled, but she knows better than to comment on my voracious appetite.

Not so Charlie.

Lily's stepbrother saunters over to our perch sometime after my third plate, face bright red from the sun. He's wearing plaid shorts and a pink polo a size too small with a sweater draped around his shoulders. Beads of sweat pearl at his balding temples.

"Oh, God," Lily mutters under her breath. "Here we go."

"Ladies." Charlie tips a make-believe hat to us in greeting then leans in to kiss Lily on the cheek. "Or should I say *Gents*?" He winks at us, seeming very satisfied with his clever joke.

"Funny." Lily bares her teeth in a grimace that doesn't even begin to reach her eyes. "Because I'm gay." Lily punches him in the shoulder. "How've you been, Charlie? Business booming?"

"Always is," Charlie says, and then he launches into a twenty-minute spiel about his sales ranking, record commissions, and famous clients. He basically sells cars, but to hear him tell it, it's the most important job in the world, and he emphasizes three times it's not a regular car dealership, it's "Italian, baby. Only the best." He even hands me his card, as if somewhere underneath my bargain garments I'm hiding my weight in diamonds.

Another twenty minutes later, I've learned he's forty-two, single, building a house down the street, and recently went on a yacht with a celebrity I am sure to know but whose name he can't divulge. I'm desperately trying not to yawn in his face, and I keep hoping to catch Lily's eye to signal it's time to make our escape, but she's zoned out. The minute Charlie started talking, her mind went elsewhere. I imagine anyone subjected to this man regularly would benefit from learning that skill.

Charlie is in the midst of relaying in detail his latest trip to Cabo when Lily's dad calls for her. She startles back to the present, and with a quick "be right back," she takes off. To her credit, she does send me an apologetic glance as she leaves. Not that it does me any good. I look after her, longing to escape, too, and temporarily block out Charlie's droning. It's not until he nudges me with his elbow that I snap out of my daze with an internal groan over the fact he's still there.

"She looks good, doesn't she?" he asks.

I squint. "Who? Your sister?"

"Stepsister." He wipes a palm across his bulging middle. "Damn shame," he says. "You're not like that, though, are you?" He locks his porcine eyes on me.

"Like what?" I cock my head to the side, chin up. He can't be saying what I think he is?

"Like, homo." He lets his gaze sweep over me, head to toe. "You don't look it."

My heart beats faster, the tingling need to punch something rushing across my shoulders. "And if I was?" I look him straight in the eye, daring him to answer.

He doesn't sense the danger. "Eh." He rocks back slightly on his oppressed loafers. "I bet all it would take is a real man to set you straight, if you get my meaning. Fairies and dykes—equally make-believe. If you ask me, it's all that feminist bullshit ruining girls these days." He nods as if to underscore the gravitas of his words.

I'm speechless. I lock my arms to my sides, afraid if I move, my fist will find a way to connect with his ugly face. Satisfying as that would be, it might also break my hand.

"So are you?" he asks. "A leeesbian?"

I can't explain what happens in my head when his lips form the word and spit it out in that slow-motion jeer. All I know is I'm on Lily's side. I want to protect her from this idiot and all the other idiots here and elsewhere who don't get her. I look down, my thoughts racing, and then they click in place.

"Of course I am. Why would I not be? Guys are pigs controlled only by their egos and the dumb stick between their legs, but women?" I settle my features into a coy guise. "Women are soft and warm." I let my hand drift up to my neck and across my collarbone. "They know how to—" I giggle. "Sorry, I'm getting carried away here."

Charlie looks like he's been struck by a sudden aneurysm. His mouth opens and closes a few times like that of a fish before he coughs into his fist.

"So you and Lily?"

"What?" I ask, feigning innocence.

"You're a... a couple then?"

I beam at him to show exactly how proud I am of him for reaching the right conclusion. Then I have a bright idea and let my hands move to my belly, cradling it between my palms so what was concealed by my blouse a minute ago is set on full display. "Soon to be three," I say, and I swear he takes a step backward as if the baby karate kicked him from inside me. I take that as my cue to leave. "Very nice to meet you, Charlie. I have to go find my girlfriend now."

I weave between the guests, high on myself. *The look on his face.* Lily will love this, and I can't wait to tell her. I find her seated between her dad and a fit man about our age resembling Charlie enough for me to guess this is Steven, the other stepbrother. They're deep in conversation, and I don't want to interrupt, but I also don't want to stand around like a target for the lonely. Without them noticing me, I veer left and go inside to seek shelter from the sun.

Cynthia looks like someone who would have a fabulous pantry.

CHAPTER 25

It's late afternoon by the time Lily finds me next to the panoramic windows in the sitting room. I would have stayed in the pantry with its upholstered bench, glass canisters, moving ladder, and megatub of Nutella had the hired hands not gawked at me, but this window seat with a view isn't too shabby either.

"I've been looking all over. I thought you'd gone upstairs," she says.

"Here I am. What's going on?" I swing my legs over the edge to face her, but that eagerness sputters when she approaches.

The light from the window hits her forehead at an angle as she steps closer, revealing a severe set of her brows. Her glower matches the edge to her voice as she says, "I was hoping you could tell me."

If I didn't know better, I would say she's mad at me, but all I've done is sit here and—

Oh.

The realization hits at the same time she says, "I overheard two of the neighbors talking about how if God wanted two women to have children together, he'd have made it biologically possible, and then Steven's wife congratulated me on your pregnancy." She looks over her shoulder as if worried someone's listening. "She said Charlie told her all about it."

"I... I only wanted to help. He was being a jerk saying all kinds of things about lesbians, and it just came out. I didn't think—"

"Right." Lily cuts me off and starts pacing. "You didn't think. Period. What makes you— How—" Her fists clench at her sides, and she stops. Draws a shaky breath. "This is my family. People I have to see again. You can't go around telling people lies like that."

"I thought it would help. To show we're in it together."

"We're not, though. That's my point." She hangs her head, shakes it a few times before looking up again. "When you leave here, what do you think these people will say? Now I'm not only the deviant in the family but someone who's not sticking with her pregnant partner. Or do you plan to come back and keep the charade going?"

Her words sting, and I want to defend myself, but at the same time I know she's right. I went too far. "I'm sorry. I got so mad at him I couldn't help myself. I know it's no excuse."

"No, it isn't." She's still glaring at me, but her voice is softer.

"I did stuff in college, you know," I say, my voice almost a whisper. "With a girl, I mean." I don't think it's necessary to tell her it happened once and only because I was too drunk to react before her tongue was down my throat, even though I *am* pretty sure I kissed her back. And then there was Alice...

Lily scoffs. "You and every other girl who didn't have a coed campus."

Ouch. "I'm still allowed to find Charlie's words offensive."

"Oh, please. College experimentation does not make you queer." She takes a seat next to me. "I need you to understand this, Kris. You and I, we lead different lives. You can't pretend to be like me for the sake of a prank, no matter how well intended, any more than you can pretend to be of African descent. It's inappropriate, and when you leave, I'll be the butt of that joke. It diminishes my identity."

Now it's my turn to get riled up. "But you're missing the point. Yes, maybe I shouldn't have said what I said, but I did it out of concern for you, to show them I'm on your side. Doesn't that count for anything?"

"You still don't get it. Just—" She runs a hand across her slicked-back hair. "Please try not to tell any more stories, okay? Now I've got to get back out there and do some damage control."

She starts walking away, and I need to stop her, make this right. I don't want her to be miserable the rest of our visit. "If you're going to tell them I made it up, why not wait until after we leave? At least then you don't have to see their reactions."

Lily stops, and I go to her. "Look, I know you don't like the idea of lying, and I promise I won't say anything else. But we could, I don't know, act as if..." My stomach flip-flops as I say the words.

"Act as if?" Lily looks skeptical.

"Remember you told me how Cynthia reacted when you brought Max here. Wouldn't it feel at least a little bit good to stick it to her again? By now everyone must have heard, and there's really no reason to set them straight. Yet."

Lily looks like she's thinking hard.

"I'll write them myself after we leave if you want. Say you had nothing to do with it."

"But my dad—"

"I'll call him. Explain in person. No matter how much he loves his wife, I'm sure he doesn't approve of how she treats you."

"To be honest, I don't know if he even notices."

I arch a brow at her, waiting.

"Fine," she says eventually. A reluctant acceptance creeps across her features. "I guess the damage is already done. And I do like sticking it to stepmother dearest." She shakes her head at me. "Definitely never boring," she mutters. "But let's not make it any worse. Nothing blatant. We simply won't correct what they're already saying about us."

"Right. I'm a teacher, remember. That makes me an expert in deflecting questions."

She holds her hand out to me, and I take it. "You sure? Not afraid you'll get hooked on playing the role?" When she says it, her forefinger graces my knuckles like an afterthought. My mind sputters to a stop as a jolt of electricity shoots up my arm and down my back.

For a moment, her eyes are serious, locked on mine, but then she bursts out laughing. "Gotcha! Ah, payback feels good."

Somehow, I manage to get my features sorted by the time we reach the patio doors.

"Ready?" Lily asks, placing a hand on the small of my back to steer me outside.

The fine hairs at the nape of my neck rise in response. "Su-sure."

It's past midnight when we finally climb the stairs back up to the east wing. I trail a step behind Lily, intent on how the fabric of her dress skims her hips. I've watched her like this all evening as part of our charade. Our eyes have locked and held across tables, her hand has entwined with mine leading me from one end of the patio to the other, my fingers have brushed a stray tendril of hair out of her face. Aside from the expected side-eye dished out by some, we've had a great time. Turns out most of the guests, once presented with our *situation* as fact rather than speculation, were able to find other things to focus on. Lily even has a lead for a job in London later this month.

I know I should feel relieved we pulled it off, happy it's over, and that we didn't let them best us. But as we're walking up the stairs, all I'm thinking is I want to take her hand again. It's hanging there loosely at her side, fingers inclined toward her body. I know how they'll feel if I do, and that knowledge makes my palm tingle. Because the make-believe was so easy—as if it wasn't make-believe at all.

A knot has formed in my throat by the time we reach the second floor. Like this is the end. I don't know what's wrong with me—maybe it's the pregnancy hormones again—and I keep my eyes on my shuffling feet as we walk down the hallway, trying to make sense of my thoughts. Then Lily yawns with a soft gasp, and at that moment, there is a sudden quake in my chest like the tectonic plates of my past shift, grind ninety degrees, then settle with a sonorous boom that forces my subconscious to acknowledge the truth. Really look at it. My step falters as light-headedness engulfs me.

I have *feelings* for Lily.

I nearly walk into her when she stops in front of her door.

"Whoa there," she says. "Aren't you the sober one?"

I take a step back, not confident my voice will carry if I try to answer.

"Did you see how drunk Cynthia got?" she continues. "Oh my God, that was awesome." She leans against her doorjamb. "Not that I approve of the whole lying thing still, but her passing out in the hammock in front of her highbrow friends almost justified the means."

I give a shaky laugh that I hope signals agreement.

"You okay? You look a little pale." She puts a hand on my forehead as if I'm five, and I can't help but close my eyes briefly.

"Pretty tired," I mumble.

She's studying me when I open my eyes again.

"Really, I'm fine." I scan the floor, the wall, my door, unable to meet her gaze.

"Kris," she says questioningly, taking a step closer. "What's going on?"

I'm forced to look up, and I meet her eyes, dark wells in the dusky corridor. I swallow, throat sandpaper dry. The air around us is so thick, I could reach out and grab a handful if I wanted to.

Lily's eyes widen almost imperceptibly. "Nuh-uh," she says, doing a quick shake of her head as she retreats as far as she can. She's released her hair from the ponytail, so it bounces around her shoulders with the movement. "I've seen that look before. It's the atmosphere, the ruse, whatever. It's not real."

"But what if—" I start.

"No." Her voice has bite now. "You don't get to do that."

"I haven't done anything," I say in protest, but she ignores me.

"Do you know how many times I've run into straight girls like you who feel 'a little crazy' and 'want to try something different'? Too many, okay. It. Doesn't. Work. That. Way."

"Maybe we—"

"No!" She tilts her head back, buries her fingers in her thick curls. Stands like that for some time before she looks at me again. "Kris, I like you. A lot even—maybe more than I should. But this?" She cuts a finger between the two of us. "It would end badly, and I'd be the main casualty. I don't do that anymore."

I'm not sure what to say. She did basically admit to having feelings for me, which is causing something akin to carbonation fizz in my chest, but she also left no room for bargaining. My dating history means I'm a risk. And if I told her about Alice now, I doubt she'd believe me.

"Let's go to sleep," she says, voice tired. "You'll feel differently in the morning."

I'm not so sure, but instead of arguing, I bite the inside of my cheek so hard I can taste blood. It keeps the tears at bay. "Okay." I hesitate, but when there's no yield in her expression, I sidestep to my door, one foot before the other. "Sleep."

"I'm right. You'll see." Lily opens her door. "Get some rest."

I let slip a muffled "mm-hmm," but she's already out of sight.

Fucking great.

"You're such an idiot," I mutter, scolding myself once the door is closed behind me. Now she'll probably not even want to be friends, let alone... Forcing myself not to finish that sentence, I throw myself down on the bed in a dramatic gesture that would rival any teen romance flick—minus the baby bump. Out of habit, I reach for my phone that's been charging on the nightstand since we arrived, and as soon as the screen lights up, any issues I have with Lily fall away.

I have fifteen unread messages and missed calls from Shannon, and they all scream versions of the same thing.

Mom in hospital. Come home!

CHAPTER 26

With the help of half a dose of Valium and a buddy pass, both courtesy of Barb, I find myself stepping off the plane in Chicago not seven hours later. My legs are unsteady, and I shade my eyes against the bright summer morning sun shining through the gate windows, but I'm in one piece, and I have blessedly few memories of the actual flight.

I do remember Lily driving me to the airport. Our conversation was monosyllabic at best, the urgency of the situation obviating any desire to discuss further our exchange outside her room, and it wasn't until I had boarded that I realized this was our goodbye. I would have lingered on that thought had the Valium not kicked in to guide me mercifully into oblivion.

After picking up my luggage at the carousel, I plan on taking an Uber to my house, but as I pull out my phone, a voice calls my name. It's Patrick. I want to hug him and yell at him at the same time, my mind still foggy, but do neither, settling for a "Hey." He pulls me into his arms, and I let him cradle my limp form for a moment. I hand him my bag and start walking, pretending not to notice his covert glances at my belly. I don't know if I'm going in the right direction, but I'm headed somewhere. Forward. Shannon was not entirely clear on Mom's condition when we spoke—or perhaps I was the one with a muddled understanding. All I know is it's serious enough she was admitted, but not life-threatening.

"Thomas called me," Patrick says, trailing behind me. "I admit I was a little surprised."

"He thinks we'll get back together again," I say, startling myself with such honest sharing. Shannon has told me as much. Thomas doesn't think any pregnant woman in her right mind would choose to have a baby on her own. Especially not when the father-to-be is such a "stand-up guy." I'm betting Shannon didn't relay the whole abortion convo.

"Oh."

The note of hope tingeing his response makes me cringe. It takes some restraint not to address it. When I don't speak, he continues, "Anyway, I figured, you know, maybe you could use a ride home. I can fix you some breakfast."

The mere thought of food makes my stomach roil, and I'm overwhelmed with the need to sit down. Without telling him, I veer left into an empty gate and collapse onto a seat, putting my head between my knees.

"Kris?" Pat's voice somehow cuts through the noise of the airport, but it sounds as if he's at the other end of a long tunnel. "Are you okay?"

I'm not sure how long I sit like that, breathing greedy lungfuls of stale airport air, but eventually the nausea subsides enough that I can look up. Pat is on his knees in front of me, his eyes wide with concern.

"Can you get me some water, please?" I ask, cotton mouthed.

He's gone and back within minutes, and I drink from the bottle he hands me as if I've not had a drop before in my life. Finally, the fog lifts.

"Thanks," I say. "Sorry. It's all a little much. And I didn't get nearly enough sleep."

"Can you walk?"

He extends an arm to help me up, but I shrug him off. "Yes, I'm fine." While it's nice of him to be here, it's also unnerving, and at the moment that's a distraction I don't have time for. All I want is to get to my mother.

To Patrick's credit he ignores my bitchy tone. "My car is this way," he says, leading the way.

Though it's early morning, the July sun is already climbing, forcing the temperature to do the same. The murky coolness of the parking garage comes as a relief, and I manage a discreet tug on my bra strap, which has started melding to my skin. Preoccupied with my discomfort, I walk past Pat when he stops. Turns out his way of dealing with our breakup has been to put expensive Band-Aids over the hurt. The car chirping in response to his key fob is a brand-new Audi. Because I'm feeling petulant, I don't compliment him on it, though I admit it's quite the step up from his old Nissan.

"I can take you back to the house, or we can grab a bite," Pat says once we've cleared the maze of freeways leading out of O'Hare.

"The house is fine." The flat Illinois plains speed by outside the windows. I've only been gone a little over two weeks, but I swear it wasn't this flat when I left. I turn up the AC. "And I'm going to head out right away. I want to get to Rockford as soon as possible."

Pat glances at me. "Want me to drive you?"

"I'll manage."

"I know how much you hate driving alone."

"It's no big deal." I lean my head back against the headrest and close my eyes. "Thanks, though," I add.

"Yeah, I should head to work anyway." He says it with a small lilt at the end. Like a question he's not sure he should be asking.

"Mm-hmm," I mumble, refusing to bite. The Valium is still in my system, and it would be best for everyone if I was allowed to pass out a little longer. My legs are so heavy, getting out of the car is about as tempting, and doable, as climbing Mount Everest. I may have to live in it from now on. I'll be the car lady, teach classes through a rolled-down window, though Pat might not like giving up his fancy metal box and—

The slam of a car door wakes me up. I have barely enough time to look around and take in the familiar surroundings before Pat opens my door.

"Time to wake up, sleepyhead. And I don't care what you say, but you are not driving anywhere until you've had some food."

My stomach growls in assent, but at the same time, delicate dragonfly wings flutter inside, reminding me of everything lying between Pat and me. This is not the time to have a conversation about the life we've created together. Soon, perhaps, but not now.

"Pat."

At the sound of his name, his smile dies. "What?"

"Thank you for picking me up. That was really nice. But I can't do this—pretend we're fine. I promise I'll eat, but I think you're right. You should head to work."

He stills on the path that leads to our door. My door. His fingers play with the keys on his key ring, and he changes his weight from left to right then back again. "Come on, Kris," he says. "It doesn't have to be this way."

"I'm sorry." I meet his gaze straight on. Don't waver.

He scoffs. "So that's it?"

"Why wouldn't it be?"

"I don't know. When I talked to you on the phone a couple weeks ago, you said you'd call when you got back, so I thought maybe..."

"We'd get back together?"

"Well, at least that I'd get another chance." He takes a couple steps toward me, squares his shoulders. "I'd like another chance, Kris. Please."

"So, what? You *want* to be a dad now all of a sudden?"

"I'll grow into it." He bridges the gap between us and takes my hands in his. "Come on. You'll be a nervous wreck doing this on your own." He lays one of those crooked half grins on me that used to make me warm and tingly.

"You have no idea what I can do when I set my mind to it," I say, pulling my hands free. "And we don't have to be together for you to be a dad. I've told you before you can be as involved as you'd like. But we're over. Time to move on."

Pat's eyes harden. "Is that what you've done? Moved on? Did you meet someone on your trip or something?"

An image of Lily flashes before my eyes. She's smiling, handing me a bottle of water after our ropes course. I clear my throat. "Of course not. Not that it would be any of your business if I had."

He makes a grunt-like noise but doesn't move. "So, I make one mistake, and I'm out? You'd throw everything away?"

"It's not like that."

"Then what? It sure seems that way from where I'm standing."

I consider my words carefully before I speak. "Listen, I think if I hadn't gotten pregnant, we'd still be together, but in six months or a year, or maybe even two, one or both of us would have ended it anyway. We want different things. We have different priorities. If you're honest with yourself, I think you know this. And yes, we've been together a long time, but that's not a good enough reason to stay together. People change. The spark—" I cringe at my choice of words. "I guess what I'm saying is, I want more."

An outsider seeing Patrick in this moment might think he's completely indifferent to what I've just said, but not me. The muscle in his jaw clenches, and his shoulders are set tight. I know he's barely keeping it together.

"I'm going to go inside now," I say, picking up my bag. "Thanks again. For everything." I pass him and am at the door when he speaks in a strangled voice.

"Give my best to Jane," he says before he gets in the car and drives away.

Hospitals are the worst. Beige linoleum floors, uncomfortable seating, the smell of disinfectant, doctors... I know I'm not alone in my opinion—rarely do you meet someone who enthuses about the idea of visiting a medical institution—but I still think my aversion goes deeper than that of most people. For instance, the halfway point of my pregnancy is only a month away, and I still have not scheduled an ultrasound. I know I should, but. But, but, but.

So many buts.

Mom is on the fourth floor in the monolithic gray building, and as soon as I get off the elevator, I hurry down the hallway, only stopping to ask a receptionist which room my mom is in.

In my head, I've pictured a solemn colorless space with a solitary bed jutting out from one wall, Mom's lifeless figure tucked underneath a crisp white sheet, maybe a machine beeping rhythmically in a corner. It never occurred to me she could be okay. Consequently, I pull up short when trills of laughter—Mom's and Shannon's—greet me, followed by a clever diatribe delivered by one of the more popular talk show hosts on TV.

Shannon jumps up when she sees me. "You're here!" She crosses the room in a few steps and throws her arms around me, only to draw back a moment later to stare at my belly. She covers her mouth with one hand. "Look at you. You're showing. I can't believe it."

I am not at all comfortable with the scrutiny.

"Hey, sis." I walk over to the side of the bed. "How are you, Mom?" I ask, taking the hand she holds out for me. There is a clear tube going into her nose, but that seems to be the only thing she's connected to. Her skin is paler than usual, though, and she's lost more weight in the past week than I'd like to think about. Her cheekbones look too sharp, contrasted as they are by the dark hollows of the eye sockets.

She must have followed my gaze to the tube, for she explains simply, "Oxygen. I had some shortness of breath."

"She had bronchitis, a fever of one hundred and three, and couldn't stand up on her own," Shannon says, disapproval in her voice. "If I hadn't driven down, who knows what might have happened."

"Pishposh," Mom says, but it seems to be a reflex more than a true dismissal.

"I'm glad you did," I tell Shannon. To Mom I say, "I can't believe you didn't tell us you were sick. I talked to you a few days ago, and you made it sound like you had the sniffles."

"I didn't want to be a bother." She straightens the sheets across her legs. "How are Barb and Lily? Did you have fun?"

Shannon butts in before I can respond. "Mom, we *want* to know. We *need* to know. Even if it's a runny nose."

"You're tan," Mom says, eyeing me.

Shannon groans in frustration.

"I did have fun, and we walked around a lot outside." I pull out my phone to show some pictures but hold it out of her reach at first. "And Shannon is right. No more secrecy."

She glares at the both of us as if we are her jailers but concedes eventually with a demonstrative sigh. As she does so, I show her the phone.

"That's the view from Lily's dad's house." I point to one picture as she browses through. Memories of the past week come before me—riding the hot-air balloon high above rolling hillsides and emerald forests, crazy donuts, browsing Powell's bookstore with Lily's laughter trilling beside me. Pretending to be her girlfriend. Maybe wanting to be.

I look up to find Shannon scrutinizing me. "You're blushing," she says. There's a tiny crease between her brows that I recognize from when we were kids. It's her crossword-puzzle-solving, Nancy-Drew-reading face. The I'm-figuring-things-out look.

I pull my shirt out from my chest. "It's warm in here, isn't it? No? Must be the pregnancy." I reach for a plastic cup on the table next to Mom and pour myself some water. When I've finished drinking, I raise my eyebrows and plaster on a grin as big as I can muster. "So, you're obviously doing better. Any idea when they'll let you out?"

"They still need to make sure the antibiotic and steroid treatments work," Shannon says before Mom has a chance to respond.

"Since when can't I speak for myself?" Mom asks. She turns to me. "She's been doing it since I was admitted. It's infuriating."

"Mother." Shannon gives her a look of such deep disapproval a weaker human would shake in their boots. Mom merely waves her off with a flick of her fingers.

"Dr. Brink says I wasn't eating enough. I don't have much of an appetite anymore. This stupid cancer." Her last words come out a grumble. "As long as I finish the meds they've prescribed and take care not to skip meals, I should be fine. For now."

"Mom!" Shannon chastises.

She snaps right back, "I'm not going to pretend."

"Okay. Let's bring it down a notch." I fix them both with a stern glare. "Mom, Shannon is only concerned. As am I." I face Shannon. "And she's right, she should speak for herself. It's her life, her choices."

Mom grabs my hand again, looks at me for a long moment. "You're different," she says eventually. "Shannon, don't you think she's different somehow?"

Shannon pulls out her phone from her purse. "I don't know. Sure. Maybe." She checks the screen and puts it back. "Sorry. I'm a bit tired. And Thomas isn't answering my texts."

Mom and I share a look. "You should go," I say to Shannon. "I can stay."

She glances from me to Mom, the question clear on her face.

"It's fine," Mom says. "Go home to my grandbabies. We'll be all right."

"You sure? They have swim camp every morning this week, and Thomas gets so stressed."

"I don't mind." I squeeze Mom's hand a little tighter. "I have a lot to catch her up on." This is new—Mom and me versus Shannon.

Finally, my sister relents. "Call me if there's any change," she says. "And we'll come down this weekend. Or come get you, whichever you want." She stands and picks up her purse, hesitates again in the doorway. "You're sure you don't want me to stay? It's not a problem, I—"

"Oh, for God's sake, I'll be out of here in a day," Mom snaps. But at Shannon's stumped expression, she adds a gentler "Sorry, I didn't mean it like that. I do appreciate you coming for me. Thank you."

Shannon rushes to the bedside and gives Mom a quick kiss on the cheek. Me, she hugs. "I'll call as soon as I get home. Keep me posted."

We promise we will, and then she's finally gone. I don't know why I'm so relieved. Typically, being alone with my mother is not high on my list, but now? The realization hits me with some force. I've missed her.

"Alone at last," Mom says.

"Don't be mean."

"Sorry."

We share another lengthy gaze.

"It's the list, isn't it?" she asks eventually. "You're enjoying it more than you thought you would."

A smile I can't do anything about creeps onto my lips.

"All righty, then." She fluffs the pillow beneath her head and clasps her hands together on top of the blanket. "Go ahead. Tell me what I missed."

CHAPTER 27

I get to take Mom home the next day, new prescriptions in a bag, including one for medical marijuana that she's more excited about than I would have expected. As soon as we're settled inside, she asks me to light her a *doobie*, and I comply since she's huddled underneath a blanket on the couch in ninety-degree weather.

She's been discharged from the hospital but not from the cancer.

Back in her normal surroundings, the effects of the illness appear all the more startling and crueler than in the hospital bed. Blinded by day-to-day familiarity during our travels, I must have missed the gradual decline, but in the week we've been apart, it's become clear something vicious is eating her from the inside.

And so I get my mom high like a good daughter.

After the first puff—which she takes like a pro, mind you—her head lolls back against the cushions, and she closes her eyes. I leave her be to feed the cats and put a few groceries away, and when I come back, she pats the seat next to her for me to join her.

"You good?" I ask.

"Mm-hmm." She takes another puff and blows out the smoke. "I'd offer, but—" She tilts her head toward my baby bump.

"Thanks." Seeing the pain drain from her features is enough for me. I don't need a high.

"As glad as I am that you're here," she says, "don't get too comfortable. There's still a lot left to do. *La Bohème*, Paris..."

I pull my legs up under me and rest my elbow against the backrest. "Why is this so important to you? Surely it's not the same to experience it vicariously." I run a nail along the seam of the cushion. "Lily thinks you're hiding something."

"Does she now? Cheeky girl." Mom peers at me, pupils dilated. "Tell me something. How did you feel after you got off the balloon? Or when you managed those rope obstacles?"

"Um... a bit shaky."

"Relieved?"

"I guess."

"Alive?" She exhales a cloud of smoke. "Sometimes we carry around undefined weights, unknown wells of emptiness behind secret walls, waiting to be filled, longings for places our souls know they are meant to visit, but..."

I take the joint away from her.

She grabs my wrist. "Promise me you'll finish the list, Kris. It's important."

"But you're—"

Her grip tightens. "*No matter what*. Promise me!"

"Okay, okay, I promise."

She lets go. Relaxes. "I'm sorry."

"Don't worry about it."

"No, I mean I'm sorry for everything."

What? I wait for her to continue, intent on nothing but her lips.

She looks up at the ceiling then blinks slowly and meets my gaze. "I wasn't a very good mother to you." She pauses as if waiting for me to take this in. "There's no excuse, but you... needed something I couldn't give you."

"No, Mom—"

She waves me off. "It's okay. We're good, right? I'm not too late?"

I nod and shake my head in a jumble in response, the lump in my throat choking me.

"You'll do it better," she says, shifting in her seat, some undefined discomfort needing placating. "I'm sorry for that too—that I won't be here. That's really shitty of me." A self-deprecating snort reverberates from her chest. "Can you hand me—" She motions to the joint, and I comply.

Watching her take another drag and release the smoke in a curly pillar gives me a chance to get my voice under control. There's so much I want to ask her. And I'm running out of time.

"What was it like when we were little? Was it hard?"

"Ha!" she cackles. "It wasn't a walk in the park, that's for sure. You have to understand, I wasn't in the same position you're in. I had nothing—no career, no home, no family around. Plus, there were two of you." Her eyes glaze over, and her features soften. "By anyone else's standards, you would have been considered the easy one."

"Really?"

"You slept at night. You ate what I fed you. Heck, you even pooped politely." The light from the window glints in her eye. "Shannon kept me on my toes, but as it turns out, that's what I needed at the time. She distracted me from everything else that wasn't working in my life. She consumed me, let me improvise. In a way she was my inner turmoil embodied. That, I could deal with. I had no idea what to do with you."

I can't move. I had expected an offhand comment about the toils of single motherhood at most, not this. That's what I would have gotten six months ago.

"Don't look at me like that. I cared for you both the same, still do. She was just an easier audience." She falls silent, worrying the edge of the blanket between her fingers. "Did I make you hate me?" she asks eventually.

"No!" The word forces its way out of me before I even consider the question. "No," I say again. "Of course not."

"I wouldn't blame you."

"Would I be here if I did? In a few weeks I'm traveling to another continent for you. If that doesn't say *I love you*, I don't know what does."

She smirks. "You have a point."

"Thank you for telling me." I rest my head against the pillow again, facing her. "I know it won't always be easy, but I love this baby already."

"I know."

"Maybe that's enough?"

For the first time in as long as I can remember, she reaches out her hand and strokes my cheek with her fingertips. "You'll be a great mom, Kris. *You* have nothing to worry about.

"Now, before I get too sappy, I have something to show you." She retreats and reaches underneath the side table, from where she produces her knitting needles. About four inches of knitting hang on for dear life as she thrusts her accomplishment into my face. "See, I've learned. On my own." Her face beams, forcing me to adjust my features to show only approval.

"That's great," I offer. "Well done."

"You know, once you get the hang of it, it's surprisingly relaxing."

"I'm off the hook for that one, then? No more knitting classes?"

"Honey, I know you meant well, but if I can be frank, you weren't the best teacher. No offense." Mom caresses the wonky weave before placing it back where it came from. "Is there any weed left?"

Ouch.

She gets better over the next couple of days. The antibiotics take care of the bronchitis, and the marijuana seems to dull the pain enough that she can function almost normally. She's still not eating much, though, and all her shirts hang off her shoulders like tents, so when she hints at kicking me out the following weekend, I hesitate.

"You promised," she says sternly. "The list is your number one priority. I've got things sorted here. Patti will check on me. Shannon and the kids are coming Wednesday. New York awaits!"

New York.

The Met is the only opera house in the country currently playing *La Bohème*, and Aimee was finally able to get tickets. Not an easy task since it just opened for a limited summer season.

"That reminds me." Mom pushes herself up from the couch with a grunt and disappears into her bedroom. She returns a minute later with a green garment bag that she carries over one arm.

"I want you to have this." She drapes it across the coffee table and unzips it. "I want you to wear it to the opera." She pulls out a simple, full-length gown in a flowy grayish-blue material and holds it up to me.

I take the hanger from her. The label at the neckline has the name of a department store that closed some time when I was in elementary school, so she must have kept the dress all these years. Yet, it looks brand new. "It's gorgeous. When did you get it?"

Mom's eyes fill with reminiscence as she caresses the dress. "Will you try it on for me?"

Intrigued by her deflecting my question, I take it with me to the bathroom to change. I take off my sweats and T-shirt and carefully free the fabric from the hanger before I pour the dress over my head. I say *pour* because that's what it feels like when the material skims across my skin—like liquid.

Its empire waist is decorated with tiny pearls in an intricate pattern, and as I run my fingers over them, I turn to the mirror and gape in disbelief at the person staring back. I've never ogled myself before—I've never had reason to—but now? I'm freaking stunning. Not only does the dress accentuate my currently awesome cleavage, but it manages to create an optical illusion across my baby bump that leaves me looking almost slender. I turn this way and that, admiring my reflection. I am never taking this off.

"How is it going?" she asks from the other side of the door.

I unlock it and step out, hands lifting the skirt like Cinderella. I even twirl for her. I can't help myself.

Mom's cheeks turn pink. "It's something, isn't it?"

She falls silent, and I wait for her to elaborate. When she doesn't, I ask again where she got it.

Her lips tighten. "It's a bit hard to talk about."

"Try?"

She lets out a small cough. "Fine." She studies the dress in silence, making me summon all the gods of patience until, finally, she begins.

"I was supposed to wear it to the opera with your father. I was about four months pregnant, and I'd picked it up especially for the occasion because none of my other frocks fit me any longer. I even had shoes to match. It was simple for back then—no puffy sleeves or anything—but as soon as I tried it on, I knew it was the one. It made me feel beautiful. He always had a wandering eye, and I thought—"

"Oh, Mom."

"No. Let me finish. I've never told a living soul, and I might as well get this out now."

"Sorry."

"Anyway, I'd had the dress hanging in my room for weeks. I must have tried it on a dozen times, and then the day finally came. I got my hair done, did my makeup, got ready." She pauses, hand rubbing at her throat. "He was supposed to pick me up at six. I called his office a half hour later and found out from his secretary he'd gone out for a business meeting. She asked if she could take a message."

I inhale sharply. "He didn't show."

"No, he didn't show. Not that night and not the day after. Or the next."

The realization of what she's trying to say finally hits me. "That's when he left you?"

She doesn't meet my eye. "In his defense, he probably didn't remember about the opera. Not even Beau would have been that cruel."

No wonder she never spoke much of my father. To be pregnant and have your heart broken in such a way... "I'm so sorry," I say, the words ridiculously inadequate.

"Pishposh." Mom's voice has that uncharacteristic thick cadence again that I'm not used to. "It was a long time ago, and now the dress will fulfill its destiny, thanks to you."

I want to hug her, comfort her, but the arms crossed over her chest don't invite such a reaction. "I love it," I say instead. "Thank you for saving it."

She dismisses my gratitude with a gruff grumble. "Just wear it to *La Bohème,* and that'll be enough."

"I will. As long as I manage to get there."

She rolls her eyes. "Oh, Kris, have you learned nothing?"

"I know, I know. *When* I get there."

"That's better. Now go take that off and pack your things. The world doesn't wait."

CHAPTER 28

I drive straight to Aimee's house when I get back to Chicagoland and am barely out of the car before she jumps me.

"Save me from the beasts," she hisses in my ear. "Now. Go, go, go." She all but shoves me back into the car at the same time Colin and the kids round the corner from the backyard. Aimee slams her door closed and rolls down the window. "Kris is here," she hollers. "We're going to lunch. Love ya!" She waves to her family.

"For God's sake woman, step on it," she says to me with a chuckle, pulling her seat belt tight. "I've filled up so many kiddie pools this summer, my fingers are permanently crinkled."

When we are out of her neighborhood, clear of a tail, she inhales deeply and blows out the breath as if about to start meditating. She turns to me, her head against the headrest. "My savior. Where have you been all my life?"

I laugh. "Hello to you too."

"Too dramatic?" She scrunches up her nose.

"I don't know. Depends on how bad the bad guys we dodged were."

She groans. "Oh, so bad. I was in mortal peril. Why is it every year I can't wait for summer break to come, and when it does, I count the days until it's over? What's wrong with me?"

"Selective memory?"

"Huh?"

"You hold on to the good things. In the dead of winter, summer means lazy days on the beach, piles of books to read, sleeping in—"

"Oh my God, I think I just came in my pants a little." Aimee giggles. "Say 'sleeping in' again."

I swat at her arm. She laughs harder.

"You're terrible," I say, but I'm laughing, too, and in that moment a weight lifts from my shoulders and the sky gets a little bluer. Bantering with Aimee is home. "Maybe you should write a note to yourself for next winter—*To remember: I have kids*."

She directs a pointed look toward my belly. "Right back at you."

"I'm not the one complaining."

"Not yet. And besides, they are lovely some of the time, so there's that."

We pull into the nearest strip mall with a Froyo place, and minutes later we're seated on one of the purple pleather benches, two heaping cups of goodness in front of us. After we get through the mandatory status-of-family check-in, Aimee's eyes bore into me as she stabs at the air with a spoon dripping with caramel sauce. "So," she says. "New York. Are you ready?"

I sit back against the cool wall. I wish I could stand and press my whole body against it because the seat is now stuck to the back of my thighs. "Really, you couldn't at least let me finish my cup?"

"Is it that big of a deal?" she asks. "Look at what you've already accomplished. This is simply more of the same, nothing to be worried about."

I glare at her. "Yay, more traveling."

"Unless..." She cocks her head and stirs her frozen yogurt with demonstrative deliberation. "You've decided to give up."

I resist an urge to fling a spoonful at her. "Of course not," I say with a snarl. "It's just... I don't..."

"Yes?"

My chest deflates. "I'm still scared, okay."

The challenging gleam in her eyes disappears instantly. "I know. But from where I sit— Kristin, this is so good for you. Have you looked in the mirror lately? Even your posture is different." Aimee scoops up the melted remainder in her cup. "Maybe think on that. You'll have several hours to kill on the plane."

I shiver. "Can we not use those two words in the same sentence?"

"You made it to California and back, right? Been there, done that."

"I'll be alone this time," I say, moping. "And sober."

Aimee shakes her head in disapproval. "I can't believe you took a Valium in your condition. What were you thinking? No, don't answer. Speaking of the baby, you're almost seventeen weeks and way overdue for your ultrasound." She holds up a hand. "Yes, I keep tabs."

"I wasn't going to object. I haven't been home."

"Okay, good. I'll come with you. You'll want someone there, trust me."

"I do?"

"Are you going to find out the gender?"

My mind goes blank. Of course I know that's what you do at an ultrasound, but—holy shit—*I can find out if it's a boy or a girl*! The thought hadn't even crossed my mind.

"Did you find out?" I ask Aimee.

"Heck yeah. Drives me nuts when people are like 'Oh nooo, we want to be surpriiised.'" She flutters her lashes to match the coquettish voice. "As if meeting the human being you've created for the first time isn't surprising enough."

"Right."

"So, can I come? Pretty please."

How can I say no to such eagerness? "Sure."

"And then we'll talk about New York."

I sigh. "Yes."

She sits back, a satisfied smirk on her lips. "Where to next? The mall?"

As far as doctors go, my OB, Dr. Sanders, is a fairly decent human being. She's a woman of few words and dubious sociability who I've been going to since I was in my early twenties, and she knows enough about me that I have no problem suppressing my aversion to all things—and persons—medical in her presence. My esteem for her increases significantly when she doesn't mention once that she hasn't seen me since the first checkup eight weeks ago.

"You're doing okay?" she asks. "No discomfort?"

There are many possible answers to that question, but since I'm assuming she means discomfort relating to the pregnancy, I answer in the negative.

"And you want to find out the sex today?" She busies herself at the equipment tray next to my leg.

I meet Aimee's gaze on my other side. Her grin is wide enough to rival the Cheshire cat's.

"Yes, please," I say.

"Great." Dr. Sanders opens my paper robe in the front to bare my stomach. "Let's get started."

The ultrasound gel tickles when she squirts it onto my skin, and I squirm a bit.

"Sorry, I know that's cold." She turns on the machine. The paddle makes contact, and instantly a grainy black-and-white image appears on the small screen. She moves it back and forth, occasionally press-ing it harder into my side, while adjusting focus on the monitor.

"I see it," Aimee gasps.

"You do?" I raise my head to get closer to the image. "Where?"

Dr. Sanders moves the paddle again and settles it just above my pelvic bone. "There." She points to the image and a white moving mass outlined by what looks like a zipper. "That's the spine." She drags her finger along the screen. "The head, the buttocks, the legs.

Now let's see if we can't—" She moves the paddle again, searching for the right angle. "Come on, little one."

My baby has a spine. It has a head. The image blurs, and I reach for Aimee's hand.

"There." Dr. Sanders freezes the image. "Do you see?"

Aimee squeezes my hand tighter. "Oh, Kris," she says.

"What?" I struggle to clear my vision. "Where?"

Dr. Sanders turns the monitor farther toward me. "These are the legs, and if you look along the curve here..."

I follow her finger, and then I see. "It's a girl?" A balloon of confetti explodes within me. "I'm having a girl?"

"I knew it!" Aimee hollers, jumping up and down. I bounce along with her, my hand still attached to hers.

"Here, she's showing us again." Dr. Sanders shifts the paddle to my left, and now it's even clearer. "That's a girl all right," she says, patting me on the leg. "I'll go print these for you while you get dressed."

After she leaves the room, I sit up and marvel at the fixed image of my daughter for a long time. *My daughter.* Tears stream down my face, but I'm smiling so wide my cheeks hurt.

"She's beautiful, isn't she?" I ask Aimee.

"Mm-hmm," comes Aimee's strangled response.

I cast her a glance. "You're crying?"

"No, you're crying." She laughs and wipes her nose. "Whatever. I'm so happy for you."

"Thanks." I turn back to the image. "I should get dressed."

Aimee grabs her purse from the floor. "Sure. I'll be outside."

Once she's gone and I'm alone with the image of my child, I tear my gaze from her picture and caress my belly. I'm going to have a daughter with pigtails, and scraped knees, and princess pajamas, and sticky fingers, and—I pause. *Or maybe none of those things.* Maybe she'll want short hair, dislike roughhousing and messes, and love dinosaurs. If so, that'll be equally awesome.

"I can't wait to meet you," I whisper to my belly button before I finally get off the bed and get dressed.

I leave a message for my mother as soon as I get home. She's napping a lot these days, so catching her awake is hit-and-miss, but I know she'll call back as soon as she hears. In the meantime, I steel myself for calling Lily.

She and I have texted back and forth since I've been home, but when she heard I was finally doing the ultrasound, she made me promise I'd call afterward. I am equal parts bursting with the news I've learned and antsy at the thought of talking to her again. I miss her a lot. *As a friend.* That other stuff was stupid. Downright idiotic. The only reason my heart is beating so fast is I worry things will be awkward. Yes, that's it.

Regardless, my fingers tremble as I dial her number.

"Well?" she shouts by way of greeting, and that one word brings all the relief I could ask for. She's the same. "I'm dying here. Tell me!"

I stopped pacing the moment she answered, and now I swallow back the knot forming in the wake of the adrenalin rush. "Hi," I say, cradling the phone to my ear.

She's quiet for a few seconds. Then, "Hi." Her voice is breathy, making me think of lazy mornings and late-night heart-to-hearts.

I lean against my kitchen counter and close my eyes. *Fuck.* I don't know who I'm trying to kid here, but my body is not as easily fooled as my mind. Her voice brings it all back.

There's a whoosh and a thud on the line followed by a dull echo, then, "Kris, are you there?"

I try my best to keep my voice steady. "I'm here."

"Sorry, I had to step outside. Too noisy."

"It's a girl," I whisper. *It's a girl, and I wish you were here.*

"Is it really?"

I picture her eyes widening like those of a startled cartoon character and grin, blinking back the moisture in my eyes. "It is."

Lily hollers on the other end, thankfully not straight into the phone but still loud enough for me to have to pull mine away from my ear. A laugh bubbles out of my chest, matching hers.

"A girl," she says with a squeal when she comes back on the line. "Everything look okay?"

"Ten fingers, ten toes. Aimee counted."

"And you?" She pauses. "You're okay?"

There are so many responses to that question, but I can't even. "I'm okay," I say. "You?"

"It's good to hear your voice," she says. "I mean, to hear you're not freaking out. Your mom, flying, the baby..." She clears her throat. "You sound like yourself."

"That's good, I guess."

"Oh, you know what I mean."

We're both quiet for a long while.

"So," she says at the same time I say, "I'm really sorry." When she doesn't respond, I go on. "For making you uncomfortable that night. And then I had to leave like that. I wish I could have it undone."

"Oh."

"I totally get it. I wanted you to know. It was my bad."

"Okay." She's silent for a beat. "Get what?"

"You know." My cheeks heat. Do I have to spell it out?

"I'm not sure I do."

I look around as if someone might be eavesdropping even though not even Morrison's around. Aimee and I figured he might as well stay there if I'm leaving again soon. "That we're different. You're gay and out, and I'm, I don't know, confused or something. Maybe." I suck in a quick breath. "So I get it's best we're just friends."

"I see."

Her voice sounds odd, making me paranoid. "Provided you still want to be, of course." I press the phone to my ear, waiting.

"You know I do, Kris," she says, her voice soft. "I'm sorry too. It *was* kind of a crummy goodbye, wasn't it?"

"Not the best."

"And I don't want you to worry about that night. Overall, I had a great time, much thanks to you."

Overall. As in, except when you came on to me and made everything awkward. "I haven't talked to your dad yet, but I'll call him today, I promise."

"Don't worry about it. I talked to him already. To be honest, I think he was bummed. He liked you."

"Really?"

She laughs. "Really."

Another silence, and I can't help but beat myself up over the lulls in our conversation that were never there before. Why did I have to go ruin a good thing?

"So have you thought about names?" Lily asks eventually.

I relax into my chair. "Not yet. Is that weird?"

"I don't think so. Mom always says I was unnamed for the first three days of my life. Apparently, they had two names picked out, but I didn't look like either, so they had to start over."

"What were they?"

"If fate hadn't stepped in, I'd have either been Daisy or Constance."

"Oh my." I giggle. "Not that there's anything wrong with those names, but—"

"They're not me."

"Not at all."

"If I were you, I'd pick out some favorites but keep things open until she's here."

She.

I look down at my belly. She's actually in there. I have photo proof. "Thanks. I think I might."

"On another topic, I wanted to ask—I got that job in London, and I'm flying out on the twenty-second. I could do a stopover in Chicago. If you want."

I do a quick scan of my mental calendar. *Crap.* "I won't be here. I'm leaving for New York on Wednesday."

"New York?"

I explain the whole situation with the opera while Lily listens.

"Well, that's a bummer," she says when I'm done. "Will you be okay flying?"

I'm not surprised that's her first concern considering she's seen me at my worst in such a situation. "I don't know," I say, meaning it. "Want to come with? Keep me sane?" I force a discreet cough to take the edge off my words, how much I mean them.

"You can do it," she says. "I've seen you pull through before. You'll do it again."

I wish I felt as confident.

CHAPTER 29

Mom, Shannon, and Aimee all insist on coming with me to the airport when it's time to leave for the Big Apple. Shannon and Mom spend the night and are up an hour before me, making sure I have everything—wallet, phone, keys, tickets tucked into the carry-on, laptop and chargers, the dress. Personally, I can't be bothered with any of those details. I'm sipping tea at the kitchen table, subconsciously aware I should be frantically checking off a list. Some might say I'm in denial, but it's more like an out-of-body experience where I know I'm about to travel again but my brain shouts "screw it all" over and over inside my head. It's kind of nice.

"I don't know why you two think this back-and-forth is a good idea," Shannon comments right before Aimee is supposed to come get us. "Panic attacks can't be good for the baby."

"It's a great idea," Mom says, sitting down across from me. "Isn't it, Kris?" She grimaces as she settles into the chair. "She'll be just fine."

I don't want to argue with her this close to my departure, so I bite my tongue and clutch my mug between my hands. I'm about to put it to my lips when something inside me goes *ba dum pum*. I straighten involuntarily, and my hand goes to the baby bump.

Mom frowns. "What is it?"

I turn inward, waiting. *There it is again.* "It's the baby," I whisper as if not to startle her. "I think she kicked."

Mom's drawn face brightens. "How many weeks are you?"

"Eighteen."

"What's going on?" Shannon asks from the doorway.

"The baby kicked." Mom leans forward across the table. "I think she's excited about going to New York."

I grin. "Maybe so." A new notion takes shape inside me in that instant. My center of gravity has shifted. It's no longer just about me. If I don't overcome whatever fears hold me back, I might well pass them on to my daughter. And now I know what she'll miss out on.

I can do this—for Mom, yes—but also for my daughter's future. And if I take my own advice, I don't always have to like it, but I do have to accept it.

I sit up front with Aimee in the minivan after she picks us up, and she glances at me so frequently throughout the drive I have to remind her to keep her eyes on the road.

"I'm not going to jump out of the car, I promise. I might get thrown out through the windshield, though, unless you start paying attention to what you're doing."

"You're too calm," she quips and looks to my mom and sister in the back seat. "Isn't she too calm?"

"Would you rather I scream and cry?" I give her a pointed look. "I can do that too."

"It's spooky, is all."

"*If* I die later today, which I won't, I'll come back to haunt you. *That* will be spooky."

Her response is a wide grin. "Oh good, you're still in there."

I ignore her and fiddle with my phone instead. Lily has been sending me encouraging gifs every so often, but it's been a while since the last one. I'm about to text her when she beats me to it.

Just talked to my friend Aaron in NY. Call him if u want a guide. Journalist. Good guy.

His phone number comes as a tag.

Oh. My mind scans through a whole encyclopedia of emotions, not sure where to settle. The possibilities are endless—excitement, self-consciousness, curiosity, jealousy that she thinks highly of him—but they swirl together until none can be defined.

Thanks, we'll see, I text back, hoping that doesn't sound too ungrateful.

A snore from the back seat interrupts my thoughts. Mom's head is tilted back, her mouth open and slack in a stark reminder of what really matters. Shannon and I look at each other in silent understanding of what this new normal means. She reaches out and pets the white skin on the back of Mom's hand with one finger.

"You'll look after her?" I ask in a low voice. "Keep me posted?"

"Of course."

"Get on the plane when they call boarding this time," my mother says once we reach the security line.

"What's that supposed to mean?" Shannon asks.

"Nothing." Mom winks at me.

"I think..." I look between the three familiar faces watching me with different levels of concern. "I think I'll be all right this time." My daughter and I will do it together.

Mom touches my arm briefly before Aimee pulls me into a hug. "Have fun!"

With a final beat of hesitation, I turn and join the line. It moves at speed today, and before I know it, I'm at the belt, placing my loose items in the tray, shoes removed. In the moment before I step into the scanner, I glance back toward the end of the line, and there they are—Mom, Shannon, and Aimee—in what looks like breathless anticipation. I raise my hand for a wave, and they do the same. I swear Mom looks happy.

I'm a security champion this time. I even remember to put my shoes back on. Heading toward the food court, I text Lily a running commentary of everything I'm doing, and she responds back instantly. It's almost as if she's there.

Not until I make it to the gate and see the airplane does my bravado falter. Heart galloping in my chest, compulsive math starts happening in my head. I'll be in the air for a little over two hours. That's one hundred twenty-five minutes, or seven thousand five hundred seconds, where something can go wrong. And don't people usually say bad things happen in a split second? So that's fifteen thousand opportunities for disaster.

I grab my carry-on and get up, ready to walk away to anywhere but here, but then my phone chimes in my pocket. Lily is video calling me. I sink back into my seat, press the accept button, and there she is, smiling at me.

"I have a few minutes, so I figured I'd check in for real. How are you holding up?" she asks, optimistic.

"Not awesome." My voice breaks.

"But you were doing so great."

I cradle the phone in both hands. "I know, but now I feel like I'm going to throw up."

"You won't. And if you do, please avert the phone."

That makes me smile, but it doesn't stop the tears from welling in my eyes.

"You can do this, Kris. You're one of the strongest people I know, and look how far you've already come."

I open my mouth to object, but she beats me to it.

"I love New York," she continues. "Think of everything you'll see, all those new experiences. You think you don't like this stuff, but deep down you do. You can't tell me you wish California or Seattle never happened."

"Or Portland."

She looks straight into the camera, straight into me, the side of her mouth curling up. "Or Portland."

I've stopped crying. I could tell her how much I miss her, I think, but instead I go the sensible route—the one she would want me to choose.

"What's your favorite place in New York?" I ask.

Lily is quiet for a long time, thinking. "There's a park on Long Island—Gantry Plaza—where you can walk along the riverfront and get great pictures of the skyline."

"I'll put that on my to-do list." I inhale through my nose, let any trepidation disperse together with my longing. "I'm okay now."

"You sure?"

A voice comes over the speaker, calling for boarding, and at the same time, the baby somersaults inside me, reminding me I have reinforcement.

"Yes," I say, this time with conviction flooding me. "Yes, we'll be fine."

CHAPTER 30

New York is hot and busy. My hotel room is on the sixth floor with a partial view of the Hudson River, but that is also its most distinctive feature. Everything else is your standard hotel staple, which is fine. I don't intend to hang out here anyway. Old Kristin might have, but I know deep within that the others are right—I'm not the same. Gradually, something inside me has transformed and expanded, aside from my belly, as if to make room for notions I never before knew I needed to accommodate. New ideas, perhaps. Curious thrills. The world! I'm away from home, and it's as it should be. The sunlight through the window feels like a possibility, the unfamiliar streets below promising something I can't quite put my finger on.

Taking some time to look inward, I recognize my old friends, Worry and Stress, without a problem, but they are coated now by a curiosity that wasn't there before. I'm eager to explore. That's the word. *Eager.* Only problem is I have no idea where to start. My ticket for *La Bohème* is for Friday night, but until then I'm free as a bird. I pull up Lily's text about her friend Aaron. I could reach out.

"Kick once for *yes*, twice for *no*," I tell my belly.

A single bubble pops close to my bladder. *Close enough.*

I dial Aaron's number.

He picks me up the next morning, two to-go cups of coffee in his hands.

"I come bearing gifts," he says, dimples adorning both cheeks. "It's nice to meet you, Kristin."

He's as disarming as Lily, that much is clear from the start. Plus, I won't have to worry about any muggers, with his biceps pushing the limits of those T-shirt sleeves like that.

After brief introductions, he asks, "So what do you want to see? Lily tells me this is your first time here."

"I like parks," I say as we start walking down the street. "And I'd love to see the Statue of Liberty. Other than that, you might know better."

Aaron rubs his hands together. "Creative freedom. I like it! I know some great places for food, some cool art galleries, parks, of course, and I'm going to a jazz club tomorrow night with some friends if you want to join us."

Now I see why Lily loves what New York has to offer. "That all sounds great."

"Awesome! So what do you say we get the statue out of the way first? It's still early enough in the morning we might avoid the worst crowds."

The baby flutters gleefully in agreement. "Lead the way."

"I appreciate you doing this," I say once we've made it onto our first subway train. "You'll have to let me know when you need to go. I'm sure you have other things to do."

Aaron takes hold of the armrest to counter the jerky moves of the train. "Not really. I'm a freelancer like Lily, so I set my own hours."

"Is the summer slow?"

"It depends. I just finished a job, so she called with perfect timing."

An inkling of suspicion that's probably overdue trickles into my mind. "So you're doing this out of the goodness of your heart?"

"I guess you could say that. Why?"

"In my experience, most people don't, unless there's something in it for them."

Aaron shifts in his seat.

Aha. Here comes the ulterior motive.

When he looks up, he has the saddest puppy eyes I've ever seen on a grown man. "Well, the thing is," he says in a low voice that forces me to lean forward to hear better, "I kind of owe her a big one. We were working in Africa a few years back, and there was this wildlife rehab center we were covering. I fell and scraped my knee, and the smell of blood, I don't know, it must have attracted the lions because when I looked up, I was surrounded. I know I'm dead, right? They're ready to pounce." He smacks his palms down onto his thighs, making me start. "Then Lily comes running at top speed, yelling like a banshee and waving her tripod around like a propeller. And here I am."

I can picture Lily, her dark curls flying, face lit up with determination, coming to Aaron's rescue. "She saved your life." I shake my head. "Wow, I can't believe she did that."

"Yeah, she totally didn't." The puppy eyes are gone, replaced instead by a toothy grin. "I'm joking with you, Kristin. I've never been to Africa."

I gawk at him. "No lions?"

"Nah. Lily told me you have an interesting story to share about this trip, and she knows how much I love those. Plus, you know, she said you were cute." He gives me a quick wink.

I want to be mad at him, but something about his aspect makes that impossible. He's like a big kid—impulsive, jolly, enthusiastic. He and Lily as friends make perfect sense. I gnaw at the inside of my cheek.

"I promise. This is fun for me." The dimples come out full force. *As if Mario Lopez and the Rock had a love child.*

I sit back in my seat. *Keep an open mind,* I tell myself. I may never go to New York again, and this is the best way to experience it—with a local. With deliberate effort, I push the last misgivings aside and smile at him. "If you say so."

Aaron is a great guide. He's lived in New York his whole life and knows everything there is to know about the city—or so it seems from my outsider perspective. He gives me a crash course in the history of the city, and I tell him about Mom's bucket list. I'm not sure which one of us is getting the better deal, but we're both enjoying ourselves. Like Lily said—having some company is nice.

After a touristy morning, Aaron takes me to see his favorite spots in the city. I try a mystery spicy meat with sesame seeds and pickled vegetables off a food truck for lunch, pose in front of colorful murals, and even let him teach me how to take a ramp on a scooter we borrow from a kid at the skate park who has more control over his limbs than is fair. I laugh more than I have in a while, and when the sun passes behind a cloud, the world doesn't dim because there's light inside me now. The confines I've built around me have cracked enough that even I can see it shine through.

By the time we get back to my hotel, it's nine in the evening, and I'm exhausted. All I want to do is shower and go to sleep. The skin on my shoulders is burnt, and I've caught unfortunate whiffs of my armpits more than once throughout the day.

"There's a bar around the corner if you're not ready to tuck in yet," Aaron says when we stand in the lobby, about to say good night.

"Thanks, I've had a great time, but I'm beat." I dig in my purse for my room key. "If Lily really had saved your life, you'd be even now."

"It was no big deal. I enjoyed it."

"Good. Then I won't feel like I took advantage."

"I'm pretty sure I would have enjoyed that too."

Oh my God, is he flirting with me? I keep my eyes peeled on the carpet in front of us as he walks me to the elevators. I could be reading too much into it. Not that it matters. I'm only here for a few days.

"So, I'll see you tomorrow?" I ask, pushing the call button.

Aaron shoves his hands into his pockets and clears his throat. "Yeah. Noon. More street art."

"Thanks again for today." The elevator arrives, and I step inside.

"Hey," he calls before the doors close.

I stick an arm through to make them open again.

"I was wondering—how would you feel about going to the opera together Friday? I know you already have a ticket, but one of my job perks is getting into shows, so..."

He *is* flirting.

My cheeks heat. Sure, it's flattering—he's a solid nine to my seven-on-a-good-day—but he's not hitting any of those buttons for me. My heart has stakes elsewhere at the moment, no matter how futile. "Um..."

"Before you say no, have you ever been to the opera before?"

"No."

"I have. Lots of times. People dress up, they go in pairs and groups, rarely alone. I would be your buffer. You know, so you don't feel out of place."

"A buffer. That's all?"

"Well, it's no secret I enjoy your company." Another grin spreads across his face.

"Aaron, I—"

He holds up a hand, interrupting me. "I know."

I startle. *What does he know?* "You do?"

"Well, yeah." He gestures to my belly. "You're pregnant and leaving in a few days. I'll come with you as a friend. Promise."

Again, I waver. It was a lovely day and I'm not overly excited about this opera thing as it is. Could be fun. "You'll take me to dinner before?"

His expression brightens further. "Of course."

"As friends."

"Barely acquaintances."

I extend my hand. "Deal."

He shakes it. "Excellent."

CHAPTER 31

On the day of the opera, I call Mom, expecting to get her voice mail as I have every other day, but instead Shannon picks up.

"She has a doctor's appointment this afternoon. I'm taking her," she explains. "We need to adjust her pain meds again."

The distance between us seems insurmountable. Here I am, having a good old time while my mother is dying back home. I know it's on her request and she'd be furious if I was anywhere but, and still it makes no sense. I should—

As if Shannon can read my mind, she says, "She wants you to be there. It's all she talks about. She's printed out your balloon photo and keeps it on her nightstand."

Oh, Mom. My chest aches. "Is she—is there any change?"

"She seems okay. She sleeps a lot, but she's still herself, if that's what you mean."

"Except she needs new meds."

"The doctor wants to see her before she ups the dosage, is all." She lowers her voice. "Personally, I think the problem is she's supposed to take the pills with food, and she doesn't eat enough. Don't tell her I said so."

"I heard that," Mom says in the background. "Don't be talking about me like I'm not here." There's a rustle, and she comes on the line. "If anything, you'd think the drugs would work better when not diluted by food, wouldn't you? They're not giving me enough, that's the real problem. I'm nothing but a dying old lady. They don't care if I'm comfortable or not."

"I'm sure that's not true," I say—a mistake, it turns out. She launches into a long speech of discontent, and not surprisingly, that makes me feel better. If she still has energy for griping, things can't be too bad.

We end our conversation with her making me promise I'll take lots of pictures.

It's late afternoon already, and since Aaron is picking me up for an early dinner, I hurry out of my shorts and T-shirt, put on my good bra, and slip into the dress. It's as transformative as I remember, but eventually I manage to tear myself away from the mirror to take care of hair and makeup, and I'm only five minutes late down to the lobby, where Aaron awaits.

"Wow," he says when he sees me. "You look—wow. I feel underdressed."

We actually look very nice together. He's wearing a gray suit and a blue tie that echoes the same notes as my dress. Plus, he's tall and muscular. With dimples.

"Thanks. I try to clean up from time to time."

"You did a great job tonight."

"Here." I hand him my phone. "You have to take my picture. For my mother."

He obliges, and then we ask the receptionist to take one of us together. I instantly text both Mom and Shannon. I consider sending it to Lily, too, but something that feels more complicated than a texted glam photo stops me. I tuck the phone into my purse.

"Ready to go?" Aaron asks.

"Ready."

We arrive at the Metropolitan Opera twenty minutes before the show is supposed to start. I'm extra grateful for the draping on the dress because I'm so full from dinner I'm sure in any other garment I would look pregnant even if I wasn't. Aaron, of course, knew the owner of the restaurant we went to, so the dishes kept coming. I certainly took advantage. The strawberry tart I had for dessert nearly made me cry.

As soon as we've entered the palatial opera building, I excuse myself to the ladies' room. There's a line, of course, because fancy clothing does not negate nature's calls, and I tiptoe in place until it's my turn.

I get more admiring looks for my dress as I make my way back to Aaron. I tilt my chin in the queenliest way possible in response to the appreciation, but to my surprise, Aaron looks supremely uncomfortable when I reach him.

"Everything go okay?" he asks, cheeks reddening.

"Sure." When he doesn't say anything else, I ask if we should head inside.

"Do me a favor and come a little closer."

"Why?"

His eyes dart around the crowd before returning to me with a whisper. "There's something under your shoe."

"Wha—" I look down, and sure enough, I've walked through the whole lobby with a long length of toilet paper trailing out from under my dress. I want to sink through the floor.

"I was trying not to draw attention to it. I'm sorry."

Right then another much more pregnant lady passes us, leans in, and says something in rapid New Yorkian that I don't catch.

"She likes your dress," Aaron explains. "And she said she wishes she was one of those cute pregnant women like you."

"Must not have seen the classy toilet paper accessory, then."

"My guess is no." Aaron smiles. "You won't see any of these people again anyway. Let's go inside, what do you say?"

I can't help but laugh. "Let me walk a few steps ahead of you so you can make sure there's nothing left."

Aaron agrees, and so we walk into the theater, him trailing behind me, until we're ushered into our seats.

I saw *Rent* in Chicago several years ago and loved it. It doesn't take me long to realize *La Bohème* is a fancy Italian version of the same, or, rather, *Rent* is a gritty modern take on *La Bohème*, and this makes it much more enjoyable than I thought it would be. I already more or less know the story.

Come intermission, I'm high on all the impressions. Aaron parks me in a corner of the lobby and disappears to concessions only to appear back in a few minutes with a glass of champagne that he hands me.

"It's nonalcoholic. Can't go to your first opera without bubbles." He clinks his glass to mine and drinks. I do the same. "Don't move. I'll take another picture with the opera as a backdrop." He whips out his phone, and I pose.

"Very regal," he says. "Too bad there's no prince."

"You sound like my mom."

His eyes glitter in the light of the sconces. "I think I'd like to meet this mother of yours. She obviously has a good head on her shoulders."

"You promised no flirting."

"Sorry, I can't help it. It's the opera... Don't tell me you're not having fun."

I cock my head to the side, thinking. "What exactly did Lily tell you about me?"

"Um." He takes another swig of his drink. "Well, she mentioned the traveling, of course. Broad sweeps. And about you and your boyfriend breaking up."

"I left him," I correct.

"Right."

"Anything else?"

His gaze darts away. "Not really."

I glare at him from under lowered eyebrows.

"Fine." He mutters something under his breath. "She said she thought you could use some company. Some male company, specifically. Nothing sordid, mind you. I'd never. We just met, and you're, you know." He gestures to my belly. "And I already told you why I said yes. I like meeting people and having a good time. And I was. Am."

My skin prickles. I can't believe what I'm hearing. Lily has set me up. She wants Aaron and me to have a good time, maybe even a *very* good time. Probably thinks it'll make me forget what happened in Portland. I can only assume that's what she wants, and the assumption stings. It means she's not willing to see me as anything but a friend.

"Hey." Aaron rests his hand on my shoulder. "You have to believe me. I wasn't going to take advantage or anything."

The gong sounds, announcing the second act, so I down my faux champagne. "No worries. Let's go back inside." I put my glass down on the table next to us a little harder than necessary then arrange my features to mimic someone excited to be here. I'll deal with Lily in the morning. Who does she think she is, setting me up with anyone?

I try hard to focus on what's happening on stage the rest of the evening, but Aaron's presence is distracting now. I know it's not his fault—he has no idea what he's ended up in the middle of—but every time he addresses me, I think *male attention*. It's so stupid. I'm stupid. Did I really think there was still a possibility of something—anything—happening with Lily? Time to get over myself.

Distracted though I may be, the opera is fantastic. I save one of the programs, and Aaron sneaks a photo of the stage. He really is a through-and-through decent guy.

"So what did you think?" he asks as we walk back to my hotel.

"It was amazing."

"Right? I love the opera."

Despite the hour and the fading light, tons of people are milling about, and I'm not ready for the night to end yet.

"How about some ice cream?" I ask.

"What the pregnant lady wants, the pregnant lady gets." He offers his arm, and I hook mine through it.

We find a bench by the river, and he buys us two cups from a small gelateria. My scoops are strawberry and Oreo, his chocolate and pistachio. We eat in silence.

When we finally get back to the hotel, it's completely dark outside, the lights from the buildings bathing the city in neon streaks. Aaron walks me to my room this time, carrying the shoes I shed in the lobby. Pregnancy and heels don't go well together. Turning to him to say good night, I'm reminded of a similar situation not long ago in a hallway not that different from this.

"I had a wonderful time. Thank you."

"The pleasure was all mine." He hands me my shoes.

Maybe it's the memory or the evening or what he said about Lily, but when I take the shoes, instead of stepping right back, I get up on my toes and place a kiss on his cheek. He looks momentarily startled but then collects himself and grins.

"Not completely immune to my charms, then?" He takes one step closer to me so there's barely a hand's width between us. "Only, that's not how I'd choose to kiss good night."

I force myself not to look away. "No?"

"Can I show you?"

Even as I nod my consent, I'm not sure why. I don't necessarily want to kiss him.

But kiss we do. It's a good one too. Soft yet demanding and with the right amount of tongue. I kiss Aaron and think of Lily. She wants this. Assumes this is right for me. But even though my lips tingle when we finally part, it doesn't go any further. My body is not involved. Now if Lily asks, I can tell her I gave it a shot, and she was wrong. I don't need "male company" at all.

"When are you going back home again?" Aaron asks.

"Tomorrow."

"Can I take you to the airport?"

I take a step back, freeing my hand from his. "I don't think that's a good idea."

He watches me for a long moment as if searching for something in my expression. An explanation perhaps. "You're right," he says eventually. "But if you're ever in New York again, let me know. I've had a great time. For real."

I unlock the door to my room and offer him a one-armed hug. "Good night, Aaron. Thanks for everything."

I don't wait around to watch him walk off.

CHAPTER 32

I call Mom from the cab to the airport the next day. It's past eleven in the morning there, but she sounds like she's still in bed.

Sure enough. "You woke me up," she says after the first tired greeting.

Good to know my deductive reasoning still works. "Did you get the pictures?"

"I printed them. I'm looking at them now. That Aaron guy is a handsome fellow."

Good kisser, too, I almost say, but of course I don't. It's a moot point.

"And you looked nice," she continues.

I smile. "Are you giving me a compliment?"

"I guess I am."

"It was the dress."

"Only in part."

The driver takes a sharp turn, and I bump into the door of the cab with a small grunt. I anchor the phone to my ear so as not to lose it or miss anything else she might say, but she remains quiet.

"So," I say when the ride gets smoother, and the silence becomes too poignant. "How are you doing? For real."

Mom's breath is a snort in my ear. "It's not important."

"Of course it is. What did the doctor say yesterday?" I scan the buildings that rush past my window at breakneck speed. "Hello?"

"Dying is not something I recommend," she says eventually, adding a humorless chuckle. "And that's all I'll say about it. When are you going to Paris to finish my list?"

Knowing I won't be able to get anything else out of her about her condition, I tell her my plans. I'll get home today, drive to Rockford to see her tomorrow, repack, and then I'll leave for Europe Thursday. It's coming up so fast, I've hardly had a chance to think about it, but that's mostly a good thing. Arrive in Paris Friday morning, eat crepes and chocolate croissants, scout the Louvre, then plant her painting in chosen location.

"I packed it in Bubble Wrap and have it waiting for you in the hallway," Mom says when I ask. "It's that small one of the covered bridge, if you remember."

The painting she's referring to is one she did well before Shannon and I were born. It's in oil and on a mounted canvas about six-by-six inches in size. The weathered wood of the bridge stands out against a canopy of fall foliage, the sun reflecting in the stream below. It's a nice painting—not my favorite of the multitude she has lying around but still good.

"Why that one?"

"I did it during my Monet phase. Seems fitting. Plus, it's small enough."

As the courier tasked with illegally displaying it in the most famous museum in the world, I am thankful for this foresight.

There's a rustle and then Mom's voice again. "Oh, there's my pretty girl."

It takes me a second to realize she's talking to the cats, my cue to end the conversation.

Right as I'm about to hang up, she says, "I love you, Kris. Be safe."

I yank the phone back to my ear, breathless and not sure I heard her right. "What was that?"

She repeats herself, and for a long moment I sit stunned, staring at the seat back before me. It's not that I haven't heard her use the L word before. She coos it all the time to her furry companions. The novelty is, she's directing it to me.

"Love you, too, Mom." I say it just in time before we enter a tunnel and I lose her.

I have one more call to make before I get on this flight. I want to ask Lily about the whole Aaron thing, if she meant to set me up with him and why, but at this point I've sat staring at my phone at the gate for fifteen minutes and can't make myself dial her number.

On the one hand, there's hearing her voice—after everything that's happened, I'm conditioned for it to calm me before a trip. Also, extending the benefit of the doubt, she may have set me up with Aaron merely as a friendly gesture, since she knows I'm such a reluctant traveler, and if that's so, I'm doing all of this overanalyzing for nothing. Maybe she'll laugh at my silliness and tell me she'll stop in Chicago on her way home once I'm back.

On the other hand, maybe she really did set me up with Aaron because she wants me to leave her the heck alone. She's probably out partying since it's Saturday night in London and won't even *want* to talk to me. That's disappointment waiting to happen. There's also the fact of me kissing Aaron. With the spiteful curiosity gone, I don't know that I want Lily to find out. Unless she *already* knows...

The inside of my cheek was already raw from gnawing on it earlier. Now it's starting to taste like blood. I still have an hour until boarding, so I put my phone away temporarily and go to find a coffee shop in the food court. Once seated, I pull it out again and start a text.

Heading back to Chicago, I type. It's neutral enough. I open a magazine as if I'm not waiting for her to respond.

It takes less than a minute for the three moving dots to appear. *How did you like New York?*

I write back that it was interesting, I did a lot of walking, and the opera was great. Then I add, *Aaron was a good guide.*

It takes a while for the dots to appear this time. *Glad you hit it off.*

Hit it off. I close my eyes and rub hard at the bridge of my nose. Does that mean she's talked to Aaron? I should have called instead. Damn you, impersonal texting. If I could only hear her voice, I would know.

I look out across the sea of people, my fingers drumming an uneven rhythm against the tabletop. Fuck it, I'm going there.

Was that the intention?

I force myself to put the phone down next to my plate and finish my soda.

No response.

I pull out my ticket and verify on the huge screen on the opposite wall my gate number hasn't changed.

Still no response.

I'm about to give up and return to the magazine when my phone rings. The number on the screen is a random series of digits I've never seen before, but I know it's her. Slowly, my finger moves toward the accept button.

"Hello."

"Hey." Lily's voice is tentative, without its usual straightforwardness.

"Where are you calling from?" I don't know why I ask. It's not like it matters.

"I'm at a pub."

"Okay." I wait for her to say something else, but the silence stretches until I start thinking we might have been disconnected.

Then she says, "Are you upset about Aaron?"

"Well... It's not that I didn't enjoy the company," I start, trying to put words to these complicated emotions.

"Then what?"

"It feels a bit like you were setting us up."

"And if I did? You're both single. It's summer. You're on vacation. Carpe diem, etcetera."

My shoulders slump. Aaron *was* her attempt at pawning me off on a guy, any guy, then. To achieve what? Distraction? "That's pretty presumptuous."

"I thought you said you had a good time."

"That's not the point."

"Then what is?"

I seethe, my face heating. I keep it turned down and my voice low so other patrons won't notice I'm on the verge of ugly, angry tears.

"Tell me. I want to know," she says, her voice clipped in a way that further nags the sore spot in my heart. "Aaron is one of the coolest people I know, he wasn't busy, he likes meeting people—"

I scoff. "You told him I was cute and could use some male company! You were playing matchmaker."

The woman at the table next to me turns her head and looks at me disapprovingly for raising my voice. I apologize and hunch closer around my phone. "I'm pregnant, and we live in different cities. Even if I was looking for a guy, which I'm not, he would be a terrible choice."

"I didn't force you to call him."

My retort gets stuck in my throat. She's right. I did choose his company. "Still," I say, for the sake of sticking to my guns.

"Really, it's not a big deal, Kris. If it makes you feel better—sorry for fixing you up with a local guide who happens to be handsome and charming."

"Because that's who you see me with?" I huff. Then I ask the most nagging question of all. "Is this still about Portland?"

"Kris, come on."

"No, I want to know."

"You like guys!" she yells loudly enough that I have to pull the phone away from my ear.

In the echoing emptiness following her outburst, my heart crumbles anew. "Which you decided to prove by sending Aaron my way. Well, it didn't work."

"Oh yeah? My sources say differently."

I grow cold. She knows about the kiss. Aaron must have told her. Only she doesn't know how for me it only served to prove my feelings are still otherwise engaged.

"Then you've been misinformed," I say under my breath.

"What was that?"

I'm suddenly exhausted by this back-and-forth. It's like we don't speak the same language anymore. "Nothing. I can't do this over the phone."

"Fine. I have to go anyway. My friends are waiting for me."

"That's not what I mean. I want to see you when you head back to the States."

She's quiet for a bit. "I don't know if that's a good idea." Another pause, then with resignation, "We haven't known each other very long. Maybe we should leave well enough alone. Enjoy the memory, you know."

My chest tightens. "What, and that would be it? No."

"Kris."

"No, that's a terrible idea." I know I'm whining like a petulant child, but I don't know how else to express the panic I feel at the thought of never seeing her again.

She sighs. "Listen, I've got to go. I'm sorry about Aaron, okay. Let me know you get home safely."

Before I can say anything else, she hangs up. I've never been hung up on in my life—not counting Mom's strange phone manners—and it stings something fierce. I sit staring at my phone as if willing it to ring again, and when it doesn't, I only reluctantly tuck it back into my bag. It's time to catch a plane anyway.

I grab my carry-on and head for the gate again. This time, I don't have the energy to fret. My thoughts are otherwise occupied.

CHAPTER 33

I pull into Mom's driveway before noon the next day. I've brought her dress back and a box of gourmet macarons from Aaron's favorite pastry shop, and I set both down on the low bench in her foyer after navigating the front door with my elbow. The wrapped painting is there like she said.

"Mom?" I call into the house.

One by one the three cats come traipsing into the room to greet me, meowing loudly.

"Hi, kitties. Is she sleeping?"

Claudine strokes her body against my ankles and meows again.

"Let's go see, shall we?"

Mom's bedroom door is closed, so I knock before opening it and peering inside.

"Mom, are you awake? It's me, Kris."

She doesn't stir, so I push deeper into the dim rom and turn on the bedside light. The first thing I see is three of her yellow medicine canisters open and empty on the nightstand. I pick one up as I turn to the bed but drop it as if it's on fire at the sight that greets me. She's in her nicest dress on top of her covers, face ashen.

The room tilts on its axis, blood draining so quickly from my head that my vision blurs.

"Mom?" I grapple for her arm, finding it limp yet oddly substantial. "Mom!"

When her head tilts impotently to the side at my jostle, I scream.

I don't remember calling 911 or the paramedics showing up. All I know is that someone has wrapped me in a blanket and deposited me on the couch in the living room with a glass of water in my hands. Footsteps pound up and down the hallway, and strange voices rise and fall in dissonant harmony with a high-pitched alarm that squeals every couple of minutes.

Random phrases reach my ears.

"I've got a pulse."

"Get her stabilized."

"Lift on three."

Eventually, a uniformed man joins me.

"I need to call my sister, but I don't know where my phone is," I say.

He crouches down to my level. "I'll get it for you shortly. We're taking your mother to the hospital. Do you know where Swedish is?"

I nod. Rockford is not that big.

"Good. Go straight to the ER when you get there."

He moves to get up, but I grab his sleeve. "Will she make it?"

"She's stable right now. That's all I can say." He frees his sleeve from my fingers. "I'll go get your phone. You should put some shoes on."

Again I nod, and he disappears.

Driving forces me back to the present. I have one mission only—to get to her as fast as I can. Colors blend together outside the window, and there's a loud buzzing in my head that I can't shake. Gas, brake, turn, red light, fingers tapping on the steering wheel. *Come on!*

I put off calling Shannon until I'm in the underground garage at the hospital. Her reaction mirrors my own, but as I'm faced with her tears, a new calm settles in me. One of us needs to stay sane, and of the two of us, I have always been the more measured one. This is not the time to change that.

I make Shannon promise to drive safely before we hang up.

"I'm here for Jane Caine," I tell the receptionist in the ER. "She was brought in just now."

"Right, you're next of kin?"

"Her daughter."

"Have a seat, and I'll have someone come get you as soon as possible."

I join two other women a little older than me in the waiting area. The large clock on the wall shows 12:39, but its second hand moves so slowly I wonder if it's not going backward. I can't take my eyes off it.

Twenty-five minutes later I'm convinced the clock's been tampered with.

"Why has no one come for me yet?" I ask the receptionist. "I want to see my mother."

She looks something up on her computer monitor and dials a number on her phone. A few mumbled phrases later, she looks at me again. "They say she's in surgery. It'll be a little longer. I'm sorry."

"What kind of surgery?"

"I really can't say."

"Is there nothing you can tell me?"

"Ma'am, it's not my place. The doctor will speak to you as soon as he can."

I drag my feet back to my chair and sit, leaning my forehead into my hands. How is this happening? We were supposed to have more time. I'm not done with the list.

Do not go gently...

I push myself off the chair and pace through the room. If my fellow compatriots are looking, I don't notice. Adrenaline courses through me as I walk back and forth. I'm not stupid. The empty medicine bottles, her choice of clothing—Mom meant for this to happen. She made a conscious choice to end her life now rather than later. Why? Why now? With what little time she has—had?—left, why not make the best of it?

I'm still pacing when Shannon rushes through the door thirty minutes later. As soon as she sees me, she bursts into tears and flings her arms around my neck.

"I'm sorry," she wails. "I shouldn't have left her alone. This is all my fault."

I comfort her as best as I can, and when she finally settles down, I explain what little I know.

"She tried to kill herself?" Shannon's wide eyes are locked on me.

"Has she said anything to you?" I take care not to sound as if I'm blaming her.

"No." Her eyes dart to the side as if she's searching her memory. "At least I don't think so. I mean, I know the pain was getting worse."

"Maybe she didn't want us to try to talk her out of it?"

Shannon's face scrunches up, warning of another imminent breakdown. "Your baby." She moans, placing a hand on my belly. "How can Mom do this to you?"

This is a path I'd rather not go down if I'm going to be able to stay sane, so I cover Shannon's hand with mine and say as calmly as I can, "She wasn't going to be here for that anyway. You know that."

She sniffles but straightens up.

"Kristin Caine?" a voice says from the doorway.

I jump to my feet and drag my sister with me. "Yes?"

"Hi, I'm Dr. Standish." He shakes first my hand then Shannon's. "If you'll come with me, we'll have a little chat."

I don't like how he says the word *chat*. The "t" is too sharp and energetic, not befitting the topic at hand. Nevertheless, we follow him down the hospital corridor and into a small exam room that's currently vacant.

"Your mother is stable for now," he says, sitting down at the narrow wall-mounted desk. A double crease between his brows betrays there's more to come.

"Is she awake?" Shannon looks at him like an eager puppy.

"I'm afraid not," Dr. Standish says with a regretful head tilt. "When someone overdoses on these types of medications, the brain rapidly experiences oxygen deprivation. We don't know how long she'd been unconscious when you found her, and therefore it's impossible to tell exactly what damage, if any, she'll sustain. We were able to relieve some pressure caused by the brain swelling, and she's on a respirator, but we can't know for sure what the outcome will be. Then there's the issue of the cancer, which I understand is quite advanced. Her liver values are significantly elevated, which could be due to the overdose or the possible presence of metastatic tumors. Either way, she wouldn't make any transplant list, as I hope you understand."

"Why not?" Shannon asks. "She's paid her taxes all her life. If she needs a new liver, shouldn't she get one?"

"Shan," I say, placing my hand on her arm.

"That's not fair. She should at least be given a chance."

"A transplant is a major surgery and highly stressful for the body. Even if she was of perfect health, at her age—"

"No." Shannon stands, glaring at the doctor. "I won't have it. I'm a nurse. I know she could make it."

"Sit down." My voice is sterner than I intended, and I think it surprises her enough to make her do as I say. "Since you are a nurse, I'm sure you're aware he's right. Even I know that."

She looks ready to rebut, but instead she returns her gaze to the floor.

"So what are we looking at?" I ask Dr. Standish. "Will there be permanent damage to the brain? Will she recognize us?"

He clasps his hands in his lap, lips pressing together briefly before he answers. "If your mother regains consciousness, yes, there will likely be some form of brain damage. But I have to be honest with you. In light of her age, her general state of health, and the extended oxygen deprivation..."

"She might not wake up at all?"

"It's too soon to tell, but, yes, it's possible."

I sag into my chair, mind going blank.

"Where is she now?" Shannon asks, panic creeping into her voice. "I want to see her."

"I'll take you up to the ICU momentarily." The doctor scans the papers he's holding. Pauses. "There is another matter I need to discuss with you first, however. Do either of you know if there's a living will?"

A chill runs down my spine, and I grasp Shannon's hand. "A what?"

"She has one—a DNR," Shannon responds. To me she says, "Her instructions for her care... in the end."

"What?" I wish they would both stop speaking in riddles.

"Do Not Resuscitate," the doctor clarifies. "I see. I'll enter it into her file. Of course, she's already intubated at the moment."

I look from one to the other. "She doesn't want to... So if something happens we're supposed to stand by and watch?"

Shannon's dejected expression is answer enough.

With drawn-out movements I rise out of my chair, hands shaking. "Please, take us to her."

Thomas comes, and Aimee and Patti and even Patrick, but I don't pay them much attention during the short periods of time they're allowed in the ICU. I sit in the chair next to Mom's hospital bed and listen to the rhythmic beeping of the machines, watch the subtle rise and fall of her chest, ignore the tubes going into her. Her hand is cool in mine, skin paper dry, but at least the limb is alive. She's still in there, and I focus my every effort into silently pleading for her to please, *please* come back. I'm not ready.

Nurses come and go. They tap machines, clear tubes, and check vitals while Shannon and I hover around the perimeter of the room, hand in hand, until they clear out. We don't speak much, intent only on the bed and its inhabitant, so unfamiliar in her unnatural slumber, a poor wax imitation of the woman who gave us life.

Thomas comes for Shannon sometime in the evening, but I stay, certain in my conviction she'll wake any moment. The sun sets outside the window, one of the nurses brings in a blanket for me, and I rest fitfully through the night with my head on the edge of the bed.

The sun rises. More waiting. The sun sets.

Shannon and Thomas return each morning. I don't know where they've been, and I don't care. It's me, Mom, and my baby in a small, tight cocoon where no one can reach us.

"Mom, can you hear me?" I ask sometime during the second night. It's dark outside, but with constant alarms going off in the hallway outside interrupting the passage of time, I don't know if midnight has yet come and gone.

I take her hand in mine, careful not to bump the tube that feeds into her vein. "Your granddaughter is kicking. She wants you to wake up now." A sob forces its way up my throat. "*I* need you to wake up." There are so many questions left to ask, secrets to our shared past to uncover. What kind of mother will I be if I myself am motherless? I rest my forehead against her arm and squeeze my eyes shut. "We were only just beginning," I whisper. "Please."

There's no response except the quiet hiss and release of the respirator.

On the evening of the third day, Shannon enters the room with my favorite chopped salad and Aimee trailing on her heels. The doctor has just finished his rounds, noting once more no change. Mom is still stable, but her body is not yet ready to return to us. Why, no one can say for sure.

"You need to eat, Kris," Shannon says. "Let's get you washed up." She helps me from my chair and leads me to the sterile en suite bathroom. My back screams in protest after I've been sitting for so long with almost no break, but I follow her complacently and let her splash my face with cold water. I register the piercing chill with detached interest. It's refreshing yet doesn't refresh.

We return to the room, where Aimee has set out the salad on the table and pulled up a chair. There's a fork, a bottle of pop, and a napkin waiting for me, but I want to go back to Mom's side.

"No." Shannon grabs me by the elbow. "You're going to eat now. And we're going to talk."

I halt my steps while contemplating whether to object or not. She tugs on my elbow.

"You're pregnant," she says. "If you're not going to eat for you, eat for your daughter."

I blink at her a few times and look down at my belly.

What am I doing?

My lip starts trembling, and within seconds the first sob bursts out of my lungs on a sputtered note. "I don't know what to do," I wail. "How do we wake her up?"

Shannon and Aimee are with me in an instant, arms enveloping me, their shoulders shaking in time with mine. It might be five minutes or ten, but when we finally settle, I feel spent and raw and bone weary. But at least I *feel*.

I sit down at the table and push the lettuce around with my fork for a minute before putting the first bite in my mouth. My salivary glands hurt from the savory dressing, the flavor bursting forth on my tongue, and gradually the fog lifts.

Aimee and Shannon are watching me as if I'm a toddler who might choke at any moment. They exchange the occasional glance that I suspect they think I don't notice, and I'm vaguely aware something is going on here aside from feeding me.

I finish a third of the salad then push it away. "I can't eat any more," I say when Shannon awards me her sternest look. "I'm full."

Aimee pushes the pop toward me. "Something to drink?"

I take it, studying her over the rim of the can. She couldn't look more abashed if she had poisoned it.

"What's going on?" I set the pop down, look from Aimee to Shannon. "Is it—" My gaze flickers to Mom.

"No." Shannon reaches for my hand. "I spoke to Dr. Standish earlier. There's no change."

"Then what?" I pull my hand away. I have a feeling I won't like whatever it is they have to say.

Aimee poses a silent question to Shannon, who inclines her head.

Aimee turns to me, her features inanimate in a way I've never seen before. "Is this what your mom would have wanted?" she asks, head tilted. "For you to sit here day and night, forgetting yourself, your baby, everything around you?"

I struggle against the thickness in my throat, waiting for her to continue.

"If she woke up right now, what would she say?"

Shannon and I both turn toward the bed and our mother's shape, for once in the synchrony befitting twins.

"She'd think I'm making a fuss," I say under my breath.

Shannon's mouth quirks up on one side. "Pishposh," she says in imitation of Mom. "I'm fine. Everything is fine."

A snort escapes me, but then I fall serious again. "She's not fine. We *should* fuss." I search my sister's face. "If not now, when?"

"She'd say *never*. It's her pet peeve."

I slump back in my chair and have another sip of my drink. "I don't know what else to do. I *need* to do something."

Again, Shannon and Aimee look at each other, and it makes me want to slam a fist down on the table. What are they not saying?

"You have the list," Aimee says, a watchful expression on her face.

I scoff. "As if."

"Why not?" Shannon asks.

I glare at them both. "Are you serious? You want me to go to Europe now? Are you insane?"

Aimee shifts in her seat, but Shannon doesn't falter. "You promised her," she says.

"Before this happened." My objection comes out strong, but inside the echo of Mom's voice struggles to reach the surface. I rub at my temples in frustration and stand up, pace around them to the other side of the window. It's a sunny day, heat radiating off the concrete where people in pastel shorts and flowery dresses stroll next to green lawns. How is it business as usual outside this room?

"Maybe there's still time," Aimee says. "She could wake up, right? And then won't she be disappointed you gave up?"

Disappointed.

Give up.

I lean my forehead against the cool pane and close my eyes, and there it is, Mom's clear voice inside my head.

Promise me you'll finish the list, no matter what.

"No matter what," I whisper, my breath fogging the glass. Aimee is right. Mom would be disappointed. I did promise. But surely this is not the sort of situation she had in mind. And how would I even begin to—

"Aimee will go with you," Shannon says behind me.

I turn, startled.

"It's better than sitting here wilting away with her. It will give you something to do, and I'll be here. I'll let you know the minute anything changes."

"You're serious?" My heart beats faster. "You want me to leave her here like this and go to Paris now?"

"It's not about what *I* want." Shannon looks at Mom. "It's what she would want. I know you know this."

My palms are turning damp, and my head spins. "But—" I return to my seat. "But—"

"If we leave Thursday as planned, we can be back this weekend. It's only a few days." Aimee tries a look of reassurance.

I finish my pop in two deep gulps. The sugar settles the impending panic attack, but I still take another few breaths to let what they're saying sink in. The baby does a slow turn, distending the taut rounding of my belly further for the briefest of moments. My daughter. If I ask a favor of her one day, will she do it for me, no questions asked?

"We'll leave Thursday, get back Sunday?" I ask Aimee.

"Not a day later," she says a little too eagerly.

My hand strokes absently across my midsection, tracing the movements of the mystery therein, while my gaze rests on the one who once carried me.

"Let's do it," I say finally, mind made up. "Let's finish her list."

CHAPTER 34

I emerge from the hospital lobby into the world of the living Wednesday morning, blinking like a mole in the sunlight. Aimee leads me by the arm. At first, I'm grateful, but with each step I feel my strength seeping back into my limbs, and by the time we reach my car, I'm walking of my own accord.

In twenty-four hours we'll be over the Atlantic, on to new adventures. A small thrill runs through me at the thought, to my surprise not altogether unpleasant.

"Are you sure you're okay to drive?" Aimee asks. "I'll be right behind, so if you need to pull over, do."

I place my hands on the steering wheel to try it out. My fingers close around it, finding their familiar grip. "I think I'll be fine."

She goes to close the door, but I stop her. "Thanks, Aimee," I say, peering up at her. "You're a good friend."

She shifts. "You're not mad at me, then?"

"Not a bit. See you tomorrow?"

"We'll come get you at noon. And if you need *anything* in the meantime, call me. I'll keep my cell on."

Cell. That reminds me I need to plug mine in. It ran out of battery sometime Monday evening.

I tell her I will, and then we're off. Packing awaits.

We're thirty-nine thousand feet in the air in our double-decker plane—you know, to challenge gravity a little bit more—before I allow myself to revisit any doubts about my being here. I might have held them at bay longer had the pilot not announced our whereabouts over the speaker just now—why do they feel a need to share this stuff?—which caused my autopilot to switch off, jolting me back into my body.

Aimee is in the back of the plane somewhere—since we didn't get tickets at the same time, we weren't able to get seats next to each other—so she's of no help as the image of Mom in the hospital once more permeates my senses. The lack of a connection to the mainland is driving me nuts. What if something has happened in the hours since we took flight? What if they need me there? I fiddle with my phone as if willing it to be my landline. Shannon's last text is still on my screen: *I won't leave her. Try to have fun. It's Paris!*

Fun... Nothing could be further from my mind.

I flip through my other messages, the ones I missed while at Mom's side. There's one from Aaron, thanking me for a good time, that I haven't responded to, and two from Lily, asking if I got home okay. She still doesn't know about Mom. I haven't replied to her either.

I lean back against the headrest. The plane drones on, and after a while the lights dim in an imitation of the changing time zones. I'm vaguely aware of my head lolling this way and that, which prompts me to roll up a blanket for a pillow to tuck between the window and the seat. It helps, and soon I drift into a deeper sleep from which I'm startled awake a bit later by a pointy elbow into my upper arm. The sky outside has darkened, but the clouds are lined by the glow of the receding sun. A glance at the clock reveals almost two hours have passed.

The owner of the elbow—a squat, gray-haired lady around my mom's age—is saying something to me in French and gesturing to my purse, which has fallen out of my lap and onto the floor.

"Sorry, I don't speak French," I say, reaching for it.

"Ah." Her face brightens. "Sorry to wake you," she says with a strong accent. "I did not want your things to go missing."

"No, it's fine." I right the bag at my feet and tuck it beneath the seat in front of me. "Thanks."

She gives me a kind nod then pulls out an intricate embroidery-in-progress from a homemade tote. Out of the corner of my eye, I can see her clever fingers feeding the thread through the canvas, producing a surprisingly lifelike image of two kittens playing. The sight overwhelms me as the memory of Mom knitting comes rushing back. Grief bunches into a heavy lump of shards in my chest. She will never get anywhere near this proficiency because she started too late.

I fake a cough to cover up a sob as I turn toward the window. No matter how many times I swallow, I can't stop my eyes from over-flowing. There is so little time. For all of us. Sometimes even less than we think.

And most of us waste what little we have.

"Is everything good?" the lady asks.

"Yes," I sob. "No. I don't know."

Her forehead sets in apparent concern as she hands me a tissue. I blow my nose with a loud honk then lean back and close my eyes.

"You've lost someone," she says. It's a statement, not a question, and I look up to meet her eyes. They are filled with the empathy only old ladies possess after a long life of living.

"My mother is dying. But she's still here. Sort of."

She places a hand on mine. "Ah. Yes, that transition is hard. More so for those left behind, I think."

"We were never close," I tell this stranger. "But the past few months..."

She waits patiently for me to continue, but I'm having a hard time organizing my thoughts. Mom may be the one transitioning to a different plane, or wherever it is you go, but this is more than that. The metamorphosis within me is also real, but it complicates the situation, because while I'm not ready to lose Mom, I also don't want to turn the clock back. My life as I knew it is gone, and that's a good thing. Patrick is in the past, I'm about to become a mother, I take on challenges, I voice my discontent, and I freaking fly. I've seen more of the world in the past few months than I did combined during my first thirty-five years on this earth, and I have no intention of stopping. I want to feel more. Do more. Before it's too late. My daughter will not be like me. The *old* me.

"We wasted so much time," I say, voicing my despair. "*I* wasted so much time."

The lady puts her papery hand on mine. "If there is love between you, it wasn't wasted. Love is forever and... *à trouver*, um, to be found in more than time spent."

Part of me wants to object, talk about minutes and hours, different choices, but I have no energy for it, so I only nod and smile.

It's only later, when Aimee and I are in the shuttle from the airport to the city of Paris, the rising sun illuminating the skyline, that the gray-haired lady's words sink in. I may not have had a close relationship with Mom most of my life, but in light of me shedding my old self, I have to admit she did figure out how to give me exactly what I needed at exactly the right time. And I now see the love in that.

To confirm I'm not making this up, I turn to Aimee on my left. "Do you think Mom made up the bucket list to teach me a life lesson?"

She squints at me and smirks. "Not all of it, but you are in Paris, aren't you? Old Kristin would rather have eaten hot coal. Jane's a smart woman."

The tension that's been lodged in my shoulders since I left Mom melts away, leaving a warm, prickling sensation along the back of my neck and arms in its wake. I pull out my phone and send Shannon another text to add to my more frantic ones from when we landed.

I know Mom is still in a coma and there's been no change, but now I need my sister to relay a different message, sprung both from my view out the shuttle window and these deeper realizations about our mother's love for me.

Give Mom a kiss from me, I type, fingers trembling. *Tell her I'm almost done and the Eiffel Tower looks spectacular at dawn. Tell her thank you.*

CHAPTER 35

Our hotel is a quaint row house on a cobblestoned street lined with small shops and eateries that sport red canopies, potted topiaries, wicker chairs, checkered tablecloths, and blackboards with menus in cursive, and thus could not look more French even if they tried. It's owned by an older couple, the Garniers, who clearly take pride in their establishment, for though everything is old, it's impeccably clean. Their English is not the best, but they're eager to listen as we ask about breakfast and to not be disturbed as we both need a few hours' rest before hitting the streets of Paris.

Aimee and I share a room with two twin beds not much longer than my five feet, six inches. Aimee's feet hang over the edge if she lies straight, but I don't think she notices. She's asleep as soon as her head hits the pillow.

I try to rest but find myself distracted by the clouds that rush past low beneath gray skies outside the window. The old house creaks, and there's an occasional thump of footsteps from other parts of the building, but other than these brief interruptions, I am alone with my thoughts. I pull out Mom's painting and unwrap it, rest it in the angle of my bent legs and belly. The glued wood frame is almost two inches deep, so it sits on its own without support, a fact I hope will make placing it at the museum an easier task. Since it doesn't need to hang, all I require is a ledge or a windowsill on which to place it. The paint is thick in spots, and carefully, I run a finger across it, follow-ing the brush strokes. If I could, I would ask her right now what she was thinking when she painted it, why she chose that scene. I can't believe I didn't ask when I had the chance. Now I may never know. I rub at my chest where tightness grows. This is a slippery slope I don't want to go down.

I turn on the small flat-screen TV, which sticks out like a sore thumb among the otherwise old-fashioned furnishings, mute it, and flip through the channels in search of anything of interest to distract me. My options are news or some children's show about a pineapple living in a junkyard, so I turn it off right away and head to the closet-sized bathroom. Minding my elbows, I brush my hair and apply makeup to make sure I'll look like a respectable art connoisseur as opposed to a scruffy tourist with questionable motives. Best be prepared if today is the day. I wake Aimee up shortly after noon.

"Feel better?"

"Why are you so awake?" She rolls over and curls up on her side. "A little bit longer."

"Nope." I pull the blanket off her and poke her side. "We're in Paris. You can sleep on the flight back. Come on."

To her credit, she doesn't put up a fight, and after an acrobatic shower in the two-foot stall, she's good as new.

"I need to eat," she says as we make our way down the carpeted stairs.

Lucky for her, this is France, and we both soon learn of the most miraculous of foods—the crepe.

I imagine Paris overcast is not nearly as nice as Paris sunny, but as we meander through the Tuileries Garden, I couldn't care less. Artists are scattered about on emerald lawns beneath the trees, tourists and locals intermingle at the small patisseries, enjoying a glass of wine midday, and even those not blessed with a Friday off who hurry down the sidewalks must surely feel lucky to do it against this backdrop.

The Louvre looms majestically at the eastern end of the gardens, dark and imposing against today's cloudy skies, but my steps don't falter. I march all the way up to the glass pyramid at center court, Aimee in tow, and not until then do I stop to catch my breath. The line for admissions is already long, so we take our place and wait our turn.

"Are these all tourists, you think?" Aimee asks, indicating the crowd. "Or do Parisians come here too?"

I scan the lines. There are a lot of cargo shorts, leggings, and T-shirts.

"Must be tourists. The French don't dress like this." While I've had only a brief time to form this impression, I'm already convinced loungewear is to the French what nudity is to Americans. You enjoy it only behind closed doors.

"Good. Tourists are stupid, so they won't notice what we're up to."

I raise an eyebrow at her. "We're tourists, aren't we?"

"Present company excluded." She grins.

A half hour later, we've cleared security through the main doors. I held my breath as our purses went through the scanner, but there was no need to worry. No one paid any attention to the square scarf-wrapped parcel in mine.

I know we're on a mission, but since we've paid to get in and I intend to make the most of it, I pull Aimee by her sleeve and get us swept up in the crowd moving from room to room. The place is huge, and several times we need to consult the room map in order to figure out where we are in relation to where we started. In addition to paintings—so many paintings—there are sculptures in every imaginable material, antiquities from cultures long lost, and indigenous art from all over the world. Even I, a nonartist, can appreciate the cultural treasure being preserved within these walls, and this only adds to the pressure of my task.

It takes us all afternoon to work our way from the lower ground level through the main floor and up to the first-floor Denon wing, where the *Mona Lisa* is kept. We follow our fellow museum dwellers and line up obediently to view the famed work, but I have to admit, I'm a little disappointed. She's as mysterious in real life as she is in pictures, of course, but she's also a painting among many other paintings.

"Are you nervous? 'Cause I am," Aimee says, glancing at the guards posted at every entrance of the room.

We scurry out of there posthaste.

As soon as we reach the second floor, I know this is where I'll find my spot. This level sports room after room of portraits and immortalized nature scapes, which means more privacy to set up Mom's painting and a better chance of it blending in. We come upon a guided tour in English as we enter the first room of French paintings and linger for a bit to hear what the guide has to say. We stay in the back of the group as we haven't paid, and when they disperse to view the paintings, we leave them behind and move on.

Deep in the Richelieu wing, there is a small room with Dutch, or maybe German, paintings, all smaller with dark frames. In a corner between a romantic meadow and a portrait of a boy and his dog, there is a build-out in the wall to accommodate plumbing, and this is the first promising spot I've seen. I snap a picture for consideration then move between the other spectators to the next room, where all the paintings are portraits. In here, we're alone, and I indicate to Aimee I need a break to rest on the bench centered in the space. Walking on stone floors for hours takes its toll, and I rub my back gingerly.

"You're not wearing yourself out, right?" Aimee sits down next to me. "We can always come back tomorrow."

I ignore her concern. The painting bides its time inside my purse, its presence spurring me on. "You might have to be my lookout later," I tell her, showing her the picture I took. "There were two entry points to the room, and I only need a few seconds, but it would be bad if I'm caught."

"*We're* caught," Aimee corrects. "Whatever you need."

I stretch and put my phone away, expecting the museum patrons from the other room to follow our path in here, but instead their muffled voices traipse off in the other direction, leaving us in complete silence. For one blissful moment, I simply sit there enjoying it. Then I bolt upright. We're alone. I could place my painting on the ledge right now.

My heart picks up speed as I feel the outline of the painting in my purse. I look to Aimee, and I can tell she's had the same thought.

"Should I? Now?"

She gets up, giggles. "Why not? Who knows if we'll get another chance today."

My pulse pounds at the bottom of my throat as we make our way back to the room we came from. We slow down in the doorway in case someone from the other party has lingered behind, but the room is empty.

"You take that door." I nod toward the opposite corner from where we're standing.

My mouth goes dry as I stick my hand into my purse and pull out the wrapped frame. With shaking fingers, I dispose of the scarf and carry Mom's painting to the ledge in the corner, glancing behind me every few steps. My ears tickle from the strain of trying to hear what's going on in adjacent rooms. Is someone coming?

I set the painting down as quickly as I can, back away from the corner, and wave Aimee along as we return to the bench in the portrait room. I'm sweaty and flustered, my blood roaring in my ears, but I also have an overwhelming urge to do cartwheels. *We did it.* The first part of the mission is accomplished.

"Now what?" Aimee asks. Her face looks as flushed as mine feels.

"Picture proof." I hold up my phone. "As soon as I catch my breath."

Aimee returns to the doorway and pretends to study the paintings there that put her in a direct line of view of Mom's. With her as my guard dog, I inhale slowly, exhale. On the third breath, I feel a kick similar to the pop of a giant air bubble in my belly, and it's so startling I give a small cough. My hands go instinctively to the rounded mound of my abdomen and linger there.

"Do you approve?" I whisper. "Momma is committing crimes for Grandma. How about that?"

The baby kicks again, and a raw burst of elation runs through me. These are the strongest movements I've felt so far. It's very odd. And wonderful.

I'm jolted from my literal navel gazing by Aimee hissing, "Psst," and jerking her head toward the scene of my crime. It seems the guided tour has finally caught up.

"Can anyone tell me the name of Vermeer's most famous painting?" the tour guide asks, scanning the eager faces of the group in front of him.

Aimee and I are positioned in front of a quartet of portraits hung in the middle of the wall to the left of Mom's painting. It's still sitting there in my peripheral, waiting, its colors too vivid for its surroundings.

"It's that book cover," one of the ladies in the group guesses. "The girl with the turban."

"And what's its name?" asks the guide jovially. "Girl with..."

"A pearl earring," I whisper to Aimee. Someone in the group must know their art, for a second later, the tour guide exclaims, "That's right!" He then goes on to explain that while that painting is not to be found at the Louvre, Vermeer painted many other masterpieces displayed here for the group's perusal.

I tune him out as he launches into a lecture on the life and work of the Dutch artist, not because I don't find it interesting but because my nerves are frayed with the tension of being at the ready. I have my phone in a firm grasp, occasionally snapping a photo of a painting as we move about the room.

It's taking a while for the group to get to the far corner where I want them. I really have to pee and am cursing the fact I didn't go after lunch, but just then, when I think I can't take it any longer, the guide turns and... walks right past Mom's painting.

What the what? Aimee and I share a jittery glance.

The guide strolls past the corner, no doubt moving along in his rehearsed program without much thought given to his actual surroundings. That's not what was supposed to happen. They were supposed to stop and look at my mother's masterpiece—well, *piece*. I was supposed to capture the moment, and then...

Then what?

Mom never specified whether or not she wanted the painting back. Placing it for viewing and then taking off is a vastly different mission than also taking back the picture and getting it out of the museum.

Knowing Mom, though, I'm sure that's what she would want me to do. She holds on to all her works of art. If I leave it here, someone is bound to at some point recognize it doesn't belong and dispose of it, and the thought of that makes me nauseous. This painting is important enough to Mom that she chose it for her Louvre exhibition. No, it needs to come back home with me.

"Excuse me," one of the straggling tour ladies calls to the guide. "This one is different. What can you tell us about it?"

I freeze. As if in slow motion, every head in the group turns toward the ledge in the corner, the group fanning out to let the guide pass.

"That's odd," he says.

I have the phone up and am snapping a picture before I'm even aware what I'm doing. Then I sidestep closer to the group, pretending to admire an interior scene from a busy baroque kitchen, and take another couple of photos. These will look great. The whole group stands in rapt attention in front of the colorful fall scene on the ledge while the tour guide leans closer as if to examine the signature.

I step back toward the far doorway and capture the whole scene, making sure the other paintings are visible, too, as proof of where I am.

"Excuse me," the tour guide calls. "There is no flash photography in here."

Oh crud. In my hurry to capture the scene, I've completely forgotten to turn it off.

"Sorry," I say with a squeak, backing away farther. "I forgot."

"Turn it off, please." He sounds as if he wants to roll his eyes at me, and I'm not sure if it's because of his French accent or because it's the millionth time today he's had to remind people of the same thing, but I'm not about to pick a fight. I've got what I came for, and so I tuck the phone back into my purse and clasp it to my hip.

"Close call," Aimee whispers under her breath when our circling puts us back next to each other again. "Did you get a good picture?"

"Yeah. Now we have to get it back. Then we can go."

"I'll keep watch as soon as they leave."

I smile at the back of Aimee's head. If I'm not mistaken, she's enjoying this.

Perhaps distracted by my flash, the tour guide moves on, Mom's painting at least temporarily forgotten. I wait until the group moves into the portrait room with the bench, then emboldened by my recent success at being stealthy, resolutely step up to the ledge and grab the picture. In that moment, a couple from the tour group returns, arguing in the primmest British English the merits of seventeenth-century versus eighteenth-century artistry. I stiffen, my back toward them and the painting pressed tightly against my torso. As long as they don't come closer, they won't see what I'm doing.

With slow, deliberate movements, I pull the strap until my purse hangs front and center. The couple is still conversing somewhere behind me as I unzip the main compartment tooth by tooth. To my high-strung ear, each snap echoes against the tall ceilings, but I keep going until the opening is wide enough to accept my loot.

There. Done.

I let out a lungful of air. I did it. *I am Catwoman.* Though, come to think of it, that doesn't quite have the same ring to it when you're in fact a middle-aged woman with a cat, does it?

"How strange," the man says behind my right shoulder. "Where did the little one go?"

I retreat two steps as his wife joins him, and they examine the now-empty ledge.

"Isn't this where it was?" he asks.

The woman turns and looks at me, eyes round and sharp like an owl's.

"Good afternoon," I say, attempting casual politeness. *Act normal, Kristin.*

"Did you see the pretty little one with the bridge, miss?" the man asks me.

I frown as if I'm thinking hard. "No. Can't say I did. Sorry." I spin around, my only thought now to get the heck out as fast as I can. I'm about to clear the doorway when the woman says, "I think she took it, Merl."

Wide-eyed, Aimee hisses, "I'll distract them. Meet you outside," and then I'm running down the stairs.

The funny thing about being pregnant and needing to pee badly is that running does nothing to alleviate the feeling. After only one flight of stairs, I have to slow down lest I want to create a wet avant-garde installation on the floor. Should someone be following me, I can only hope they are equally pregnant and in need of a bathroom.

Slowly but surely, I make my way through the thick crowds to the nearest exit. The hallway is packed, but I'm too busy glancing behind me to notice the bottleneck until I'm upon it. I come to a full stop against the shorts-clad behind of a squat man about my age.

"Sorry, so sorry." I try to squeeze past him at the same time I spot a guard approaching, walkie-talkie pressed to his ear.

"Do you mind?" the man says in an unusually high-pitched voice.

Several other tourists turn at the squeak to stare at me. So, too, does the guard. I face forward and squeeze my eyes closed. Nothing to see here.

Not a moment later, a heavy hand lands on my shoulder. "*Pardon, Mademoiselle.*"

No, no, no. I plaster on a smile and turn. "*Oui?*"

The guard glances pointedly at the purse I'm clutching to my belly then looks straight into my eyes.

"A moment of your time, please?" He says something else in French into the walkie that I can't make out.

Gone is confident, rational Kristin. My legs don't work. I know what's about to happen, but I can't move. I'm going to jail. French jail. I'll disappear into the justice system, one of those sad tales covering the tabloid front pages back home. The American embassy will get involved, maybe the Chicago mayor if my friends make enough ruckus back home.

He takes my arm.

Oh God, I should have stayed home.

CHAPTER 36

I dream of a labyrinth chase through Daliesque landscapes and Rapunzel locked in a tower but wake with a start when someone shakes my shoulder and says, "Your ride is here, Mademoiselle."

The female officer who's been checking on me ever since I was finally deemed harmless an hour ago is crouched in front of my chair in the holding room where I've spent the evening. The combo of stress and jet lag has me delirious with exhaustion. No wonder I nodded off.

I run the back of my hand across my mouth. "Who?"

"I don't know. Whoever you called."

I rouse myself enough to have a sip of the tepid water on the table in front of me. The liquid brings back the memory. *Aimee*. Aimee has come for me.

I follow the officer through yellowed linoleum hallways to the reception area of the understaffed police station they brought me to. The space is quiet and the light muted, but a few people are still at their desks in the room beyond.

The indignant voice of an angry, sleep-deprived American demanding to know where I am reaches me before I see her.

Aimee rushes me and pulls me into a tight hug as soon as I'm within sight. "Oh my God, are you all right? I've been so worried. These *idiots* wouldn't tell me anything."

"We speak English," the officer next to me drones, but she doesn't seem too offended.

"I'm so sorry about this," I say to Aimee. "I should never have put you in that position."

"You're sorry?" Aimee balks. "*I'm* sorry. It took me forever to find out where you were. I would have had you out sooner if I'd known."

"It's fine. I'm fine. It's been a long day."

"Can I go?" I ask the female officer.

"Oui, Mademoiselle. Good night." She turns away but then stops and calls for my attention again. "I almost forgot," she says in accented English. "You may have this back." She picks up a parcel from the reception desk and hands it to me. The painting.

"I can keep it?"

"There was no crime, and we have no use for it, but I strongly recommend you keep it at home from now on."

I thank her and comply with Aimee as she steers me out of the police station. A slap on the hand, that's all. I would laugh from relief if I wasn't so tired.

"Are you sure they treated you okay?" Aimee asks after we get into the cab she has waiting.

"I'm sure." They did. Mostly. There was one officer who seemed determined to uncover my secret terrorist motives early on— *"There could be a bomb in the frame. How do we know this was not a test run? We've requested an Interpol data search."* Fortunately, the other interrogators were better judges of character and assured me they were doing whatever they could to verify my story. The security footage from the museum made all the difference. The fact that I hadn't thought of the cameras actually seemed to help convince them I wasn't a criminal mastermind, after all. I would have been out of there faster had I had my passport on me, but as it was, I didn't, and so it took them a while to reach Aimee at the hotel and confirm my identity. In the end I wasn't charged with anything, only banned from entering the Louvre for the foreseeable future. It's okay. Been there, done that.

"Do you want something to eat?" Aimee asks.

My stomach rumbles, but I decline. *Sleep*, is all I can think. Glorious sleep. My feet are leaden from the stress and anxiety of the day, but with the last bit of effort I can muster, plus Aimee's guiding hands, I make it up the stairs to our room.

Still fully clothed, I collapse onto the white coverlet, nose buried deep into the soft pillows. My whole body tingles as if my limbs are already asleep, my brain the only organ yet to catch up. It doesn't take long. Before I can turn off the light, wave after wave of dreamlike images pass before my eyes. And that's the last thing I remember before the shrill ringing of my phone startles me awake.

Confused, I peel my cheek off the pillow. At first, I'm not sure where I am, but as the features of the room come into focus, I remember. Bright sunlight shines through the window, the sun already high in the sky, and a peek at the alarm clock on the nightstand shows the inexplicable numbers 11:08.

The phone stops for a minute but soon starts up again.

Aimee emerges from the bathroom, a towel wrapped around her head. "Are you going to get that?"

I push my hair out of my face and clear my throat then reach for the merciless device. "Hello?" It comes out a croak.

"Kristin?"

It's a male voice, and in my groggy state I can't quite place it. "Who's this?"

Aimee mouths the same question from across the room, but I ignore her.

There's a pause on the line then, "It's me, Thomas."

The first chilly trickle of foreboding starts somewhere between my shoulder blades and makes its way up toward my neck. "Thomas? What's going on? Is everything okay?"

Aimee takes a step closer to me, the strangest combination of emotions flickering across her face.

Thomas seems to hesitate, and that brief silence knocks the air out of me. I know what's coming. I know, but I wish I didn't.

"I'm so sorry, Kris, but your mom is gone."

I hear Thomas say the words, but they don't compute. The language center in my brain has stopped working. I know he said *sorry*, and *Mom*, and *gone*, but put together that makes no sense. Mom can't be dead. I'm not done yet. We still have to climb the Eiffel Tower. Everyone said there would be time.

"Kris?"

"Mm-hmm."

"Did you hear me?"

"Mm-hmm." Details previously obscured by the normalcy of life come into sharp focus, like how thin the carpet has worn underneath the legs of the beds and the dance of the dusty speckles in the ray of sun shining through the window. Somewhere in the background, muted voices rise and fall.

Aimee sits down next to me on the bed and takes my free hand in hers, and that's when I know I was wrong. My mother *is* dead.

The phone slips out of my hand and somersaults against my lap, the bed, the floor. A muted "Hello?" reaches me from far away then Aimee picks up the phone, exchanges a few words, and ends the call.

My pulse bangs at the base of my skull. "Mom's dead," I say, my voice barely a whisper.

Aimee's eyes fill with tears. "I know." She reclaims my fingers. "Thomas said she wasn't in pain. There was nothing more to be done."

I stare at her blankly.

She leans forward, seeking my gaze. "Do you understand, Kris? She went peacefully."

I nod as carefully as I can because something terrible is coming. Something hatching deep within me. It's writhing, moving, swelling in my chest, its black tentacles reaching up my throat, choking me. I swallow, but the movement doesn't make it past the knot restricting my airways. I gasp, panicking. There's no air, and I'm deflated. My mouth is open, my eyes burning, and I try again and again to breathe with little success.

I'm vaguely aware of Aimee pushing off the bed, of her rummaging through her suitcase. Then she's at my side with a paper bag that she holds in front of my mouth. It smells of old books.

"You're having a panic attack," she says as I clasp her arm. "Breathe in and out. In and out."

I follow the cadence of her voice, and after what seems like an eternity, the fist squeezing my lungs relaxes its grip.

She removes the bag, eyeing me with a worried brow. "You okay? You're not going to faint on me, are you?"

I shake my head, calmed for the moment by the feel of my lungs working again. When the yellow spots on the inside of my eyelids go away completely, I want to open my eyes but find I can't. A jumble of disjointed thoughts acts as glue, keeping the world shut out. A handstand on a grassy lawn. Mom's painting next to the *Mona Lisa*. Claudine purring in my lap. Arguing with Lily. Being pushed into a swimming pool. Riding on a dolphin into the sunset. Mom knitting with giant needles. Nothing makes sense, and I grab onto the edge of the bed to steady myself.

Mom's gone.

I press the heels of my hands into my eye sockets, and a strange keening rises around me, muted somewhat by the sheets and the carpet to resemble hollow echoes from deep within a cave. It's the oddest sound, at the same time human and not of this world. Not until Aimee places an arm around my shoulders do I recognize it as me. The noise is coming from me.

"Shh, it's okay," Aimee says, stroking my arm. "It'll be okay." She pulls me toward her, and when she wraps me in her arms, the creature within breaks free, and I lose it completely.

Sometime later I lie tucked into bed in a room made blue by a towel covering the window above me. I'm on my side, staring at the swirls and curlicues of the wallpaper, counting them, comparing them, and trying hard not to allow any other thoughts into my mind. I'm not sure if I've slept. My body is heavy as it might feel from rising early, but that could be the aftermath of all the crying.

So much crying.

Turning my head into the pillow, I find it damp and cool. A shaky breath escapes me. "I want to go home," I say, trying my voice. It carries better than I thought it would.

The bed dips as Aimee sits down next to me.

I roll over on my back and look up into her face.

She sucks in her lips. "Are you sure? We could still finish it."

The list. The final task. *Climb the stairs of the Eiffel Tower.*

Something akin to rage explodes within me at the thought, a pleasant contrast to my sorrow. How could Mom do this? If the list was so important to her, why not wait until I was done? Why make me go through all this trouble? I shove myself into a sitting position and hiss, "What's the point? It's not like she'll ever know."

There are so many things she'll never know.

I clamber off the bed and start throwing clothes and toiletries haphazardly into my suitcase. "Did Thomas say how Shannon is doing?"

Aimee eyes me warily. "We didn't talk about that. She's a nurse, though. It's possible she saw it coming. Um... what are you doing?"

"Packing. I'm going to the airport."

"Our flight isn't until tomorrow morning."

"So I'll sleep there. Or take an earlier flight if there's room. Whatever. I'm not staying here. I'm done doing things for other people. I'm going to do me now."

"But, Kris—"

"No. Do what you want, but I'm leaving." At her expression, my anger falters. "I'm not mad at you," I clarify. "I'm sorry. I can't stay here."

Without a word, Aimee gets off the bed and goes into the bathroom. She returns with my toothbrush and toothpaste, which she hands me, and then she pulls out her own suitcase too.

"I understand," she says. "Let's go home."

CHAPTER 37

We land in Chicago on the last day of July, when the air above the concrete vibrates with heat. I'm mushy-headed and wary of what's ahead but also at some stage of acceptance after eight uninterrupted hours in the air contemplating Mom's at least partially self-imposed demise. As heavy as it weighs on my shoulders, and no matter how many times in my life I've disagreed with her, I know she typically had good reasons for her actions. She wouldn't have chosen to end her life unless she felt that was her only option. It's a small comfort but a comfort nonetheless.

Passport control, baggage retrieval, customs, and then we push through the swinging doors to the bland atrium where Aimee's husband, Colin, waits. It's a subdued welcome committee, but I don't mind. I stand off to the side while he kisses Aimee hello, and I trail behind them to the car. They hold hands, which makes me pat my pockets to ensure my phone is there. I texted Lily before we boarded the plane, letting her know what's happened, but there has been no response.

When we get to my house, Colin helps me with the suitcase, and Aimee walks me inside. "Do you want me to stay? Colin won't mind."

"No, I'm okay. I'll stop by tomorrow for Morrison." I brush a strand of hair out of my face. I want nothing but a shower and a nap right now. Also, Shannon is expecting my call.

"The funeral is Thursday?" Aimee asks.

I nod.

"We'll drive you."

I nod again. "Thanks. For everything."

Aimee looks as if she wants to say more, but I turn away, eager for solitude. Their car pulls away at the same time I close the front door behind me and sink onto the stool by the entry. I stretch my legs out before me, roll my neck, and inhale the silence, and in doing so am granted one precious moment of tranquility before my gaze falls upon my unfinished painting from Butterfly Beach, and the cycle of despair starts from scratch.

My distress ebbs and flows as I go about my homecoming chores. Every time I think composure is within reach, I'm overcome by something—a scent, a color, an innocuous item in my path—that reminds me of my mother, and eventually I can't take it anymore. I've dreaded calling Shannon, not knowing what state I'll find her in, but now I dial, hopeful to hear her voice.

It's Zach who answers with a timid "Hello."

For the first time in I don't know how long, I smile. "Hi, bud. It's Aunt Kristin."

"Hi, Auntie. Guess what? I have two whole dollars."

I roll with it. "Wow, you're rich. Did you win the lottery?"

"What's that?"

"Oh, never mind. Are you having a good summer?"

"I had ice cream for breakfast today."

"I'll take that as a yes."

Keep it going, I think. The longer this conversation lasts, the lighter my heart. Every word out of my nephew's mouth is like balm to my soul.

"Are you playing nice with your sister?"

"Mm-hmm, I am. *She* told me I was a dummy when I didn't want to play tag."

"I don't like tag either. Does that make me a dummy?"

Zach's laugh trills into my ear. "No," he says as if that's the silliest thing he's ever heard.

"So what are you doing instead?"

"Legos. Mommy was going to build me a car, but she's resting because Nana is gone to heaven, and Daddy is cutting the grass. Again."

My response sticks to my tongue. "Hmm," I say, reaching for a glass of water. "And," I croak, "could I maybe talk to your mom, please? She won't be mad at you for waking her up, I promise."

"Okay," Zach hollers. "Later, gator." From the sound of it, he runs up the stairs, banging the phone into the handrail every few steps. A door opens, and I hear Shannon's voice in the background then a crackle before she comes on the line with a crisp "Hello."

"It's me," I say.

"I was wondering when I'd hear from you."

"Zach said you're resting."

"Yeah, well, head's killing me. Too much crying."

"I know what you mean."

We're quiet for a long while during which I scrub at a stain in the kitchen sink.

"Was it hard? To be there?" I ask eventually.

Shannon sighs. "Yes. And at the same time, it might have been harder for you being far away. She wasn't there anymore. I could tell. Not sure how to explain it."

I don't respond right away, but when I do, what comes out is not what I expect but something that must have been lurking deep beneath the surface ever since we left Paris.

"I didn't finish it," I say.

"It?"

"The list."

"Oh."

With the first words out, the rest follows unbidden. "I can't get it out of my mind. I was so close, and I promised her—promised I'd finish *no matter what*. I think she knew she wouldn't be here. I think she had planned it. Why didn't she tell us? And why couldn't I suck it up enough to climb that damned tower? Now I picture her looking down on me with that expression she always used to have when we'd done something she didn't approve of."

"Yeah, that was the worst."

"I feel like I failed her. It was her final wish, and no matter the differences we had in the past, in the end we..." I shake my head in frustration and sit down in one of the chairs. "We were just beginning to..." I rub my brow with some force, not sure how to end the sentence.

"For what it's worth, I think she felt the same," Shannon says. "She was really proud of you."

"Pfft."

"*I'm* proud of you. I didn't think you'd go through with any of it."

"Well, I didn't finish, so..."

"Maybe one day you will."

I glance out the window at the receding light. The sun is far enough set that it's hard to tell the color of the trees. "Who knows? At least I know I can now. That's something. But work starts in a couple of weeks, and then the baby..." I caress my silent companion, who's growing by leaps and bounds every day, it seems. I'm halfway there, halfway to meeting my little girl. Maybe Shannon is right, and one day I will take her to Paris. "Thanks for making the arrangements for the funeral, by the way."

"It's all Thomas. He's been great."

For the first time, my immediate reaction is not a snarky "Of course he has" or an eye roll. Instead I think, *Good for her*. She's got what she needs. It's not what I need, but I'm happy she's content.

We chat a few more minutes until the conversation fizzles out. I make myself some chamomile tea that I bring to the couch and turn on the TV. I want to not feel anything for a little bit; I need a break. It works for a half hour until my phone chimes with the text I've been waiting for, and it's even better than I hoped.

I'm so sorry, Kris. I have a few things to wrap up here but will be there Wednesday unless you tell me not to.

Lily is coming.

CHAPTER 38

Lily shows up at my doorstep the day before Mom's funeral, bright-eyed and with a large bag of duty-free chocolates. After the obligatory condolences, she looks me over and smiles.

"Pregnancy suits you."

I glance down at my growing belly, so different now from when last I saw her almost a month ago. "There's no hiding it now, is there?"

"Nope."

And with that she's somehow managed to set the tone for the evening as one of life and future instead of death and past.

She orders takeout while I lay out clothes for the service, and we eat side by side at the low coffee table.

"Tell me everything." Lily hooks me with her gaze over a plate of pad Thai. "What have I missed? How was the opera? Do you have pictures? Did you end up going to Gantry Plaza? What did you think of Paris?"

I put my fork down and hold up a hand to make her pause while I swallow the first mouthful of noodles. "One at a time. Here." I pull out my phone and flip to the picture of me at the Met.

Lily grabs it from my hand, eyes widening. "Holy sh— Kris, that's some serious garb!"

Her unabashed admiration of the photo makes my face flare. "Well, I... Mom had good taste, what can I say?"

Lily looks up from the picture. "Good taste? You're gorgeous."

I blush even harder. "Thanks." I snatch the phone back and tuck it next to me on the rug, far from her reach. "So... um... Did I tell you I was arrested in Paris? It was nuts. Aimee was about to lose it. Pretty sure she wished she'd never volunteered to come with."

Lily looks at me, a quizzical expression playing across her features. "You didn't have any more pictures from New York?"

As if I'm going to show her the one of Aaron and me together. I don't know that this is the time to reopen that can of worms. "Nothing interesting. Want some more food?"

"I'm good." She frowns. "Wait, did you say you were arrested?"

"Yep." I smile, tension releasing its hold on me. I talk until I'm hoarse, and soon she's laughing hysterically at the story of my faux heist.

"Sorry you didn't make it to the Eiffel Tower," she says when I finish my tale.

I shake my head and push my plate away. "I couldn't. I should have. Maybe. But I had to get home."

"Makes sense. I'm so sorry this happened. And Mom sends her love, by the way. She really feels for you. She... um... her brother, my uncle, killed himself when I was little." She watches me, perhaps gauging whether or not to go on.

"What happened?"

"He was an alcoholic. His liver gave out, and he needed a transplant to survive, but of course he wasn't high on the priority list."

An involuntary shiver runs down the back of my legs as I recall Dr. Standish saying something similar.

"The Christmas when I was eight, he announced to everyone it was the last holiday he'd ever celebrate. It didn't go over well with the adults, as you can imagine, especially since I was present. I remember being ushered out of the room by my grandmother, but before I got away, I heard him yell, 'The kid should know there are things worse than death.'"

Her last word hangs suspended between us before dissolving into nothingness.

"It stuck with me. He was still young, and he hurt a lot of people, but he *was* already dying. At times I think that was a comfort to my mom."

I make a low sound of acknowledgment at her words but take my time before responding. "I've thought the same thing. I miss her—" My voice falters, so I pause, conjuring the strength from my core I now know is there. "She did everything else in life on her own terms. Why not this too? Selfishly, I wish she hadn't taken away what little time we had left together, but at the same time I'm thankful she didn't have to suffer more than she already did. Does that make sense?"

Lily reaches out and takes my hand, the warmth from her palm a reassuring caress in itself. "Perfect sense," she says, accompanied by a quick tightening of her fingers that leaves a ghosting trail of tingles on my skin when she retreats.

I rub it with my other hand then let it fall to the right side of my belly, where there's intermittent resistance from within. "I'm going to do everything in my power to make sure my daughter knows from the start she's loved. I'm going to listen to her, and share myself with her, and not waste any time. That's the hardest thing." I look up at Lily. "Thirty-five years, and we spent all but three months as virtual strangers. I don't know if I'll ever forgive myself."

"Do you forgive her?"

I answer without a thought. "Of course."

Lily shrugs. "Then that's your answer."

Simple, effortless, unquestionable—that's how the truths of the world appear when I'm with this woman. And she's here. She flew all this way just for me.

"What? Why are you looking at me like that?" She runs a hand over her hair as if to smooth it down.

Mom would want me to be brave. "I shouldn't have kissed Aaron," I blurt. "I wasn't into him like that."

She stills, and for a moment I think she's going to deflect, but then she asks, "Then why did you?"

I shift in my seat, lift one shoulder up and release it. "Because I was mad at you for wanting him and me to 'hit it off.'" I make bunny ears around the expression she used. "And to prove to myself that I was right, and you were wrong. Which I did, by the way. He was perfectly nice, and yes, handsome, and charming, too, and it didn't change anything. I still felt what I felt. Feel what I feel. For you."

"Kristin..." She looks down.

"No, I want it in the open. I don't expect it to change anything, and I don't really have the emotional bandwidth to care what it means for tomorrow or next week, but I want to at least be honest. With myself and with you."

She's quiet for a beat as if checking that I'm done. "Can I speak?"

"Yes." I exhale then put a finger up. "But if you tell me I'm straight again, I'll scream."

She smiles. "Noted." Her fingers worry the edge of one of the takeout napkins while she seems to contemplate where to start.

"I have been someone's first before, and I've been burned. I just don't know..." The napkin rips, and she balls it up. "The timing is all wrong. My assignment in London is being extended into next year."

"And I'm having a baby."

"Right." A small laugh ripples past her lips. "I'm sorry." She meets my gaze directly and extends her hand across the corner of the table.

I take it. The caress of her thumb against my skin makes my throat knot, but I blink against the stinging in my eyes.

"You mean so much to me, Kris," she says, emphasizing the words with little squeezes against my palm. "And I desperately hope you'll still want to stay in touch. It would break my heart if we didn't."

"Of course," I manage to choke out. "I'll always want to be your friend."

She entwines her fingers with mine and tugs gently. "Hey, don't cry. Not over this."

I force a smile as she wipes a stray tear off my cheek. Pure instinct makes me lean into her touch, and when I do, she lets me. Ten seconds pass. Twenty. Neither one of us looks away. I know I'm not imagining it. She feels exactly what I'm feeling.

But I also know she's right—the timing couldn't be worse—and that's what finally allows me to release her.

She'll be gone tomorrow. We'll stay just friends.

At least for now.

The day after the funeral, Shannon and I meet at Mom's house for our private goodbyes. The service was not as bad as I expected, held at a nondenominational church even though my mother, to my knowledge, hadn't set foot in a church since we were born. Like so many other things about her life, this, too, will forever remain cloaked in mystery. The pews were packed with mourners in colorful summery outfits per her request, and though there were no fireworks, there was a very nice-looking bagpiper in a kilt, saluting us with "Amazing Grace" as we exited. Also per her instructions.

I didn't cry then, in front of so many unfamiliar faces, but as soon as I see Shannon in the midst of garden ornaments and sunflowers, we fall into each other's arms, and no one could say where her tears end and mine begin.

I haven't been back since that awful day when I found her, but Shannon leads me inside without hesitation and sits me down in the sunniest spot in the living room. It helps scare the monsters away.

"I can't believe she's gone," she says, pulling her knees up next to me. She hands me a can of sparkling water, which I open with a *fizz* and a *pop*.

As I sip slowly, my eyes trace the rugs, the canvas-adorned walls, the outlines of furniture I've never not known, the cats' climbing tree, the plant collection. They speak of her, a comforting eulogy of a life well lived.

"Do you remember that time you got stuck in the grandfather clock, playing hide-and-seek?" I ask, admiring the imposing floor-to-ceiling mahogany giant.

Shannon's eyes widen. "That wasn't me. That was you."

"Was not."

"Was too. I would have never fit in there."

"Hence *getting stuck.*"

Her brow wrinkles as she considers this. "Maybe you're right. She was not happy, though, that's for sure."

"No, she wasn't."

"What about when we tried making her breakfast and nearly set the kitchen on fire?"

"*That* was me," I concede. "You took the blame with me, though."

"I cracked the eggs. It was the least I could do." Shannon smirks.

Our conversation lapses into silence for a while until Shannon says, "The church was pretty crowded yesterday. I didn't know half of them."

When I don't respond, she goes on, "It was nice to meet Lily finally. Mom talked about her a lot." She fluffs the pillow next to her, averting her eyes for a moment. "I was surprised to hear she came all the way from London."

The corner of my mouth quirks up. "That's Lily, I guess." I have another sip of water to cover my expression. I have no reason for it other than the fact that Lily and I have made up and now she knows the truth. Deep down, I still wish for more between us, but at least I didn't mess things up this time. She's on a plane back to England as we speak. She's promised to text as soon as she lands.

Shannon is quiet for so long, eventually I have no choice but to look up. She's eyeing me, her expression inscrutable.

"Why are you looking at me like that?"

She cocks an eyebrow.

"What?" I put my water down.

"Nothing. It's cute how you think you can keep secrets from me."

"What secrets?" I ask, my voice higher in pitch than I intend.

"You tell me." Shannon swirls what's left in the can before setting it down.

I press my lips together, willing my face to return to its normal color. There's no way she knows, so whatever she thinks I'm hiding, it must be something completely made up. "I don't know what you're talking about."

She lets out a dry chuckle. "Fine. Be like that." She leans back then reaches out to let her fingertips brush one of the buds on the big hibiscus—my favorite of all the plants. "I saw Patrick last week," she says after a while.

I'm only partly listening, my thoughts still lingering with Lily. "Okay."

"He said he's dating someone."

"Mm. Good for him."

Out of nowhere, Shannon shoves me hard in the shoulder like she used to when we were little.

"Ow, what did you do that for?"

"I just told you the father of your unborn child has moved on and is dating again, and you have no reaction?"

"I said good for him. What more do you need? I ended it, re-member? And since I've moved on, why shouldn't he?" *Uh-oh.*

"Aha!" A triumphant grin illuminates Shannon's face. "I knew it! You have feelings for Lily. No, don't you dare deny it. I have eyes to see with."

I open my mouth, but nothing comes out.

"You know she does, too, right? For you, I mean."

Shannon is practically jumping up and down in her seat with glee, so I hold up a hand to settle her. "It's complicated."

"Only if you make it so."

Escape is my only option. I get up from the couch and stalk down the hallway to Mom's room. Too late I remember this is the bad place and find myself face-to-face with her bed, her nightstand, her closet, her jewelry box. Unprepared. The bedding has been stripped off, and there are no traces of that day to be seen, but underneath the barren surface is a note of her perfume that hits me square in solar plexus. I sink to the floor in almost the same spot where the paramedics must have found me, only this time Shannon is the one who comes for me.

"Hey," she says, sitting down next to me. "I'm sorry. I know it's none of my business."

"It's not that," I sob. "It's the stupid room and her stupid perfume and everything else stupid about this stupid situation."

"Oh." She pulls my head to her shoulder and holds me until I'm spent. "Here, she always kept tissues underneath—" She reaches under the bed and pulls out a half-full box. She hands it to me but immediately tilts her head forward to peer deeper into the darkness. "There's something—scooch." She shoves at my leg so she can lie down and get her whole arm under the frame.

When she emerges with dust bunnies stuck to her skin, she has two envelopes in her hand. Two letters, one for each of us, addressed in Mom's neat cursive.

CHAPTER 39

Saturday, July 23, 2016, Rockford

Dear Kris,

If you're reading this, I'm dead. Hopefully the service wasn't too drab and dreadful, and Patti got me the right color flowers. I swear that woman is surprisingly bad at color coordination for someone who calls herself an artist.

I'm sitting here at my desk, looking at the photo you sent from the opera. I'm not much of a crier, but I admit my eyes turned damp at seeing you in my old gown. Like I said, it has now fulfilled its purpose, and in a way, so have I.

I've always seen so much of myself in you. Don't laugh. If you had known me before you kids came along, you'd understand. I, too, grew up fearful of the world, not knowing how to listen to my inner voice, always expecting the worst. Shannon is a different beast but a beast all the same. Yes, like I said, she was easier for me at the time, and yes, I know you think she's my favorite, but that's like comparing a resilient snake plant to a finicky moth orchid. Anyone—even a beginner—can handle the former because it's okay if you wing it, but the latter needs time, patience, and care to get right. I'm sorry I didn't always spend the time. I'm sorry what I had to offer was better suited for a snake plant when you so clear-

ly needed someone who knew orchids. I guess I saw Shannon being happy in that way I never was, and I wanted it for you too. I didn't want you to mess up like I did, falling in love once, then twice, and then getting them muddled together so they both disappeared because I knew nothing of life. If there's one thing I regret, it's that I didn't find myself before finding love. I would have handled myself differently then, or so I'd like to think.

So good riddance to Patrick (unless you're taking him back, in which case I give you my blessing IF and only if you really love him) and may this last of my meddlesome ways have sent you on a journey not only of the world but of yourself so you can welcome life for yourself, your daughter, and whoever else comes into your life. Aaron would not be a bad choice. Imagine what that would do to our gene pool! Or Lily. (I have eyes to see with.) Or someone else. But don't mess it up, Kris. Don't settle.

I'm so proud of you. I did worry at first I was pushing you too far, but I hope you see I had no choice. Failing you is my only real regret, and I'm out of time. This plague is getting harder to bear each day, and I have no intention of letting it consume me. Death is but another journey.

I'm tired now and need a rest. Please finish the list.

See you on the other side.

I love you,

Mom

P.S. There's a present for my new granddaughter in my nightstand. I finished knitting the blanket yesterday.

EPILOGUE

"Ow! Fuck, that hurts!" I squirm on the bed where I'm lying prone on my side, clasping Lily's hand in a vise.

"Language, please." Lily's stern voice quivers with suppressed laughter, and it takes everything I have not to call her out on it. She *did* make the trip here from England to come see me. We've been planning it for months.

"Make it stop. Please."

She laughs. "No can do. You knew what you were getting yourself into. You've had enough time to prepare."

"This is cruel and unusual punishment."

"For a worthy cause."

"Whatever." I give her an angry glare, which she doesn't see. She's busy exchanging an isn't-she-ridiculous glance with the needle-wielding man behind me.

"Oh, come on. You've given birth, but you can't take getting a small tattoo without screaming like a baby?"

As if to mark her words, my four-month-old daughter, Maya, gurgles from her perch in the harness strapped across Lily's front.

"Isn't that right?" Lily coos to her, bouncing in place. "Mommy needs to get over herself."

"There are"—I twitch—"nerves." I dig my fingers into my palm.

Yes, I know this is my idea. Since we're in Paris to finish the list, I figured why not? Surely it couldn't hurt as badly as did giving birth. So today, on my mom's birthday, I'm getting her artist mark tattooed on my left shoulder next to a sunflower. Guess the laugh is on me.

"Almost done," the guy behind me says in a heavy French accent. He's said that twice already, so I'm pretty sure he's full of it.

"It's looking good," Lily says. "Makes me want to get another one."

"Masochist. Ow!" I jump when the needle hits a particularly sensitive spot.

Lily sits back, a satisfied smirk on her face. "Serves you right, calling me names."

Eventually, the torture does end, I get patched up with instructions for how to care for my new work of art, and we're sent on our way.

In typical May fashion, the Paris air has warmed up with the day, hinting of the summer to come.

"Do you need to call home?" Lily asks as we stroll down the sidewalk toward Champ de Mars.

I've taken over the harness, and Maya holds on to my fingers as if she's the one steering us. She does have a way of getting the people in her life to do her bidding, my little Christmas miracle. Even Patrick. He's made me promise to check in every once in a while so he'll know she's safe. Despite how Maya's journey into our lives began, the moment Pat looked into her brown eyes—mirror images of his—he was a goner. We're slowly getting into a routine of co-parenting.

"After," I say. "Right now, we've got places to be."

The Eiffel Tower is about a thousand feet tall, but as we stand beneath it, the airy structure appears at once shorter and stouter and more infinite—an optical illusion brought on by its wide base and needle-sharp tip.

We approach from the north, crossing the Seine by the Grand Palais then following it west until we reach our goal. The crowds grow denser as we near it. Between tourists struggling to get the perfect picture, locals enjoying the large parklike area behind the tower, and merchants peddling souvenirs, the air fills with a cacophony of sounds that on any normal day would make me rethink this venture and come back during slow season. Today, I don't have that luxury.

Pushing through the throngs of people, Lily tight on my heels, I get in line for admissions. For a spring afternoon, even the walk-up line is impressive, though not quite as intimidating as the lift line.

"Are you sure you want to take the stairs?" Lily asks, gazing upward.

"You know it's what she wanted."

She must notice my expression for she simply says, "Walking, it is."

Slowly but surely, we approach the ticketing booth, me with money in hand. I know the rush is imagined, but it's there all the same. I need to get up there now—should have been there months ago.

Once we have our tickets and I set foot on the first step, a rush of anticipation surges through my body. If not for the wide behind of the woman in front of me, I'd run up, taking two—no, three—steps at a time. I could not be in a greater hurry if Mom was up there on the second floor, waiting for us. It is with the greatest restraint I force my feet to pace themselves.

Many people stop on the first floor to look around, have a rest, and shop for souvenirs, but not me. Lily makes a vague sound of protest, which I ignore as I dash toward the second staircase. I need to get as high as I can. *Climb the stairs of the Eiffel Tower*—that's what the list says, and that's what I'm doing. Not even Maya's now sleep-heavy weight strapped to me is going to get in the way.

Almost there, Mom. I'm almost done.

"I lost count at six hundred," Lily pants behind me. "Are we there yet?"

The second floor opens before us, and I come to a sudden stop. My heart is a hammer in my chest, as much from the exercise as from reaching the finish line, and the people around me melt away.

"Excuse me," someone calls from behind.

"Kris, you're blocking the way." Lily grabs my arm and tugs me to the side. "Sorry," she says to our fellow climbers.

"Look at that." I point toward the windows.

Lily follows my gaze. "Wow."

Together we approach the glass panes that supposedly will keep us safe up here. With clear skies, the sprawl of Paris is laid out before us, a seemingly random grid of streets, parks, and the glittering river.

"It's like when the plane takes off except we're still on the ground."

"I don't know about that," Lily mutters.

"You know what I mean." I start moving, trailing the perimeter of the huge space, the view shifting a little with each step. Back where we started, Lily grabs us a couple of chairs, and we sit down by the window to watch life as it unfolds far below us.

"You finished the list," Lily says after a long while.

I let her words sink in. "I guess I did."

"She knew you would."

I follow the bows and bends of the Seine with my gaze, my throat working to keep the threatening emotions at bay. "She knew more than me," I say, barely managing to get the words out.

Lily takes my hand and pulls it into her lap, but she doesn't respond, and for that I'm thankful.

We sit there long enough for the light to start changing outside, making shadows stretch across the ground. I think about my mother, about her life raising two kids on her own, about her art, her friends, Bart. How I always thought she didn't get me. Maybe that's the curse of the child—to not understand the nature of a parent's love. Don't get me wrong; I know she wasn't perfect. But neither was I.

"I wish..." I say to no one in particular.

Lily looks up. "What?"

"I wish she had waited a little longer. I know it's selfish, but I could have sent her a picture. The list checked off."

"It would have made you feel better." Lily turns so she's facing me.

I nod.

"She knows." She tilts her head, forcing me to make eye contact. "Don't you feel it?"

A smile I didn't expect creeps over my lips. "You're going religious on me?"

Lily raises an eyebrow. "Hard not to, this close to the sky."

I squeeze her hand tighter. "Thank you for being here."

"Of course." Our eyes meet, and for a brief second, I think she's about to say something else, but then it's gone. "Of course." She pulls me into a one-armed hug that ends too fast.

I free my hand and stand, again turning toward the safety of the view. Maya digs her fist into my chest, a sign she's about to wake up. "Well, this one is getting hungry, and so am I. I don't think I've eaten enough today. Should we head down?"

Lily pulls two lift tickets out of her pocket. "Not yet. Did you honestly think I'd let you visit the Eiffel Tower and not go all the way up?" She gestures toward the elevator, where a line of people is already waiting to go up. "You game?"

I snatch one of the tickets from her hand. "So that's what took you so long at the admissions counter."

My ears pop as we ascend to the top of the tower. One of the men in the elevator is sweating profusely, and I can't say I blame him. The confined space alone is enough to fray one's nerves, not to mention the awareness of being high enough off the ground that the slight sway of the tower is noticeable.

Lily gasps for air as soon as we exit, fanning herself with an information leaflet she must have picked up along the way.

"Oxygen," she pants. "I need oxygen, stat."

I chuckle at her antics, which I know are meant to lighten my introspective spirits, and follow her to the outdoor observation deck. A gust of wind promptly knocks the air out of my lungs. The exposed skin on my arms prickles in response to the unexpected chill, and I instinctively wrap my arms around Maya.

Lily grins into the breeze. "Let's go around to the other side. Might be more protected."

I don't attempt to answer, certain the words would evaporate before reaching her ears, but I follow her when she sets off, eager to get my hair to stop whipping my face.

Lily is right. The other side of the tower is a little better, though still on the cool side for my light outfit. But whatever discomfort I feel is soon forgotten as I take in the blazing horizon, here even farther away than below—buildings smaller, sky bigger.

We stand shoulder to shoulder, pointing out the places we recognize and how ant-like the crowds seem below. The wind is refreshing, almost cleansing after a while, and finally the pressure that's had my chest in a vise lifts and floats away. The sadness is still present, but as I stand there, it uncoils and settles, its corners no longer sharp and threatening.

I suck in a deep breath and let it out. Press my lips to my daughter's head.

Lily nudges my elbow but keeps her eyes on Paris. "You okay?"

"I will be."

"Good."

Another silence stretches out between us.

"Thank you for, you know." I gesture at the expanse of air before us.

She turns her head to look at me, lips slanted. "You keep saying that."

"Well..." The corners of my mouth quirk up. "I keep thinking of that day at O'Hare—what a mess I was. Without you, the journey might have been over before it began."

"Right place at the right time." Lily's eyes twinkle in the setting sunlight.

"You think so?"

"I do. You've come a long way, moving past all those limits you'd set for yourself."

"I know."

"Good." She turns to me fully. "Your mom was one of a kind, and I'm glad I met her."

I let this sink in, the reel of the past few months playing like a movie before my eyes—every daring step into the unknown I've taken, every fear conquered. The freedom I've gained for myself and my daughter.

I meet Lily's gaze, unbridled joy quivering in my core. Letting that feeling guide me, I lean in and kiss her. Her lips are soft and warm, the scent of her skin familiar like Christmas morning. And the miracle is that there, at the top of the Eiffel Tower, she kisses me back.

The wind tangles our hair together, two strands like one caressing my cheek as she pulls me closer. When we part, I search her face for regret but find only a mirror image of the wonder filling every part of me.

"Hmm," she says, humor playing at the corners of her mouth. She pushes a stray lock of hair behind my ear only to have it whip loose again before her hand is back at her side.

"I'm not sorry," I say, watching her carefully.

"Okay."

"And this is not because we're far from home."

"Understood."

I shift, self-conscious at the intensity of her gaze. "You're not an experiment to me."

Her smile widens. "I should hope not."

"But?"

"No buts." She reaches for my hands, threads her fingers through mine. "I realized just now I've set limits for you too. I won't do that anymore. I promise. Plus, I'll be back in the US in two months. Maybe I'll find a gig in Chicago this time."

My pulse gallops, and my knees turn progressively more jellylike each moment. "So does that mean—" I can't finish the question, and as it turns out, I don't have to.

Lily runs her thumb across the back of my hand. "Will you mind terribly if I kiss you again?"

To do before I die in any order:
1. ~~Learn to do a handstand~~
2. ~~See~~ La Bohème ~~on stage~~
3. ~~Learn to knit~~
~~(4. Get a tattoo)~~
5. ~~Climb the stairs of the Eiffel Tower~~
6. ~~Do a ropes course~~
7. ~~Paint the sunset at Butterfly Beach~~
8. ~~Apologize to Bart~~
9. ~~Have a painting displayed at the Louvre~~
~~(10. Fall in love again)~~
11. ~~Ride in a hot-air balloon~~

Acknowledgments

This is the book that made me a writer. It's not the first book I ever wrote—in fact, it's book number four—but up until this one I had not dared to think of myself as a "writer." I wrote books, yes, and I'd even queried them ever so slightly, but it still felt like something I was dabbling in. So, what changed, you wonder? Well, this is the book that got me into Pitch Wars (class of 2017, yeah!) into a writing community, and into a headspace where dabbling became plotting, drafting, and revising with intent.

So, if I'm going to go in order for this book, I have to first thank Brenda Drake for creating PW way back when. I know it's no longer around, but I'm forever grateful for the platform and the connections it introduced me to. Thank you also to my PW mentor, Vanessa Carnevale, who picked my manuscript out of the many and put me through a crash course in editing that was probably the single most valuable lesson I could have received at the time. You were instrumental in putting me on a path to becoming the writer I am today.

Thank you to my agent, Kimberley Cameron, for seeing enough in this manuscript to take a chance on an unknown writer when my query came across your desk some six months after PW. Your tenacity ensured it found a home.

And with that, thank you to the team at Red Adept Publishing—Lynn, Erica, Sara, Darlene, and the proofreaders—for finally bringing Kristin's story to readers wrapped up in a neat bow. She's been waiting very patiently, so I appreciate you all.

Even though I really wrote this book before I had found my writing community, there were a few people who either read early versions, answered questions, and/or were especially vocal in their support. Jessica Holt, Teresa Rosenberg, Layne Fargo, Katie Osterhage, Megan McGee, and Tobi Iott—thank you so much for all the ways you contributed to the existence of this book.

Also, shout-out as always to Rompire—Amy, Em, Julia, Lana, Lexie, Lisa, and Megan—another PW 17 jackpot. I love you all. Let's keep the bookshelf expanding.

To my husband, for believing I was a writer before I did and for loving me for me. I'm so lucky I found my person in you. To my kids, for teaching me more about life than I thought possible on a daily basis. To my parents, for making it okay for little me to be bookish. By the way, Mom, sorry I keep writing about dysfunctional mother-daughter relationships. I promise you are not the inspiration for that. You are the very best mom a girl could have.

Lastly, a thank-you to anyone who has shared news of this book on social media, posted reviews, and generally spread the word, and also to you, lovely reader, who keeps supporting me and my messy fictional casts of characters book after book—thank you, from the bottom of my heart. I couldn't do this without you. And if I could, I wouldn't want to.

About the Author

Anna E. Collins was born and raised in Sweden, where she spent her early years hounding the local librarians for new reads. One American husband, two children, and two international moves later, she realized she had her own stories to tell, and once that proverbial lid was opened, there was no closing it again. She put her master's degree in educational psychology on the shelf and picked up the pen.

Anna currently resides in the Seattle area, where she writes about the lives and inner workings of women—their hopes, dreams, journeys, and relationships. Her goal is to make readers both laugh and cry. In 2019, she was a Golden Heart finalist.

When not writing, reading, or raising humans, she can be found exploring other creative pursuits like painting, woodworking, and baking as well as endlessly brushing her mini goldendoodle, Archie, who is a Very Good Boy.

Read more at www.aecollinsbooks.com.

About the Publisher

Dear Reader,

We hope you enjoyed this book. Please consider leaving a review on your favorite book site.

Visit https://RedAdeptPublishing.com to see our entire catalogue.

Check out our app for short stories, articles, and interviews. You'll also be notified of future releases and special sales.

Made in the USA
Monee, IL
06 July 2023

38724400R20189